Staffordshire Library and Information Services
Please return or renew by the last date shown

BIDDULPH
01782 512103
11/15

KINVER

If not required by other readers, this item may be renewed in
person, by post or telephone, online or by email.
To renew, either the book or ticket are required.

24 Hour Renewal Line
0845 33 00 740

Staffordshire
County Council

A Christmas Kiss

A Christmas Kiss

Vicky Pattison

sphere

To everyone who has enjoyed a
moment under the mistletoe

SPHERE

First published in Great Britain in 2015 by Sphere

1 3 5 7 9 10 8 6 4 2

Copyright © Vicky Pattison 2015

Edited by Faith Bleasdale

The moral right of the author has been asserted.

A CIP catalogue record for this book
is available from the British Library.

ISBN 978-0-7515-6136-4

Typeset in Baskerville by M Rules
Printed and bound in Great Britain by
Clays Ltd, St Ives plc

Papers used by Sphere are from well-managed forests
and other responsible sources.

MIX
Paper from
responsible sources
FSC® C104740

Sphere
An imprint of
Little, Brown Book Group
Carmelite House
50 Victoria Embankment
London EC4Y 0DZ

An Hachette UK Company
www.hachette.co.uk

www.littlebrown.co.uk

PART ONE

Chapter One

Beep. Beep. Beep.

An incessant beeping interrupted my dreamy sleep. I reached for a pillow and buried my head under it. *Sshh, man. I'm sleeping.*

'Amber,' a familiar voice said.

Nope.

'Amber, get up.'

Definitely not. If I stay really still and pretend to still be asleep maybe she'll go away.

'AMBER!' the voice shouted.

I sat bolt upright.

'What the hell?' I said to Jess, my flatmate, rubbing my eyes. 'For God's sake, Jess! I was sleeping! What's your problem?' I am not a morning person. Through bleary eyes, I took in Jess's immaculately fitted suit, her neatly styled long red hair, her perfectly applied make-up.

She tutted disapprovingly. 'Mate, didn't you hear your alarm clock?' She waved it in my face.

'No. Now kindly go away and let me go back to sleep. I was dreaming that Tom Hardy took me to the cinema. He was just buying me Haribos and Ben and Jerry's when you interrupted.' I screwed my eyes shut, pulled the pillow back over my head and willed my subconscious back to the confectionary queue at the cinema with Tom.

'What flavour were you going for?' Jess was not giving up.

'Cookie dough, obvs.' Ridiculous question, but I thought I might as well humour her.

'Amber, now that I have your attention through the power of ice cream . . . '

I started to drift off again. Jess grabbed my pillow and hit me over the head with it.

'What the—'

'AMBER!' Jess interrupted. 'You need to get up. Now. It's six-thirty a.m.!'

'WHAT?!' Suddenly, it hit me. *How could I have slept through my alarm?* Oh shit!' I jumped out of bed, stubbing my toe on the bedside table in the process and shouting more expletives. *Balls!* I tore out of my bedroom and ran straight to the bathroom, Jess's laughter ringing in my ears.

Ten minutes later I was back in my room. I threw on the outfit I'd picked out the night before, and grabbed my make-up bag. I'd have to do my make-up in the cab. I couldn't really afford a cab, but it was the only chance I had of making it to work before Diana, my boss. I rushed into our open-plan living area and Jess handed me a mug of coffee and a piece of toast. While throwing things into my huge, but somehow already full, bag, I shrugged myself into my jacket, ate a few bites of the toast and washed them down with as much of the coffee as I could – burning my mouth. *More balls!* I ran to the door, flung it open and I was about to run down the stairs and into the street when I heard Jess calling my name.

'What?' I said impatiently. 'What is it?'

'You've only got one shoe on,' Jess said, holding up my other wedge. 'You're going to need this, I think.'

I looked at my feet. *How can a person not realise that they are only wearing one shoe? Who does that? I need to get my life together. I'm a twat and Jess is a wedge-wielding angel sent by God. Balls again!*

'What would I do without you?' I said to Jess. 'Thank you!' I threw the last comment over my shoulder as I ran down the stairs, hurriedly putting the wedge on, so of course, I fell over. *Balls.* My fourth set of balls for the day and I wasn't even out the front door yet.

'You OK, Ambs?' Jess called down the stairs through stifled giggles.

'Yip! Yeah, just fine. Bloody shoes. See you tonight!' I scrambled to my feet and ran out the door.

'Good luck!' she called after me.

A crisp February sun was shining. I love wintery sunny days like these. I glimpsed the golden light of a free cab, waved my arms and sent a silent prayer of thanks to the taxi gods when it stopped immediately.

'Where to, love?' the driver asked as I clambered into the back of the cab.

'Somerset House, please,' I replied.

'You off to London Fashion Week?' he said. 'Are you a model then?'

'Nope,' I replied, 'Just a fashion assistant.'

As the cab wound its way with snake-like skill through the London traffic, I started applying my make-up. I'd mastered how to do this in taxis, on trains, on buses, without blinding myself with a mascara wand or painting my cheeks with lipstick years ago. It was a CV-worthy skill that saved me time on mornings like this one, of which, I'm not going to lie, there are many. Did I mention I hate mornings?

I smiled as the cab driver chatted about all the models he'd had in his cab since London Fashion Week had kicked off. It wasn't the first time someone had asked me if I was a model; whenever it happens I always roll my eyes and tell them no. It's probably my height that does it – at just under six feet, I've got long enough legs for it. Though not the grace: my ankle was still slightly sore from the tumble down the stairs. I scrutinised myself in my compact mirror. My eye make-up made the most of my chocolate-brown eyes, I'd pulled my long caramel-coloured hair into a messy bun so I slicked on a bit of MAC nude lipgloss to complete the look. A model I was not, but I'd do for backstage at today's shows – hopefully. The adrenalin, the running around, all those beautiful clothes, amazing new prints and trends – I couldn't wait. This was what I lived for. I'm a total clothes perv. And I am not ashamed.

As a kid growing up just outside Newcastle city centre in Walker, I spent all my time sketching and drawing clothes. My mam taught me how to use her sewing machine when I turned thirteen and that had been it. If I hadn't been addicted to fashion before, I definitely was after I'd made my first skirt. The hem had been wonky and one of the buttons had fallen off after a week but you would have thought I'd created a classic Chanel piece the way I treasured it. The only way was up after that. There was no getting me off that bloody sewing machine and I had more holes in my fingers and thumbs than a second-hand dartboard, but I didn't care. I'd found my passion and that was it.

Now, just like any other twenty-four-old, I love shopping but have developed my own style over the years and often customise the things I buy. And here I was on my way to work at London Fashion Week . . . not exactly in the capacity I'd always imagined, but I was still going. And that was the main thing, wasn't it?

I was still a far cry from my dream of designing my own fashion line. Right now, I was a lowly assistant to the formidable Diana Grant. I'd idolised her for years and had been so excited when I'd landed the job as her assistant – her designs were some of the most unique and timeless in the business. To work for and learn from someone like that was the opportunity of a lifetime, so despite the appallingly low salary (it barely keeps me in gin) I'd accepted the job without hesitation. In reality Diana is such a grade-A cow she makes Cruella de Vil look like Mary Poppins. She isn't interested in mentoring anyone and she doesn't waste any compassion or warmth on her employees. She's still a genius, yes, but she is also mean, small-minded and unkind to anyone she deems beneath her. Which is almost everyone. However, I know that to make it in this industry, you have to pay your dues and so I've stuck it out. I've taken care of her dog, let her shout abuse at me for things I haven't done, and for the first six months of work I allowed her to call me Amy. She didn't like the name Amber, you see, though thankfully now it has grown on her 'like a cancerous cell'. I still had hope that one day Diana would take me seriously and look at my sketches.

She'd better, or I'll set her car on fire. I laughed evilly to myself at the thought of her precious Porsche going up in flames and caught the taxi driver looking at me in his mirror like I was a fruit loop.

'Erm, we're here, love.'

Great, now he thinks I'm insane.

The cab pulled up outside Somerset House, which even at this time was beginning to crowd with similarly harried-looking assistants. I threw my make-up back into my bag, paid the driver, thanked him profusely while trying to look as normal as possible – the weird cackle had obviously freaked him out – and jumped out.

I immediately felt the buzz around me as I rushed to the Edmond J. Safra Fountain Court, where Diana's collection was being shown. I love London Fashion Week. It's glamorous, fast-paced, fun and has such a significance within the industry all at the same time. It had cast its spell on everyone here, and no matter how hard we had to work, how difficult it could be, every single one of us was powerless to resist its charms. I fancied London Fashion Week. It was the David Beckham of Fashion Weeks.

As I squeezed myself backstage, showing my staff pass through all the security checks, I looked around and let out a breath I hadn't realised I'd been holding – Diana wasn't here yet. I had made it! *Jess, you legend! You have saved my skin once again.* I had the chance to make a quick mental note to buy her a lifetime's supply of gin and Pop-Tarts before the extent of the chaos hit me smack in the face. Models were everywhere in various states of undress, hair stylists were working furiously while make-up artists were trying to do their thing at the same time. Diana's team of designers was shouting, shrieking and sweating about God knows what. It was madness. And I had to try to coordinate it before the maddest hatter herself arrived.

No one took any notice of me. I dumped my bag in a corner and went to find Portia, the headline model of today's show. I spotted her in one of the hairdresser's chairs so made my way over to her.

'Hey, Portia,' I said. I liked her a lot, despite the fact that she and Diana genuinely appeared to be friends.

'Hi dahling,' she said in an accent which made the Queen sound common. 'What do you think of my hah?'

'Eh?' I asked, frowning.

'You know, my hah style.'

Oh, hair, I thought. Honestly, sometimes I needed subtitles to understand what Portia was saying – though she probably thought the same about me and my Geordie accent.

'You look a beaut, babes,' I replied. The tiny plaits that were being piled on her head looked uncomfortable but she smiled through the pain like a pro. Eat your heart out, Cara Delevingne.

'Everything all right here?' a Mancunian accent said behind me. I turned to see a face that seemed very familiar to me. It couldn't be . . . ? She nodded at the stylist and I realised that it really *could* be – she must be supervising the hair stylists.

'Er, are you Issy Jones?' I asked before I could stop myself. 'From *Can You Cut It?*' I'd been obsessed with the hairdressing competition/reality TV show when it had been on the telly and Issy had been hands down my favourite contestant.

'Yeah, hun, that's me,' she said, smiling. 'I'm in charge of hair for Diana today.'

9

'I had no idea, she never told me,' I said. 'I'm one of her assistants, Amber Raey.'

'Nice to meet you,' Issy said, giving me a warm hug, completely unlike the usual fashion world air-kisses. She gestured to Portia's intricate hairstyle. 'What do you think?'

Diana's collection was highly tailored this season, so the dramatic hair would be perfect to show off the sharp, crisp angles of the clothes.

'It's perfect,' I gushed. 'You're a genius. I loved you on *Can You Cut It?*' I knew I was fangirling so hard but I couldn't help myself. The room might be full of A-listers, but reality TV star turned celebrity hair stylist Issy Jones was making me lose my shit more than any of them.

'Thanks, babes,' she laughed. 'It didn't exactly go to plan, though, did it?'

'I thought you were great. What's been happening since? I didn't see you in the papers much after the show finished.'

Issy shook her head. 'That kind of fame wasn't for me in the end. I took some time, figured things out and decided what I really wanted to do. I've opened a couple of salons now, one back home in Manchester and another in Shoreditch.' She looked around. 'And I get to style hair for shows like this. Life's good,' she finished with a big smile.

'It means a lot to people like me,' I said, 'to see someone, you know, *normal* make something of themselves. It gives the rest of us hope.'

Issy reached out and squeezed my arm. 'If this is really what you want then stick with it, work hard and good things will happen.' As she pulled her hand away something on her finger caught my eye.

'Hey!' I caught her left hand and looked at the elegant ring

on her third finger. 'This is beautiful. So you and Ryan . . . ?'
One piece of scant information I had read in *New* magazine
was that Issy had fallen for a fit sound man who worked on
her show. I knew they were dating but I hadn't realised they
were this serious. *OMG. I sound like a stalker.*

Issy nodded, a happy look on her face. 'We're getting married in the summer. It can't come soon enough.'

'Congratulations,' I said. 'That's great news.'

'Thanks, babes. Anyway, I better get on. I've got a lot to do
before Diana gets here, and we don't want to be on the
wrong side of her, do we?' She threw me a knowing look
before wandering off to check on another model's hair while
I stood there grinning like an idiot, completely starstruck.

There was a commotion near the door to the backstage
area and I hurried towards that section, knowing what was
coming – the temperature in the room had dropped a couple
degrees. It could only mean Diana was in the building. An
eerie silence descended over the chaos as she appeared. She
was a striking figure. She was about six foot tall, an inch or
two taller than me, and her slick bobbed hair was midnight
black, a striking contrast to her pale alabaster skin and post-
box red lips. She was carrying her pug, Lulu, while behind
her Paddy, her first assistant, shuffled along carrying Diana's
Hermès bag. As first assistant, Paddy was with Diana all the
time, and as far as I could tell his main job was to continually
stroke her ego. As lowly second assistant, I was lucky if I got
to say hello to Diana most days. Or should that be unlucky?
Whichever way you look at it, I thought to myself, *when we do talk
she's normally too busy shouting at me or barking me her lunch order to
even let me even open my mouth.* I braced myself for her worst as
she approached me.

11

'Amber,' she shouted unnecessarily.

I'm right here mate, no need to shout whatsoever. I'm literally in front of you.

'I'm right here, Diana,' I said.

She thrust Lulu at me and pushed me aside as she strode into the middle of the room. 'Paddy, coat,' she yelled. Paddy hurriedly slid the coat from Diana's shoulders and scurried off with it without a word.

Diana was wearing a pristine white suit, so tight it could've been sprayed onto her bony frame. Glaring at me for unknown reasons, she clicked her fingers and she was immediately surrounded by her designers.

For all her loathsome ways, Diana was innovative and creative when it came to fashion and that was why I had been so desperate to work for her. From Hollywood A-listers to British royalty, she had dressed the best and the most elite people in the world. She'd even once refused to dress Angelina Jolie – she'd been Team Aniston, you see. Diana wasn't called the Queen of British Fashion for nothing. I so badly wanted to learn from her but the sad truth was the only thing she seemed to be willing to teach was how to develop a bad attitude.

Lulu was squirming in my arms, growling. I looked down and shot her a look of loathing. Lulu and I aren't friends; I'm convinced she hates me as much as Diana does. The dog is better dressed than me for a start – she has a diamond-encrusted collar which probably costs my yearly salary. And don't get me started on her wind.

'Paddy,' I hissed, when he had returned from coat-hanging duty. 'What am I supposed to do with this?' I held Lulu out to him.

'Amber,' he said, raising a skinny eyebrow. 'Your one job today is to hold on to Lulu and take her out for pee-pee at regular intervals. Surely even you can manage that?'

Once again, I wished that Paddy would be a bit of an ally to me. The problem was that I was the only person he was allowed to talk down to, so he made the most of it. It was never going to be a case of the two of us against Diana.

'Welcome to the world of high fashion, darling,' I said to Lulu as Paddy walked away.

She farted on me in response.

Chapter Two

I was heading back inside after taking Lulu for another 'comfort' break, and in the fifteen minutes I'd been gone the show had finally got under way. The chaos backstage had increased and Diana's voice was reaching heights that would shatter glass, but I couldn't help but be infected by the excitement and buzz. I looked out at the audience, spotting A-lister after A-lister ... I could see the Olsen twins, Rosie Huntington-Whiteley, Alexa Chung, and I'm pretty sure there was a Kardashian in the mix as well. A shiver of ambition went through me. I didn't want to put up with Diana's ridiculousness, I didn't want to look after Lulu, and I certainly didn't want to have to look at Paddy's horrendously over-waxed brows any more. I wanted to be showing my collection. I knew I could do it, I just needed someone to take me seriously. I'd worked for Diana for over a year now – it was time to make her look at my sketches properly. And I'd make sure she did, as soon as London Fashion Week was over. I had to.

'What the hell have you done?! It's ruined!' Diana's screams shattered my ambitious thoughts.

'I didn't do anything, it just broke,' an Eastern European voice stuttered.

'What. Is. Your. Name?' Diane shrieked.

'Natasha.' The girl was on the verge of tears. The other models, who were being ushered onto the runway, shot her sympathetic looks but weren't able to offer anything else in the way of support. Paddy was hovering nearby, looking between the girl and Diana, a panicked expression in his eyes. I looked at Natasha. Her outfit was a one-piece designed to look like a tailored trouser suit, but her nipple was poking out from behind the lapel and the one of the trouser hems was trailing on the floor below her stacked heels. *Shit. This is going to go off.*

Diana was pacing back and forth, screaming incomprehensibly at whoever happened to be standing closest to her. All of the designers, plus Paddy, were running after her doing their best to placate her. No one, however, was doing anything to fix Natasha's outfit – Diana's bitch fit was obviously being deemed the main priority. I rolled my eyes. We had about five minutes until we had to either send Natasha onto the catwalk or pull her, which I knew would devastate the show. We didn't have time for all this drama.

Still clutching Lulu, I retrieved my bag. I looked around and saw a man standing on the sidelines. Without thinking, I thrust Lulu at him.

'Pet, do me a solid and hold Lulu please,' I said quickly, throwing him a smile. 'It's an emergency.' I ran over to Natasha, who was looking shell-shocked and distraught. 'Hey, babes, don't start crying, it'll mess up your make-up.' I gave her arm a squeeze. 'We'll fix all of this in no time.' I pulled some tit-tape out of my bag and deftly attached some to the inside of the collar so that her exposed nipple was firmly tucked back into place. I then crouched down, grabbed my needle and cotton and sewed a couple of stitches into the hem. It wouldn't last forever but it would do for the next ten minutes.

Natasha's face broke into a relieved smile. 'My God, thank you.'

'No worries,' I said, standing up. I gently pushed her towards Diana who had stopped frantically pacing. She looked Natasha up and down and waved her hand dismissively.

'You'll do,' she said. She shoved Natasha towards the cat-walk. 'Go, go, go.' She turned to me and fixed me with an icy glare.

'You're welcome,' I said brightly, before she could say anything. Diana stared at me for a moment, then turned back to show and I was forgotten.

'Your doggie,' an Italian accent said behind me. I turned and saw the man I'd left Lulu with. I'd forgotten all about him and that stupid mutt.

'Thanks for that,' I said, taking the dog back. 'I'm Amber Raey, by the way,' I said, 'Diana's assistant. Well, one of them,' I explained. The man was about three inches shorter than me, with a glowing tanned face, a bald head and thick black-rimmed glasses. He looked familiar, but I couldn't place him.

'Alessandro Rossi,' he said, sticking his hand out toward me and raising a perfectly plucked eyebrow.

'Oh shit,' I said before I could stop myself. How had I not recognised him? I had just made the head of House of Rossi, one of the most successful fashion houses in the world, hold

17

Diana's smelly, arse-faced dog. I wanted to die – but I shook his hand instead. *Best thing is to style it out, play it cool. You work in the same industry here. I mean, he's practically a colleague.*

'I'm so sorry. I'm a huge fan of your work, I love it! And you! But with the chaos I just didn't ... I can't believe I didn't realise. I really am sorry. I feel like a right knob. I can't believe I just said knob in front of you. And again. Oh God. I'm just going to shut up.'

Yip, cool as a cucumber in a bowler hat, Amber. Way to act cool. Bollocks.

Alessandro smiled kindly. 'Thank you,' he said. He gestured at Lulu. 'Is the dog yours?'

'No, it's Diana's. I'm on dog-sitting duty today.'

'Really? It looked to me like it was your job to rescue the show.'

'I wouldn't go that far,' I said. 'But I couldn't sit by and watch everyone else run around like distressed teenagers at a 1D concert.'

'Is that an English saying?' Alessandro looked perplexed.

I shook my head, laughing. 'No, sorry. 1D, One Direction. Have you heard of them?'

'Ah, of course,' Alessandro said. 'I'm not familiar with the phrase, what did you call them, 1D? But they are lovely boys.'

'Yeah, they seem it. I like Harry, he's dreamy.' I said, before I could help myself. Desperately trying to move the conversation to more professional and less 'dreamy' territory I racked my brains for something to say.

'So,' I asked, 'which part of Italy are you from?'

Well, it's a start.

'Tuscany. Is very beautiful there. Have you ever been to Italy?'

'Nope, but I'd love to one day.'

'Maybe you can go to the Milan shows?'

'That's the dream,' I said, 'though it depends on Diana. She usually only takes one assistant with her. And I'm her second assistant so it's not usually me.'

'I see.' Alessandro looked at me steadily. *Do I have something on my face?* I thought. 'I admire her work,' he went on.

'Me too. She's a genius.' I sighed sadly. 'But . . . ' I paused.

'But?' Alessandro said, tilting his head to one side.

What are you doing here, Amber? This isn't one of your mates and you aren't down the pub slagging off your bosses together over an over-priced G&T. This is Alessandro Rossi and he doesn't want to hear your sad little sob story about how your boss is an über-bitch. He could be best mates with Diana, for God's sake! Stop talking. Now.

'What I really want is to be a designer. When I got the job with Diana I thought it would be the first step on that road but it hasn't exactly turned out like that. I'm not sure dog-sitting and coffee-fetching is going to get me where I want to be. I don't mind hard work or paying my dues, as long as there's genuine scope for advancement and learning, but I don't get the impression Diana sees this arrangement the same way I do.'

Or . . . just lay all your cards on the table and tell the man you barely know all your deepest career desires and concerns. Excellent, Amber.

Alessandro looked at me, an expression of amusement on his face. 'Are you always this forthright with your opinions, my dear?'

'Yeah, I suppose I am. My mouth just runs away with me sometimes. I'm sorry.'

'Don't be. I like it.' He was smiling broadly now, showing off his perfectly straight white teeth. 'As designers, I believe it's our duty to encourage young talent. You said that you were a fan of my work?'

I nodded with genuine enthusiasm. 'I love your designs! Honestly, Mr Rossi, they're incredible. Your 2012 spring/summer couture collection blew my mind. It was so creative. Was it inspired by Monet's *Irises in Monet's garden*?'

Alessandro's eyebrows shot up in surprise. 'Bella, it was! You saw that?'

'Yes, the entire collection was beautiful. I've always wanted to ask you that question but never thought I'd get the chance. You've made my day.'

'Amber Raey,' Alessandro said thoughtfully. 'You are a very impressive young lady. I have difficulty understanding some of what you say, but what I do hear is very smart,' he laughed.

'You wouldn't, man, I'm a Geordie.' I thickened my accent for effect and laughed along with him. I liked him.

'I'm not sure what that means!' Alessandro was still smiling to himself as he drew an expensive-looking black wallet out of his inside pocket. 'Here's my card. Give my assistant a call and make an appointment to see me next week.'

'Really?' My hands were shaking as I took the card. I stared at it like the golden ticket it was. There they were – Alessandro Rossi's contact details. I shoved it in my pocket before Lulu ate it. Alessandro smiled, kissed both my cheeks, and then he was gone.

Diana was walking down the runway, basking in the glory of another successful show, and the sound of rapturous applause filtered backstage. I was so buzzing after my encounter with Alessandro that I was grinning from ear to ear. She came off the catwalk and when she started walking towards me I thought it was me she was making a beeline for and panicked, until I realised I was still holding Lulu.

'Mummy's back,' she cooed, taking Lulu and walking away without so much as a look at me.

'You're welcome,' I called after her.

'Why do you keep saying that?' Diana said over her shoulder. She carried on walking, but not before I heard her mutter, 'Such an odd girl.'

'I'm dying,' I said, collapsing on the sofa. I'd had had the wonderful job of packing up after the show and had only just got home. Jess handed me a glass of cold white wine.

'Of course you are, hun,' Jess said, an amused look in her green eyes.

Jess was lovely and she never takes any of my melodrama seriously. She was from Surrey, straight-talking but fair and with a heart of gold and the largest tolerance for white wine I had ever witnessed in a human being. Along with the lovably irresponsible Tom, our other flatmate, we made a tight little trio – they were my London family and I would do anything for them. I had met them right after I had graduated and was working for a pittance for an obscure fashion magazine. I was even more of a dogsbody there than I was now and was constantly knackered, running around all hours, learning the business and missing home. I had been crashing on friends' floors, but in searching for a place I'd been to see so many ropey flatshares that I was seriously thinking about giving up and moving back to Newcastle when I'd spotted Jess's ad on SpareRoom. It had been friendly and well-written, and the flat had sounded so perfect and affordable that before I'd even met Jess and Tom I'd decided that I had to have the room.

I'd arrived to the appointment ten minutes late – practically on time for me – and Jess had opened the door with a look of resignation on her face. Tom works at a bar, Jalou, and had been called in to cover a shift at the last minute so she'd spent the last two hours interviewing one hopeless prospective flatmate after another. She'd been losing the will to live, but after a few minutes she'd clearly decided that I wasn't as much of a weirdo as the rest of the people she'd seen that day and cracked open a bottle of Prosecco. We'd bonded over the miserable time I'd been having looking for a decent flatshare, which had included meeting a man from Dalston who'd said I could live in his spare room for free if I let him wash my feet once a week. And Jess had shared her stories about the 'fruit cups, loons and utter bellends' she and Tom had seen. We worked our way through the Prosecco pretty quickly so started on a bottle of rosé. By the time Tom returned home from work, we were smashed and practically in love with each other. I would've let Jess wash my feet any day. Tom had been so happy to see that I was also a 'pisshead' that he had offered me the room there and then. No flatshare was perfect, but I was grateful every day that I'd found this place and the two of them. We were completely different but it worked. Jess, so career-driven and serious, was clearly the mother of the group, and so it was our job to help her see the funnier side of life when her responsibilities at the law firm she worked at weighed her down too much. Out of the two of us, I liked to think of myself as the cool older sister and Tom, with his scruffy and laid-back ways, as the naughty younger brother. But he had a heart of gold and I couldn't imagine my life without him either.

'Jess, you're wasted becoming a lawyer,' I said, taking a much-needed gulp of wine. 'You should stay home and be my housewife.'

'I'm all right, thanks,' Jess said, sitting down next me. 'So you really met Alessandro Rossi?'

'I did! And he told me to call his assistant and set up a meeting for us. I don't know what he wants to talk about, but that must be a good thing, right?'

'Definitely,' Jess said. 'After the blood, sweat and tears you've put in working for Diana, it's time you had a bit of good luck. You've earned it.'

'I hope so.' I stretched and let out a yawn. 'Anyway, I'm knackered. I'm going to take my wine and have a soak in the tub. See you in a bit?'

'Actually, I'm just heading out for a quick drink so I'll probably see you in the morning.'

'OK, cool. Who are you meeting?' I asked. Like me, Jess was single, but she was going out on dates all the time. Her and Tom's obsession with online dating meant I'd christened the flat 'Tinder Towers', and I bet tonight's chap was no different.

'This guy I met on Tinder.'

Knew it.

'Jess, I told you, you need a back-up plan if you're seeing someone you met online.'

'Don't worry,' Jess said, 'we're heading to Jalou so I'll be perfectly safe.'

'In that case, have fun, and have a tash-on for me.'

After a steaming bath I literally crawled into bed. I was

bone tired and I couldn't wait to go to sleep. I didn't often get the flat to myself so I should probably have made the most of it and watched something on Netflix while eating cocktail sausages with ketchup or some equally disgusting concoction, but my eyes wouldn't stay open a second longer. I set my alarm for the morning and drifted off to sleep immediately.

'Argh!' I shouted, startled awake as the duvet was pulled off me and a body crashed into my bed.

'Argh!' Tom shouted back. I flicked on the bedside lamp. My drunken flatmate was lying next to me fully clothed, clutching a pizza box and with a confused expression on his face.

'Tom!' I sat up and hit him over the head with my pillow. 'You're in the wrong room. Again. This is my bed, you helmet!'

Tom had a habit of coming home in the early hours, completely steaming, and forgetting where his room was. Usually he ended up in my room, though there was nothing romantic about it. All he wanted was a warm duvet and his pizza. It had earned him the loving nickname the Pepperoni Prat.

'Sorry, mate,' Tom said, slurring slightly. 'I thought this was my room.'

'Yeah, pet, you always do,' I sighed. I climbed out of bed and pulled him up. 'Come on, back to your room.'

He mumbled something incomprehensible and lumbered towards the door.

'Don't forget your pizza,' I said, thrusting the box at him.

'Thanks. Do you, hic, want someth? It isch stuffed crustsss.'

Even half-cut Tom was still a gentleman, if barely understandable, and despite the unwelcome wake-up call, I couldn't be mad at him for long. Especially not when there was an offer of stuffed crust on the table.

'Go on, just one slice then,' I said, 'but I'm going back to bed now, mate. I'm shattered.' I nabbed a slice, then gently guided him through the door, turned him toward the direction of his room and set him free into the night. I settled back into bed, inhaled my cheesy delight, and as I slowly drifted off to sleep for the second time that evening I did so with a smile on my face.

Chapter Three

My bedroom looked like a bomb site. There were clothes, shoes, bags and belts everywhere. I'd spent the past few agonising hours trying to select the perfect outfit, and had finally settled on a pair of wide-leg white trousers, a cropped blue cashmere jumper and my nude courts. I'd been shooting for sophisticated but current, and after emptying the wardrobe and trying on everything at least twice, at last I had hopefully achieved it. Even though I was a bag of nerves thinking about the meeting ahead, I looked the part and that would do for now. *Fake it 'til you make it,* I thought.

I'd phoned Alessandro's assistant the day after the fashion show and had managed to make an appointment to see him three weeks later, when the chaos of London Fashion Week would be over. It seemed such a long time to wait, but obviously Alessandro was incredibly busy, and I knew how lucky I was to be able to see him at all.

And now, finally, today was the day. I'm a terrible liar and I knew I'd never be able to come up with a convincing excuse to disappear from work for a few hours. My mam thinks it's because I have an honest soul. Even if I do, lying is too complicated and I get confused and flustered when I try. Instead, I'd taken the entire day off as a 'personal day' – whatever the hell that meant. As it was Friday, that meant three completely Diana-free days in a row. Bliss. I picked up my sketchbook, kissed my gold feather necklace and left the flat.

The necklace is my most treasured piece of jewellery. My dad, David, gave it to me for my eighteenth birthday. I'd loved it instantly and it was now even more important to me. Two years ago my dad died in a horrible car accident and – I know it sounds silly – wearing the necklace makes me feel closer to him. It's like there's a small part of him that's still with me, watching over me, looking out for me. He may not have been my biological father but he was my dad in every way that mattered and I miss him every day. I don't think that dull ache will ever go away completely, and I don't know if I'd want it to either. I never want a day to go by where I don't think of him. He was an incredibly special man.

I've never met my natural father. My mam, Angela – Ange to her mates – fell pregnant with me when she was just eighteen and my 'father' disappeared not long after he found out. My grandparents tried to convince Mam to get rid of me but she wasn't having any of it. I don't think their relationship ever recovered, and as a result I only see them once or twice a year. It wasn't easy for my mam, I know that. We lived with my grandparents until I was two and when the two of us moved out into a crappy little council flat in Walker. It was a hovel but it was ours, and it was a happy place thanks to her. She got a job as a sales assistant in Fenwick's in town and she's worked her way up over the years to become one of the general managers on menswear. And it was in the shop that Mam first met David.

I was five at the time. He came in looking for 'something smart'; Mam sold him a shirt. He'd come back the next day, and the day after that. It was only when she sold him his fifth shirt in as many days that the penny finally dropped and she realised that maybe it wasn't the clothes he was interested in.

The fact that Mam had a kid hadn't put David off at all. They'd got serious quite quickly and he'd insisted on meeting me as soon as things were official. I'd fallen under his spell as quickly as Mam had. He was a good, kind man – even five-year-old me could see that. And my mam came alive around him, she lit up, it was beautiful. They were married a couple of years later, we moved into a nicer place and David adopted me. As far as I'm concerned he was my dad, and though I was too young at the time to fully understand how big a deal the adoption was, I get it now. He wanted the whole world to know I was his daughter, that me and Mam were his family. I was ten when Mam got pregnant again. And out popped my sister, Ruby. She was born 7lb 4oz, screaming bloody murder and with a bright red face. Mam joked that's why they named her Ruby. And with that, our little family was complete.

Dad dying changed all of us, and I don't think it's some-thing we'll ever get over. I don't know if it would have been easier if he'd been ill and we'd seen it coming, had time to get used to the idea of life without him, to adjust mentally, but I have to admit to myself that the unfairness of the way he was taken from us is never far from my mind. He had been driv-ing home from work, home to his girls, when another car had run a red light and ploughed straight into him. The policeman who came to our door that night had said he'd died instantly so he wouldn't have felt any pain, but that was little comfort. The other driver had died too and it turned out he'd been high on a cocktail of drink and drugs. That's why he'd run the red light, and that's why my dad was dead, and I hate drugs as a result. I can't stand to be around them or around anyone who takes them.

I'll never forget the sound that came out of Mam's mouth when she found out. My mam is a fighter, always has been, but hearing that the love of her life was gone undid her completely. She's still one tough lady, fiercely protective of me and Ruby, but some of the light behind her eyes has gone and I'm not sure it's ever coming back. As for Ruby, well, the last two years have been tough on her too. She was only twelve when Dad died, too young to know how to cope with pain, but old enough to know that it still hurt like hell. Over the last two years I've watched my happy, charming little sister turn into a surly, almost mute, angry teenager. A teenager who I couldn't get close to at the moment. She pushed me and Mam so far away I never knew what was going on with her. It was a fact that really hurt me.

I shook my head, trying to clear away all the sad thoughts of home. I curled my fingers around the pendant again. 'Wish me luck, Dad,' I whispered.

The House of Rossi offices were in an old factory building in Shoreditch. It was cool, edgy and the complete opposite of Diana's pristine Mayfair premises. In many ways, House of Rossi's studio was more cutting edge than Diana's, but it was also high-end so the building suited it perfectly. The other huge difference was that Rossi had different labels within his house, and he encouraged his designers to work under his umbrella, whereas Diana simply had 'Diana Grant' and nothing else. It was all about her – there wasn't room for anyone else to shine.

I pushed open the door and approached the reception desk. The two women sat behind it looked like they'd stepped straight out of the latest issue of *Vogue* – tall, leggy, immaculate and with the superpower of making regular women feel like inadequate, chubby hobbits. *Self-esteem zero. Thank you, glamazons!*

'I'm Amber Raey, I'm here to see Alessandro Rossi,' I said more confidently than I felt. One of the girls nodded at me, and whispered something into the phone. A few minutes later another gorgeous modelesque girl approached. *Is there anyone in this building who couldn't walk for Victoria's Secret?*

'Hi Amber,' she said with a smile. 'I'm Laurie, Alessandro's PA. We spoke on the phone.' She stuck out a perfectly manicured hand.

'Of course, nice to meet you properly,' I said, shaking her hand.

'Follow me, I'll take you up to Alessandro.'

We got into one of the lifts and Laurie pushed the button for the top floor.

'Is the whole building yours?' I asked.

Laurie nodded. 'Yes, all five floors are House of Rossi.'

I thought about that for a moment. Five floors filled with designers, all working for the creative genius that was Alessandro Rossi. It sent an excited fizzy feeling all through my body. I felt like a human Tangfastic. *Mmm, Haribos. Stop thinking about sweets, you gimp, and start concentrating. This is your dream here. You can't get distracted by sugary goodness. Not today, Amber,*

31

not today. Now focus! Whoa, my subconscious was a tough bitch. But she was right; if I wanted to work here, to be one of these designers, I needed to act like it.

We reached the top floor and Laurie led me to one of the empty meeting rooms. I walked past people running around, shouting things to one another about colours and textures and samples. It was a buzzing hive of activity and already I wanted to be part of it more than anything.

'Take a seat,' Laurie said. 'Alessandro will be along in a minute.'

After Laurie left, I did my best to calm my nerves. I leafed through my sketches, wondering for the hundredth time if I'd picked the right ones to bring along.

'Ah, bella Amber,' Alessandro said, walking in. I stood up and Alessandro kissed me once on each cheek. I had to bend slightly so he could reach me but we managed it without any weird awkwardness. He was obviously used to kissing giraffe-like models. I must have seemed like a baby hippo in comparison.

'Hi, Alessandro. Thank you so much for seeing me.'

'Of course,' Alessandro said. 'And I'm understanding you better this time!'

It was a crap joke but I laughed anyway. Not only because I wanted to impress him, but because he was likeable and he made it easy. I felt more comfortable with him after just a few minutes than I ever had with Diana over the last year.

'So, bella, let's see what's in that book of yours.'

We talked through each sketch, my inspiration behind the looks, which fabrics I'd use. Alessandro wanted to know every detail and I was more than happy to give them all to him. I loved this world and the more I talked with Alessandro, the stronger my excitement and passion became – two things that had been slowly disappearing since I'd been working for Diana.

I looked up at the clock on the wall and gasped. An hour had flown by. 'I'm so sorry,' I said. 'I didn't realise how long we'd been in here. I didn't mean to bore on so much.'

'Bore on?' Alessandro frowned in confusion.

'Harp on, go on, talk too much.'

'No, not at all. I love the passion, the heart you have. Your designs are *impressionante*.'

'Eh? Does that mean you like them?'

'Yes, they are *molto bene*.' He stood up. 'Now come with me. I want to show you around.'

We were about to step out of the room when a thought suddenly occurred to me. In amongst all of our talking, not once had I asked if there was actually a job going at House of Rossi. How had I not thought to ask the most basic question?

'Er, Alessandro? Can I ask, I mean, is there, you know, is there a job here with your house?' *Idiot*, I thought to myself. *You sound like an utter melt.*

Alessandro stared at me for a moment before slapping a hand on his forehead. 'Why do you think I asked you here, bella? I thought I saw something in you that I liked when we met backstage at Diana's show, and after seeing your sketches today, I know I did. We've just confirmed with Selfridges that we'll be opening a new concession with them. The clothes will be aimed at young women, women your age and perhaps a little younger. It's a new challenge for us, a market that we don't yet design for and I need to bring in some fresh blood to help me with the range. I need someone who knows what women that age want to wear.'

My mouth fell open. 'Wow.' That's all I could manage. *Nice one, Amber. Very eloquent. This is your dream opportunity, don't ruin it. Say something clever, or witty, or inspired.*

'So in theory you would be interested?' Alessandro looked amused.

'In theory, mate, I'd bite your fucking hand off.' *Balls. Should have stuck with 'wow'.*

Alessandro looked taken aback but he recovered well. *A true professional,* I thought.

'I hope that won't be necessary but I will take this to mean you are keen, no?' he said, laughing. I nodded vigorously; my subconscious had obviously decided I could no longer be trusted with the spoken word. 'Now, come. Let me show you around the offices.'

I tried to take in everything Alessandro was saying as he showed me round each floor but I was having trouble concentrating. This was my dream job. The thought that Alessandro might give the opportunity to someone else ... Well, that couldn't happen. I wouldn't let it.

We came to the end of the tour and Alessandro walked me back to the reception area. 'It was a pleasure to see you again, Amber,' he said warmly. 'I will be in touch with an answer very soon.'

'Thank you,' I said. 'House of Rossi is amazing and I'd love nothing more to work here, with you. It would be my dream come true.'

I meant every word and I just hoped I'd done enough to convince Alessandro to take a chance on me.

I phoned my mam as I made my way to the Tube station. She answered after a couple of rings.

'Hiya, love. How was it?'

'OK, I think. Oh, Mam, the offices are amazing, Alessandro is amazig, the job sounds amazing. It's all—'

'Amazing?' she interrupted.

'Very funny,' I said. 'Mam, this is it. This is the job I've been waiting for.'

'Pet, take a breath,' she said. 'Now tell me everything.'

I filled her in on my afternoon, anxious to get her take on things. My mam always cut to the chase – I knew I could count on her to be honest.

'You're right,' she said when I'd finished. 'It does sound amazing. And if it means you don't have to work for that demanding old witch any more, I want this for you as much as you want it for yourself. What happens next?'

'Alessandro said he'd be in touch soon, so I guess I just have to wait it out now.' I groaned. 'I want this so badly, I don't think I can wait too long.'

'If Alessandro really is as nice as you think he is, he won't keep you waiting any longer than he needs to.'

'I suppose.'

'And don't go drinking your nerves away while you're waiting,' Mam said, a note of warning in her voice.

'You know me so well. All I can think about is Tangfastics and gin now that's over,' I said, smiling.

'Oohhh no. You want Galaxy and white wine, man!' Our confectionary and tipple of choice were two of the only areas our opinions differed. Otherwise, we were like two peas in a pod. 'But seriously, missus, I'm your mam, of course I know what's going through your head. And listen, just call me if you find yourself worrying too much.'

'I will,' I promised. 'And I'll be home next weekend for your birthday anyway.'

'Hmm, I don't think turning forty-two is anything to celebrate.'

'Yes, it is,' I said determinedly. 'Me and Rubes are taking you out for dinner.'

'Now that sounds perfect – an evening with my girls.'

'So I'll see you next weekend, then. I better go – I'm at the Tube now.'

'All right. Call me as soon as you hear from Alessandro.'

'I will. Bye, Mam. Love you.'

'Bye, pet. Love you too.'

I hung up and pulled my coat a little tighter. The wind was picking up and there was a definite chill in the air. There was only one thing for it – I was going to ignore my mam's advice and spend the rest of the night with the gin.

Chapter Four

I pushed open the door to Jalou, the bar Tom worked in. It was just after six o'clock but the place was already busy. Because of its location, Jalou was usually full of wannabe models, aspiring journalists, bloggers and vloggers, and people like me – assistants struggling to get their first proper break. Jalou was downmarket enough that none of our bosses would ever think to come here, but trendy and edgy enough to suit the next generation of up-and-comers who were for the most part pretty skint. So for London, it was reasonably priced and did some great offers. Tonight was 2-4-1 mojitos and I intended to get two – one for myself now and one for me in fifteen minutes' time. #happyamber. It was the one place I knew I could just turn up to and find people who understood what it meant to work for someone liked Diana. We were all in the same boat and this was the place we gravitated towards to let off steam at the end of all those bad and horrible days. And having a personal in with one of the barmen was the icing on the cake, or, in tonight's case, the mint on the mojito.

I spotted Tom behind the bar and made my way straight over. I waved at him and he grinned back. The girls he was serving shot me a look that clearly told me to back off. I smiled to myself. Tom was not my type in the slightest but I could see how his lazy smile, floppy hair and toned arms had girls coming back to the bar night after night. He seemed oblivious to it all though, which was another part of his charm. He came bounding over to my end of the bar once he'd dispatched the girls with their drinks. Where he got his endless supply of energy from was beyond me.

'So?' he said. 'How was it?'

I dropped my voice. 'I'll tell you later,' I whispered, gesturing at the crowd. Fashion thrived on gossip and around this way there would definitely be some industry types about. I couldn't risk Diana finding out about my meeting, at least not until I knew what the outcome was going to be. She would set fire to my arse if she thought I was entertaining the thought of leaving her, despite her still not really knowing who I was.

'Right, of course,' Tom said. 'Do you want a drink?'

'Mojito please,' I said, nodding. 'Two.'

Tom cocked his head to one side. 'Ahhhh, making the most of the old 2-4-1, eh? Is it that bad?'

'Nope, potentially that good,' I said.

'Oh? So celebratory rather than commiseratory drinking? My favourite type of drinks. But, ssshhh, don't tell the other drinks, I don't want them to get jealous!'

A few minutes later I was pulled into a conversation with a couple of assistants I knew, but I was distracted. Jess would be here soon and I kept checking my watch. I needed to catch her up about Alessandro and that afternoon's meeting.

'Hey, Amber.' I turned round to see Silvia, an editorial assistant on the magazine I used to work for. She was a nice lass and I hadn't seen her for a while.

'All right, hun. How's it going?' I asked, giving her a hug.

'The same,' Silvia sighed. 'You know how it is.'

'I'm sorry.' I gave her arm a squeeze. She looked so dejected and I knew exactly how she felt. 'Just hang in there. One day, things will change and putting up with all this will be worth it.'

'I hope so,' Silvia said. 'It's a long time coming. I sometimes worry that when I do get a break, I'll be so grateful that I'll forget what it was like to be on the bottom rung and I'll turn into a super bitch in stilettos just like the rest of them.'

'Embrace it, mate. It's beyond your control, law of the land, order of the food chain. I can't wait to be a great white, chomping up Nemos like us for breakfast.' Silvia laughed along with me and relaxed a little. 'In all seriousness, babe, that's never going to happen. You and I haven't got it in us.' I shook my head. 'Let's make a pact. No matter how far ahead we get, we'll never forget where we came from and we'll always, always, be nice to our assistants.'

'I'll drink to that,' Silvia said, laughing.

'Oi, oi,' a voice boomed behind me and I was suddenly enveloped in a bear hug. When I was finally released, I turned round laughing. I knew exactly who it was.

'Jamie,' I said, pretending to be annoyed. 'Can't you just say hello like a normal human being? Do I always have to be semi-accosted by you as a greeting?'

'Yes, you do,' he said, 'otherwise where's the fun?'

I'd known Jamie for as long as I'd known Tom – the two of them were friends from a short stint when Jamie had worked at Jalou. And as an aspiring model, Jamie spent a lot of time in here. Like the rest of us, he was working his way up, trying to find his big break, and I didn't think he'd have to wait too long. He was your classic tall, dark and handsome, with piercing blue eyes and chiselled features that made David Gandy look like the man who delivers my mam's milk. All of these things had meant that many a woman had found themselves susceptible to his charms. He managed to have just the right amount of stubble, and was toned and fit without being either too muscly or too thin. He was from Walthamstow, born and bred, and sounded more like a genuine London cabbie than a model but that, again, was all part of his appeal. We flirted a little but I never took him seriously. It was just his way, radiating charm and charisma, and I had strong suspicions he was like that with all the girls.

'How's my Geordio Armani doing, then?' he asked.

Oh, and that was another thing. Not long after we'd met, he started calling me Geordio Armani. He thought it was hilarious; I hadn't been convinced. But it had stuck and now that was what he called me. All the time.

'Same old,' I said. I turned to Silvia. 'Do you guys know each other? Jamie, this is Silvia. We used to work together at the magazine.'

'Hiya, babe. It's nice to meet you, Silvia.' Jamie stuck out his hand, and Silvia shook it, dumbstruck. I rolled my eyes. Was there a woman alive who wouldn't lose her it around Jamie?

'Erm, yeah. Mice to neet you too. I mean, nice to meet you. Oh God. Erm, I better go,' Silvia stammered. 'I promised my friends a round of drinks ages ago.' She threw Jamie what I think was meant to be a 'come find me later' look but looked more like an 'if you sleep with me and pie me off I'll watch you through your window and stalk your social media for months afterwards' look, and slinked off.

Jamie, completely unperturbed by his effect on Silvia or women in general, gestured towards my almost-empty glass. 'Another mojito?' he asked.

'Sure,' I said. 'Thanks.'

Jamie was served almost immediately by the barmaid and he clinked his bottle of Beck's against my glass.

'So, work still the same?' he asked. 'Is Diana still being the biggest bitch in the biz?'

'Nice alliteration,' I said and Jamie smiled that blinding, Colgate advert-worthy smile in thanks. 'I don't think she'll ever change, you know,' I said. I thought for a moment about telling him about Alessandro but quickly decided against it. The last thing I needed was for him to casually mention it to the next model he did the dance with no pants with. Then she'd tell all of her model pals on her next shoot and before you knew it the gossip would be doing the rounds and Diana would almost certainly find out about my meeting with Alessandro. *No, keep this to yourself, Amber.* 'So how's work with you?' I asked instead.

'Fashion Week was insane, and it's been pretty busy ever since. My agent has been lining up some really good go-sees, and I've had a couple of callbacks so hopefully one of them will work out.'

'No more hair loss ads on the Tube then?' I said, a wicked gleam in my eye.

Jamie groaned. 'I'm never gonna live that down, am I?'

'We all have to start somewhere,' I said, patting his head in mock sympathy.

'I can't wait for the day you ring me, begging me to be a model in one of your fashion shows,' Jamie said, looking down at me.

'Me begging *you*? It's more likely to be the other way round.'

'No way.' Jamie took a step closer to me and lowered his voice. 'But all you'd have to do is ask nicely and I'd be all yours.'

OK, too intense. Over the last couple of months Jamie had been taking the flirting a bit too seriously. I needed to change gear before he got the wrong idea. I wasn't interested in becoming another notch on his bedpost. Not that it wouldn't be the most satisfying notch of my life. Jamie was snap-your-neck beautiful and he knew it, but I was no one's one-night stand.

I gave him a playful shove, trying to lighten the mood. 'Not in this lifetime, petal.'

Jamie looked at me seriously for a second and then his face broke into a smile. 'I'll wear you down one of these days. You can't resist my charms forever.'

'Yes, she can,' Jess's voice said behind me. This girl was always saving me.

'Not you too?' Jamie put his hand over his heart. 'You girls will be the death of me.'

'Well,' Jess said drily, 'there is a group of girls over there who would be willing to give you mouth-to-mouth, should we end up killing you.'

Jamie glanced over and shrugged his shoulders. 'Not really interested, babes.'

My eyebrows shot up in surprise. 'Really? Why? They're fit. I swear one of them is in the new Rimmel Sunshimmer ad. Her legs are longer than my entire body.'

'It's not that they aren't attractive,' Jamie said seriously. 'I just wanted to catch up with mates tonight, and there's a game on soon so I'll be heading off anyway. I'm not the ladies' man you all think I am, you know.'

'Aw come on, Jamie, don't piss on my leg and tell me it's raining, man.' I laughed but I meant it. Jamie was a good friend and a nice guy but I wasn't blind to the number of women who followed him around all the time. He was like the pied piper of the slaggy models, up-and-coming designers and the general population of single women in London. His 'I'm just a normal guy looking for love' routine had me feeling sceptical.

'You'll see,' he went on. 'One day you'll realise I'm for real, but by that point it'll be too late and Jennifer Lawrence will have already swept me off my feet.'

And with a kiss on the cheek for Jess, and a ruffling of the hair for me, he was gone.

'That lad,' I said, laughing.

'He likes you,' Jess said. 'It's obvious to everyone.'

'He likes *all women*,' I corrected. 'It's not about me.'

'Whatever you say,' Jess said. 'But maybe you should go on a date with him. Or anyone else. You know, it's been a while . . . '

Serial-dater Jess couldn't understand my lack of interest in men. And actually, it wasn't because I was uninterested, it was more that I hadn't met anyone who gave me that butterflies-in-the-stomach feeling you can't explain. And I was too busy with work and keeping up with my sketching to allow myself to be distracted by just anyone. It may sound like some silly fairytale but I know that that feeling exists – I know because I saw it between Mam and Dad every day when I was growing up. Mam worries that the way my biological father walked away from us may have had too much influence on my attitude towards men but that's not the case at all. I believe in love, marriage, soul mates, the works. But I'm not convinced you can meet your soul mate at a 2-4-1 mojito bar in Islington. I'm not interested in kissing a load of frogs before I meet my prince. I'd rather wait for him, so when he does come along I don't have stinky pond breath. At the end of the day I want what Mam and Dad had and I'm not settling for anything less.

But for now I just say to Jess, 'If things change for me in the way I hope they will, then I'll think about dating, OK?'

'Deal,' Jess said. 'Now can you tell me about today?'

'I will, but not here. Too many eager eavesdroppers.'

'You're right, let's get out of here. Are you hungry? Shall we grab some dinner?'

I suddenly realised that I'd barely had any lunch and as a result I was starving. No wonder the mojitos were going straight to my head.

'There's Wagamama's round the corner. I'll tell you everything over a chicken katsu.'

'Sounds like heaven after the day I've had,' Jess said.

I took in Jess's tired eyes and felt a pang of sympathy. She worked hard too and probably needed to let off a bit of steam as well.

'Come on then, little one. Let's go.'

Chapter Five

I flung open the front door to my home in Newcastle and shouted at the top of my voice, 'I'm hoooooooooooooooome!' Mam came out of the lounge and enveloped me in a hug.

'It's so good to see you. I've missed you.'

'Are you OK?' I asked, concerned. I pulled away and looked into her face. It wasn't like Mam to be this emotional.

'I'm fine,' she said, smiling sadly. 'But, you know, birthdays always make me think about your dad.'

My mam was still the rock in my life but she had become more fragile since Dad died. I was the spitting image of her and we were often mistaken for sisters but the last two years had taken their toll and now there was this thin layer of worry and sadness that surrounded her. I worried about Mam and Ruby so much and I often felt torn and guilty, wishing that I could spend more time at home.

'I know, Mam. Would the bottle of Prosecco I've got in my suitcase help?' My attempt at making my mam laugh worked.

'We can drink to your birthday and toast Dad at the same time. Where's Rubes?'

'She's at Maisie's down the road. She said she'd be home in a couple of hours but I'll give her a ring if she isn't.'

'How's she been lately?' I asked, shrugging off my jacket.

'Oh, we have our good days and bad days,' Mam said, leaning against the wall. 'We're going through a good spell at the moment so let's hope that lasts a while.'

'Teenagers, eh?' I joked. 'Bet you're glad I wasn't this bad.'

'You had your moments.' Mam raised her eyebrows. 'Now where's that fizz?'

As if I ever wondered where I got my love of alcohol from.

Mam and I were sat on the sofa, sipping our Prosecco and munching our way through a bar of Fruit & Nut, the TV humming in the background. We'd been chatting for over an hour and the conversation had moved on to Ruby.

'I worry about her,' Mam was saying. 'She's so quiet. I don't know what's going on inside that head of hers.'

'Isn't that normal teenage behaviour? Being a bit moody and introverted? Ignoring your mam? Thinking no one understands you and all that?'

'Maybe, but Ruby isn't a normal teenager, Amber. She's been through a rough time. She never talks about your dad, never tells me how she feels or if she's missing him. If she's not talking to me I want to know that she's talking to *someone* at least. It's not good to bottle these things up, you know.'

'We have the odd conversation about Dad,' I reassured her. 'Nothing major but we do talk about him sometimes.'

'You do? That's good.'

'Maybe,' I said slowly, knowing that what I was about to say was a sensitive subject, 'she doesn't want to talk to you about him because she thinks it's too painful for you.'

'She shouldn't be thinking like that! It's my job to protect her, both of you, not the other way around, for God's sake.'

'We're a team. We look after each other,' I said. 'We're Dad's three musketeers and that hasn't changed just because he's gone.'

'So young, so wise,' Mam said, smiling. 'Enough about that. What about you, pet? Any news on the job?'

'No,' I groaned. 'I haven't heard anything. Last week was hell. I can hardly concentrate on anything but checking my phone at Diana's palace of pain. I'm losing hope.'

'Now, come on, I didn't raise a quitter,' Mam said. 'Just because you haven't heard back yet doesn't mean you haven't got the job.'

'I suppose,' I said, draining my glass dry. 'It's just the longer I have to wait, the further away it seems. I want it so badly.'

'I know you do, love. And I want it for you too. It'll happen, even if it isn't straight away. One day you'll get the break you deserve.'

Just then, the door to the lounge opened and Ruby appeared. She smiled when she saw me.

'Rubes!' I jumped up and hugged her. She hugged me back and for a moment it was like old times, before she suddenly remembered to be cool and pushed me off.

'Gerroff, Amber,' she said, but she was smiling.

'How are you, kiddo?' I asked. I was constantly reminded of Dad every time I looked at her. She looked so much like him, with her dark hair and olive skin

'Argh, stop calling me that. I'm fourteen.'

'Sorry,' I said. I didn't want this to escalate into an argument. 'Force of habit. You OK? Did you have fun at Maisie's?'

'Yeah, it was all right.'

'You going to join us?' I asked.

'Nah, I'm knackered, I'm going to bed.'

'Well, rest up because we're all going shopping tomorrow afternoon for Mam's birthday and then I've booked us a table at Fat Buddha for dinner.'

'Sure, OK,' Ruby said, sounding bored. 'Night.'

'Night,' I called after Ruby's retreating back. I looked at Mam, who just raised her arms in despair.

'Ooohh, she's an insolent little shit, isn't she?' I laughed.

'Welcome to my world, pet.'

'Amber, are you sure?' Ruby asked me, wide-eyed and looking happier than she had all day. Mam and I had dragged her from shop to shop for the past three hours and she'd barely said a word. In a last-ditch attempt to force a smile from her, I'd made her try on a few things from the Kendall & Kylie range in Topshop and now I was insisting on buying her one of the pairs of skinny jeans and a couple of the tops. Yes, I was buying her affection; no, I couldn't really afford it on the pittance Diana paid me, but right now I'd do anything to make this afternoon a success and get a smile out of Ruby.

'Of course I'm sure,' I said. 'You looked great in everything you tried on – but these were the best.'

Mam threw a silent 'thank you' at me over Ruby's shoulder. She made a decent salary now but she still had to be careful and watch what she spent. She couldn't afford to splash out on things like this for Ruby and I knew she found that hard. I was happy to do it once in a while. Maybe one day I'd be able to look after Mam and Ruby properly, and Mam could finally relax and enjoy life after all the sacrifices she'd made for us.

After we left Topshop, we decided to call it a day on shopping. It was almost five p.m. and the table at Fat Buddha was booked for eight o'clock, so we needed to get going. Ruby chatted happily on the drive home and deciding which of her new clothes to wear to the restaurant. Mam said she could borrow a pair of her heels if she wanted and I thought Ruby was going to burst. Yep, today had been a good day.

The restaurant was lovely. Mam hates being the centre of attention so I knew it would be her idea of hell to get the waiters to come out at the end of the meal, carrying a birthday cake and singing happy birthday, but I'd had a quiet word with the hostess when we'd arrived and she'd sent over a complimentary bottle of Prosecco as a birthday gift instead. The barman had even created a bespoke mocktail for Ruby so she wouldn't have to drink water while we enjoyed the fizz.

'Amber,' Mam said gently. 'If Ruby isn't allowed her phone out at the table, the same goes for you.'

I looked up guiltily. 'Sorry,' I said, stuffing the phone back into my clutch. I had developed a habit of incessantly checking it to see if Alessandro had called. 'I was just—'

'Checking to see if you'd heard about the job. I know,' Mam said. 'But it's a Saturday night and I don't get the two of you to myself that often. Besides, I know you've got your bag on your lap and you'll feel your phone vibrate if it rings,' she added wryly. I could never get anything past her; I don't know why I still tried.

49

'OK, I'm back in the room,' I said.

'What job?' Ruby asked.

I did my best not to sound annoyed. I'd spent a lot of time that afternoon talking about Alessandro and the job. Hadn't she been listening? 'I had an interview a week ago for a junior designer position at another fashion house,' I said as patiently as I could manage. 'It could end up being a really big deal.'

'Oh, right, yeah. I remember now.'

Is she trying to wind me up? Mam and I exchanged a look and I bit back my retort. This was Mam's night; now wasn't the time for me and Ruby to get into it.

The rest of the meal passed without incident and we actually had a nice time. The food was delicious, the service was impeccable and Ruby and I teased Mam mercilessly when we realised that our very young waiter was flirting with her. It had been fun, and long overdue

When the bill arrived, Mam and I argued over who was going to pay it. I really wanted to pay for everything but she wouldn't let me and in the end we compromised and split it between us. I couldn't usually afford to splash the cash as I had done this weekend but I had a little saved up and it was worth it. It had been a great day and a fab night. It felt so good to be home. Now if only Alessandro would pull his finger out and let me know about the job, one way or another, I'd be completely content. Having it hanging over me like this, not knowing, was awful.

As if on cue, I felt my bag vibrate. I pulled out my phone – it was Alessandro. Mam glanced up and she took one look at my face and nodded at me to answer the phone.

50

'Hello?' I said, hoping I didn't sound too pissed. How much Prosecco had I had? *Focus, Amber,* I thought to myself.

'Amber, bella,' Alessandro's cheerful voice said.

'Alessandro, hey, how are you?'

'I'm fine, just fine. Can you talk?'

'Of course, give me a minute.' Mam gave me a thumbs-up as I quickly walked outside. 'I'm here,' I said breathlessly, as soon as I'd found a quiet corner.

'Sorry to call you on a Saturday evening but I've just got back from Paris. I've already kept you waiting while I was away and I thought it was unfair to keep you in suspense any longer.'

'Oh, don't worry, it hasn't been that long.' *Liar. It's felt like months, years, decades, you cruel man! Why would you do this to me? OK, Amber, that was a tad melodramatic.*

'Good, good. So, I very much liked your work, and more importantly I like you. My board of directors is impressed by your sketches too and although your style is not exactly what we were thinking for the new range, we are *fiduciosi* that you can adapt and work with my team to do what we need.'

'Eh? Fid what?' I asked.

'Confident, bella. We have confidence in you.'

'Yes, I can adapt. I'm like the chameleon of designers.' *The chameleon of designers? Really, Amber? What the hell are you even saying?*

'What is this chameleon?' asked Alessandro, sounding confused.

'It's a, erm, sort of small lizard thing. Yeah, it changes colour according to its surroundings. I think it's a defence mechanism – I saw a documentary about it. They're fascinating creatures actually.' *All right David Attenborough, give it a rest*

will you? What are you doing lecturing him about the animal planet?
He's going to think you're a nutcase. Get back on track!

'Amber, why are you telling me about this lizard?'

Oh no, Alessandro was completely lost now. *That's it, you've done it now, he thinks you're a weirdo.*

'Ah, sorry Alessandro. I was just trying to explain that I'm super-adaptable and I'm pretty confident I can do what you need me to do too.' *Nice save, Raey. But wait, am I being offered the job here?* I felt my knees go weak.

Alessandro laughed. 'That's all I needed to hear. The job is yours. Welcome to House of Rossi!'

'Fuck, yeah!' I screamed without thinking.

Alessandro chuckled down the phone. 'Does this mean you're saying yes?'

'Yes! Absolutely. Yes with knobs on.'

'I am very happy for the knobs. Call Laurie next week and we will sort out your contract and start date. Welcome to the family, bella.'

'Thank you, thank you, thank you!' I couldn't believe this was actually happening. I was so happy I couldn't even think about the fact that Alessandro had just said he was 'happy for the knobs', which normally I would have found particularly hilarious.

'*Prego. Ciao* Amber.'

I ran back into the restaurant. Mam had seen me come in and was already halfway out of her seat.

'Did you get it?'

'I did!' I shrieked. 'I got the job!'

Mam hugged me hard. 'I'm so proud of you, pet. I knew you could do it, I knew it. My little superstar!'

'Yeah, nice one,' Ruby said with a small smile.

Mam looked at her watch. 'It's a little on the late side but I'm going to ring round and see if I can get a few people to come over and help us celebrate. You OK with that?'

'Yes,' I said. Right now I was OK with anything.

'Can I invite Maisie over?' Ruby said.

'Only if her mam says that it's OK,' Mam said. 'C'mon, girls, we've got some celebrating to do.'

It was two a.m. and there was no sign of the party slowing down. Mam and Dad would often have friends over and a quiet dinner would soon escalate into something more raucous, with more and more people turning up. Ruby and I would be running around as well, watching the happy, drunk adults having the time of their lives. Those kinds of evenings had almost disappeared since Dad died, but looking around now, it felt like old times. My mam's best friend Liz and her husband Billy were there. She'd hit the Pinot pretty hard already and Billy was having to prop her up. My Uncle Jimmy was throwing some serious shapes, and even Betty, our eighty-year-old neighbour, was looking rosy-cheeked as she merrily sipped away at her sherry. Ruby and Maisie had disappeared upstairs just after midnight and we hadn't seen them since. Mam was working the room, making sure everyone's drinks were topped up, and telling everyone who'd listen how proud she was of me. I clutched my feather necklace. There was only one person missing.

'Amber, love.' Betty called me over to where she was sitting. Mam was perched on the armrest. 'Your mam was just telling me about this Diana woman who work for. She sounds like a right miserable old bag.'

'She's horrible,' I said. 'But I'm not going to be working for her for much longer.'

'Thank goodness for that,' Betty said.

'How do you think she'll take it?' Mam asked.

'She'll be thrilled,' I said. 'Over the moon. Couldn't be happier for me.' *This is going to go down like a sack of shite*, I thought.

Chapter Six

'AMBER!' Jess shouted.

I sat bolt upright in bed. 'Not again?' I groaned.

'You're going to have to be a better timekeeper in your new job,' she said.

'Being on time just isn't my thing.'

'Up!' Jess pulled the duvet off me. 'Today's the big day. If Diana is going to kill you, you should at least make sure your outfit is on fleek while she does it.'

'I'm up, I'm up. And don't say 'on fleek', for God's sake. You're training to be a solicitor.' I stretched and yawned.

'I reckon I can pull it off. I'm cool, I'm down with the kids,' Jess replied, laughing.

'No, Jess. We are not "down with the kids". Face it, we're past it and therefore should not be bandying around terms like "on fleek".'

'Someone woke up on the wrong side of the bed this morning, didn't they?' Jess joked. 'Get up, get dressed and go and hand your notice in, you moody cow. And once that's over you can cheer up, please! You're about to be the next big thing in the fashion world, missus. Act like it rather than whinging about my vocab of choice.' Jess was right. I was snappy because I was nervous about today.

On the one hand, I couldn't wait to hand in my notice. But on the other, I was terrified of Diana's reaction. She wasn't exactly known for being rational. She once threw her stapler at an assistant because they brought her a normal latte rather than a decaf.

I showered and dressed in record time. Thankfully I didn't have to worry about what I was going to wear as I'd already chosen my outfit the previous evening. It was a knee-length pinafore that I had made out of some blue vintage fabric, with a little white shirt underneath. As soon as I was ready I joined Jess in the lounge. As usual, she was looking immaculate and had not only made herself a decent breakfast, but had made me eggs and toast as well. *How does she do it?* I thought.

'When I grow up I want to be just like you,' I laughed. 'What do you think?' I gave her a twirl.

'Perfect. Now drink your coffee, eat your breakfast and go tell that bitch where to stick her job – up her pretentious arsehole.'

'Strong.' I laughed and we clinked coffee cups.

I pushed open the door to the building, immediately feeling the blast of the air-conditioning. That was another thing I wouldn't miss. Why Diana insisted on keeping the air-con up so high was beyond me. We froze our bollocks off every day for no reason. *Not for long*, I thought. *I'm getting out of here.*

I stepped into the lift and hit the button for the sixth floor.

56

The lift was red inside with gorgeous Venetian mirrors. It was funny, but now I knew I was leaving I wanted to memorise everything about the place. I may have had a miserable time but I still wanted to remember my first job in a design house. I'd come here to interview for the job as the great Diana Grant's second assistant because I'd known that I had to leave the fashion magazine and work for a well-respected designer if I ever wanted to design myself. A contact had tipped me off that Diana was looking for someone, though at the same time she'd warned me that she was a total cow to work for. But I hadn't listened. I wanted the job so badly that I'd convinced myself she couldn't be that bad.

And I was right, she wasn't. She was worse.

Paddy was already at his desk, which was just outside Diana's office. My desk was a little further along, but still safely within shouting distance.

'Hi, Paddy,' I said.

'Amber,' he replied. He barely looked at me.

'I need to see Diana,' I announced. That made him look up.

'She's busy,' he replied after a cursory check of her diary.

'It's urgent,' I said firmly. I had to do this now. I'd only worry about it all day otherwise.

Paddy sighed and picked up the phone. Diana was all of ten metres away, on the other side of the door. *Would it kill you to get up and use your legs for a change?* I couldn't wait to put this place and this sycophantic little tosser behind me.

'Diana,' he gushed. *Stiletto-licker*, I thought. 'I am *so* sorry to bother you, but Amber is saying that she needs to see you urgently.' There was a silence, and then Paddy nodded his head a few times before hanging up. He fixed me with a steely gaze. 'She'll be with you in a minute, but she says if it's not urgent you're fired.'

Too late for that, I thought. *One more hurdle and then she can't hurt me any more.*

Eventually, and with a huge sigh, Paddy led me into Diana's office. Despite myself, I was still impressed by the amount of glamour this room exuded. A floor-to-ceiling window ran along the back of the room, and her desk was carved from a heavy piece of mahogany and was simply stunning. Huge canvases decorated the walls – an eclectic mix of modern and vintage. Diana had style, I had to admit that. Lulu was asleep in her dog bed – which probably cost more than the flat Jess, Tom and I lived in – in the corner of the room, snoring loudly.

'Amber, what do you want?' she asked coldly.

'Hi, Diana.' I smiled broadly. 'I am so sorry to bother you, but I wanted to tell you as soon as possible. I've been offered another job so I'm handing in my notice.' There you go. Quick and moderately painless, like pulling off a plaster. I put the letter that Jess had helped me compose down on the desk and tried to quickly back out of stapler range.

'Excuse me?' Diana looked at me through narrowed eyes.

'I'm leaving.' I smiled again.

'And why, may I ask, would anyone want leave me?'

Why don't you ask your three ex-husbands that? No, no, Amber, be professional. This is the last hurdle. You can do this.

'Like I said, I've been offered another job,' I repeated. 'And I've accepted. It's what I've always wanted – I'm going to be designing clothes for a new label.'

'What?' Diana's voice had risen to a level that Paddy was sure to be able to hear from his desk. She wasn't going to make this easy for me. 'You are my second assistant, so there is no way you can take on design work for a new label. I've seen nothing from you that would convince me you're ready for such a move. This is ridiculous. No one would take a risk on such a *nobody*, unless you're going to work for someone completely insignificant and incompetent.'

Her words stung but I wasn't going to let her see how much I was hurt by what she'd said. I had admired this woman from afar for years and I was crushed when I realised that she was actually nothing but a vicious and bitter old bint who thrived on putting others down and exploiting her position of power. Even after all this time as her assistant, being treated the way she had treated me, her complete disregard for me still shocked me and hurt me, but I pressed on. I kept my voice clear and crisp. 'When I came to work here, I told you I wanted to design. You said that if I worked hard I might get the chance to do that here one day but you won't even look at my sketches. You've never taken the time to teach me anything. Well, luckily for me a completely significant designer did look at my designs and he does want to teach me. I'm going to work for House of Rossi.' I smiled in satisfaction.

'Rossi?' Diana's voice was tight with anger. 'Alessandro Rossi?'

'Yeah, it's mad isn't it? Me, helping to design a range for House of Rossi, one of the best fashion houses in the world, with Alessandro as my mentor.' I was enjoying myself now.

'You're lying.' Diana couldn't even look at me. 'Alessandro wouldn't employ you. You're a lowly assistant. You're not even a very good one.'

I sighed. This wasn't getting us anywhere. 'Diana, it's done.

Alessandro's offered me the job, I've accepted and now I'm handing in my notice.'

Diana stood up and walked slowly around her desk, never taking her eyes off me. 'I gave you an amazing opportunity and this is how you repay me? After everything I've done for you! I knew I should never have taken a chance on someone like you.'

'What do you mean, someone like me?' I said quietly.

'Someone so *common* has no place in the fashion world.' Diana's voice was dripping with venom.

I wanted nothing more than to rip her eyes out at that moment but I'd been raised better than that. I was taking the high road. However, that didn't mean I was going down without a fight.

'I was grateful for the job, Diana, and I've always admired your talent. But I've worked my bollocks off for you and you don't let me do anything but dog-sit and pick up your dry cleaning. I saved that outfit at your show during London Fashion Week and you didn't even thank me.'

'You didn't save anything! Do you know how many would kill to work for me? You ungrateful little—'

'Right then,' I interrupted. I had no desire to hear the end of that sentence. 'As lovely as this has been, I'm going to leave. I know I should give you a month's notice, but as I'm going to a competitor's house I assume you'd rather I left straight away.'

'I don't want you anywhere near me or my work! Get out of here now and don't ever think about coming back!'

Before I knew what was happening she'd taken off one of her Louboutins and had thrown it across the room towards me. Thankfully she had a crap aim and it missed my head, but I still couldn't believe that had happened. Did she really just throw a *shoe* at me? Is that better or worse than a stapler? And why did she love throwing things so much?

'You're a fruit loop,' I said, laughing, not caring about the high road any more. 'I'm well rid of you and this place. Goodbye, Diana.'

'GET OUT OF MY OFFICE!' Diana screamed.

I turned on my heel and walked out. *Well, that went better than expected. I need a gin.*

PART TWO

Chapter Seven

I chewed the end of my pencil and cast a critical eye over the sketch I'd just finished. It was a backless playsuit in a bold print. It had a real sixties vibe but with a modern twist, I'd liked the idea when I'd first started work on it, though now I'd been staring at it so long I wasn't sure. I was just *so* tired. I rubbed my eyes, pushed my hair off my face and looked out of the window for inspiration. It was only then that I realised that it was pitch black outside – how long had I been working on this? I had no idea.

It was the second week of May and I'd been working at House of Rossi for several weeks already. Time had whizzed by without me noticing – the work was hard, the hours were long and I was exhausted all the time. But it was a happy exhaustion and I was loving the challenge. My days had purpose, I was finally doing the thing that I loved and the passion that had become almost dormant while I was working for Diana had come alive again. The new line for the concession in Selfridges was launching in the autumn and it was my job to work with the more senior designers and help them shape the range into something women in their twenties would want to wear. Alessandro had also given me the freedom to work on my own designs for the range. He kept a close eye on my work but he was never territorial or too harsh. For the first time I felt like I had a real mentor, someone I could learn from.

The office door swung open and Freddie, my assistant, appeared. Well, he wasn't just my assistant, I shared him with the whole junior design team, but still, I'd never had an assistant of any kind before. It was pretty exciting, although I tried to play it cool. Freddie was such a top bloke – straight out of university, already amazingly good at his job, and a real sweetheart. Not that he looked that sweet – he was all ripped jeans, piercings and platinum-blond hair. We had quickly established a close working relationship, and there had been many a day I wouldn't have been able to get through without him.

'Amber, have you turned into a vampire when we weren't looking? Do you need me to find you a coffin for the office?' I laughed at the stern look he was giving me. Freddie definitely kept me in check, and while I knew his job was to do all those menial tasks I'd hated, I tried to include him in the more creative side as well. He had a great eye and a sharp tongue so I knew I'd always get honest feedback from him. The memory of how Diana had treated me was still fresh and I was determined to make sure Freddie felt valued by me.

'Babes, I'm so sorry. I didn't realise you were still here. I completely lost track of time. You should've left hours ago. You don't have to wait for me.' I felt constantly guilty about the long hours Freddie put in, largely because he didn't feel he could leave when there was still a designer in the office.

'I like to get everything finished before I leave. Anyway, if I went home at a civilised time, then who would be here to remind you that there is a world outside of House of Rossi? Do you remember the outside? The blue sky? And wine, lots of wine?' He gestured to the black sky.

'That's the worst thing you've ever said to me,' I said, placing a hand over my heart. 'Of course I remember wine!' I laughed. 'And you should know by now that this is my world.' I was joking, but I had to admit that this place had become my actual world – and I wouldn't have it any other way.

'Perhaps, but it's time to leave. How about we clean up this bomb site of an office and head over to Jalou for a quick drink? You can buy me a JD and Coke to make up for being such a slave driver.'

'You're on. But, really, the mess isn't as bad as it looks.' I looked around at all the debris that covered most of the floor. To anyone else it looked like chaos, but to me it was *organised* chaos. I couldn't work at my desk. I preferred to spread out on the floor, with everything surrounding me and within easy reach. Alessandro shook his head in despair every time he was in my office. He said it was an unorthodox way to work but who was he to try to change my habits?

Freddie and I started piling things up, and as I flicked through the sketches I'd been working on that day a shiver of excitement went through me. I honestly believed this is what I was made for. Nothing else made me feel like this. For a fleeting moment I wondered if any man would come close to satisfying me like this.

Freddie nudged me out of my reverie. 'Penny for them?' he said.

I gave myself a mental shake. 'They're not worth a penny, mate. I think we've tidied up enough. Shall we go get that drink?'

Freddie cocked his head to one side and looked at me critically. 'You might want to visit the ladies first. Your hair is doing . . . ' He waved his hands above his head dramatically. I had no idea what that meant and guessing this he elaborated. 'You look like Frankie Cocozza after a mad one, love. Sort it out or I'm taking you nowhere.'

'Cheeky twat. OK, OK,' I said, laughing. 'Give me a minute. I'll meet you by the lifts.'

I looked at myself in the bathroom mirror in horror. It turns out Freddie was being kind – in reality, I looked terrible. My hair was definitely doing some weird bird's nest thing, but my face was just as bad. I was pale and the dark circles under my eyes were evident. I looked like I hadn't seen the sun in weeks – which I hadn't. I tied my hair up, pulling it back into a messy bun, and quickly slapped some foundation on. I brushed some blusher onto the apples of my cheeks and slicked on some lipgloss. I didn't look great but I wouldn't scare children any more. It would have to do.

I met Freddie by the lifts, who I'm sure visibly relaxed when he saw that I no longer looked like Frankie C, and we waved goodbye to the last few people left in the office. One of the first things that had struck me when I'd started working here was how happy everyone was. It was a million miles away from the paranoid, bitchy and tense atmosphere that Diana had created. I'd become so used to being shouted down or ignored at every opportunity that it had taken me a while to realise that wasn't going to happen here.

The designers helped one another, bounced ideas off each other, and I marvelled at the collaborative spirit Alessandro had fostered. It had been easy to make friends, and while none of us had that much time to socialise after work, I felt at home here and looked forward to work every day. I finally felt like I belonged somewhere.

Freddie and I pushed our way through the Thursday night crowd that had gathered at Jalou, and we made our way to the bar. We shouted hello to those people we knew and nodded at those we recognised. One thing I'd noticed since working at House of Rossi was that people who hadn't given me the time of day before were now going out of their way to say hello and were trying to strike up a conversation with me. That was something I hadn't been expecting but I'd quickly become adept at sidestepping those people. I was never rude, and always spent a few minutes with them, but I didn't have time for such blatant ladder-climbing. I had so little free time these days that I just wanted to see my friends, the real ones, in the precious moments I did get to myself.

I spotted Jess sitting on a stool at the bar. She was chatting with Tom, who was clearly slipping her the odd free drink. I felt a pang as I realised how little I'd seen them over the last few weeks.

'We made it!' Freddie announced dramatically, giving Jess and a perturbed-looking Tom a quick kiss on the cheek. Freddie had only met my flatmates a handful of times but he was easy to like and they'd all bonded pretty quickly. Tom wasn't quite used to the cheek-kissing yet but he was getting there.

'Hello!' I said cheerfully, giving both of them a quick hug.

'One JD and Coke, one large rosé and two shots of tequila please,' Freddie said to Tom.

'Whoa, steady there,' I said quickly, as Tom turned away to get the drinks. 'We said a quick *one*. I have a lot of work to do tomorrow.'

'C'mon,' Jess said. 'Have a proper drink with us. I feel like I haven't seen you in ages.'

Tom lined up the drinks and shots on the bar and raised his eyebrows. 'Fine, but you'll have to cover for me with Alessandro tomorrow if I go in stinking of booze and looking like I've been dragged through a hedge backwards,' I said to Freddie.

We tossed back the tequila and as soon as the sharp liquid hit my throat I felt myself loosen up a little bit. Maybe I did need this.

Freddie spotted some friends, and with a wave and another round of cheek kisses he was gone. I settled down on the empty stool next to Jess.

'I only see you in here these days,' Jess said, pouting slightly.

'That's not true,' I said. 'I see you at home all the time.' I looked at my friend closely. She looked upset and I suddenly worried it was because I'd been neglecting her. 'I'm sorry, I know I haven't been around much. I've been so crazy busy at work.'

'No, I'm sorry. Ignore me. I just had a crap day.'

'What happened?' I asked, concerned.

'Some of our notes for this big case we're working on went

missing, and my boss blamed me. I spent most of the day ransacking the building trying to find them only for them to turn up in *his* desk drawer. I barely got an apology and he didn't acknowledge that I'd lost most of the day looking for notes he had the entire time. I've got so much on, I really didn't need it today,' Jess explained. She didn't look angry, just sad and tired. I wasn't the only one working long hours.

'What a twat,' I said, giving her a hug. 'Did you give him what for?'

'Sort of. I told him I was sick of being blamed for everything that went wrong, even when it's not my fault. He looked so angry I thought he might fire me.'

'But he didn't?' I asked.

'No, but it was only after I'd made a fuss that he apologised. It wasn't exactly heartfelt, but it's more than I have been getting recently. I've only just calmed down – I was in a right state when I got here.'

'I've been helping,' Tom called over the bar as he put another couple of drinks down in front of us. He ruffled Jess's hair and I managed to dive out of the way before he could do the same to me. My hair looked bad enough as it was.

'Forget him, Jess. You work hard, you do a good job. Everyone can see that. You'll not have to put up with that forever and in the meantime, spit in his coffee. Sexist turd.' We both laughed and I sensed Jess relax a little. 'So what have I missed so far tonight?' I asked Tom, looking around the bar.

'You just missed Jamie. He left about half an hour ago – he said he was going to get an early night because he's got this big casting tomorrow apparently,' Tom said dramatically.

'Right,' I said. 'Or was he just taking someone home and he told you not to tell me?'

Tom looked confused. 'What? No, he left alone. He's got this casting . . .'

'He doesn't sleep around as much as you think, you know,' Jess said pointedly.

I raised an eyebrow. 'Did he ask you to say that to me?'

'Not in so many words,' Jess went on, looking guilty. 'He thinks you have the wrong impression of him.'

'I don't think I do, but, whatever,' I said, changing the subject. 'I haven't seen either of you properly in ages, what else has been going on?'

'Jess and I were just talking about my birthday party,' Tom said with a grin. He loved his birthdays.

My mind went blank. I knew Tom's birthday was coming up but had I been so preoccupied I'd missed the part where we'd organised a party? 'Er, what birthday party?' I asked.

'The one I've just decided to have on my birthday, Saturday after next. I've got the night off so I'm thinking house party at ours. Jess is in. Sound OK to you?'

'Sounds great,' I said. As if I'd say no to Tom or to a party. 'What's the theme?'

'We don't have one yet,' Jess answered, slurring slightly. *Ha, I love drunk Jess.*

'A PJ party!' Tom yelled. 'It's *got* to be a pyjama party!'

'Is that your way of legitimately perving on lots of women in sexy lingerie?' Even when she was pissed, Jess could get straight to the point and say five-syllable words. I could barely say them sober.

Tom grinned. 'You know me so well. It's one step away from an underwear party. You know what, maybe—'

'No way,' Jess and I said at the same time.

'Fine, PJs it is,' Tom said, holding his hands up. 'I'll WhatsApp everyone later. It's is going to be epic.'

'As long as you two don't leave me to do all the cleaning up again,' Jess said, pointing at me and Tom accusingly, and looking at us through drunk, narrowed eyes.

If I'd been less tired I might have been quick enough to fire back a response but it wasn't happening. Besides, Jess was right. Every time we had a party at our flat, Tom and I would spend most of the following day sleeping off our hangovers. By the time we emerged clean freak Jess would already have cleared everything away.

'OK, weasel eyes, promise we'll do better this time,' Tom said. 'Right, my shift is just about done. Fancy grabbing a pizza on the way home?'

'Sounds good,' I said, yawning. 'Let me say bye to Freddie.'

I found Freddie huddled in a corner with an attractive male model. I didn't want to interrupt so I caught his eye and waved to him that I was leaving. He nodded back and winked, looking pretty pleased with himself. I gave him a thumbs up and then Tom and I set off on the journey home, with a hammered Jess in between us. Jess didn't often get this drunk but she was hilariously affectionate when she was. If she told me and Tom she loved us any more, one of us would have to marry her.

I ducked into our local pizza place and grabbed the pepperoni pizzas Tom had had the sense to call ahead for. I left him outside with Jess, who was almost asleep on his shoulder. I looked at them through the window, amused. It wasn't often Tom was sober enough to help anyone home. He could barely get himself home most nights.

Back in the flat, I grabbed some plates and napkins, but by

the time I'd carried everything through to the living area Jess had already passed out, and was snoring – like a baby elephant, I might add – on the sofa.

'We'd better get her into bed, pet,' I said to Tom. He nodded, picked her up as though she was no heavier than a child, and carried her to her room. We tucked her in, and I put a glass of water next to her bed, along with some Berocca. *That should see her right in the morning.* It always worked for me. Tom and I looked down at her, like parents would a sleeping child.

'She looks so peaceful,' I whispered.

'Nice to see her without a frown on her face for change,' Tom said as we slipped out of her room and shut the door quietly behind us.

'Has work been that bad?' I asked.

'Yeah, mate,' Tom went on. 'She's been having a hard time over the last few weeks.'

'Shit,' I said. 'I should've been there for her.'

'You've been busy too. Don't beat yourself up,' Tom said kindly.

'It's no excuse,' I said. As much as I loved my new job, I needed to make time for the important people in my life. Especially the ones who'd been there when things hadn't been going so well. *I have to be a better friend,* I thought. *And I will be.*

Chapter Eight

I rushed out of my office, almost catching my heel. I was late for a meeting with Alessandro. Freddie had already had to remind me about it twice that morning. My time-keeping had definitely improved since I'd started working at House of Rossi, but I was still pretty close to the wire some of the time. Jess was having to wake me up less often, though, and that was a massive win for me as far as I was concerned.

I try to call Mam and Ruby as soon as I get into work every morning as I could usually catch them before they left the house. It had become an important part of my routine and it meant a lot that I was able to keep to it. Once I got stuck into work I lost all track of time so if I hadn't got the routine in place I'd never have spoken to Mam. That morning the conversation had been longer than usual as Ruby had actually been quite chatty on the phone. I hadn't wanted to be the one to cut it short, which was why

I was now doing my best Usain Bolt impression towards Alessandro's office.

'Laurie,' I said breathlessly when I reached her desk. 'So sorry I'm late. Has he been waiting long?'

'You're all right,' she said. 'I put a call through about ten minutes ago. He's still on the phone so technically he's keeping you waiting.'

'Thank fuck for that,' I said flopping down on a chair. 'Or rather, thank you for that, mate.'

Laurie smiled at me. She and I had become friendly quickly. She was a top lass, smart and efficient, and she kept Alessandro's life running smoothly. I'd learnt a lot from her about the business side of things. I had no idea how much work went into running a business as big as House of Rossi. All those numbers and spreadsheets made my head swim. Give me a sketchbook and pencil any day.

I'd also learnt a bit about Alessandro through Laurie. He liked to keep his private matters, well, private, so I hadn't know much about his personal life when I started working for him. I'd known that he lived with his boyfriend, Leonardo, who was drop-dead gorgeous and an ex-model. They'd been together for ten years. What I hadn't known was that he spoke to his parents, who lived in Italy, every Friday morning, that he was the kindest employer Laurie had ever had, and he had a soft spot for Ben & Jerry's Phish Food ice cream and Julia Roberts films. Who knew?

'So Amber, what's new on the man scene?' Laurie smiled at me mischievously. She always asked me this.

'Nothing has been down there in months, pet. In fact, it's probably dusty by now,' I laughed.

'Thanks for the visual, babes,' Laurie joked. 'I know I've

76

said this before, but I'm serious. My boyfriend Alex has loads of single friends. I could easily set you up with one of them. Or more than one . . . '

'And I keep saying that I'm OK for the time being,' I insisted. 'Maybe once the collection has launched, eh?' I added. I didn't want to appear ungrateful.

'I'll hold you to that.'

'What are you holding?' Alessandro asked, appearing in his doorway.

'I'm going to set up Amber with a friend,' Laurie declared.

I winced. We were all fond of Alessandro but he was still our boss. We didn't have to share everything with him.

Alessandro laughed. 'Yes, romance is important. I'll hold *you* to that, Laurie. Amber, bella, you should always make time for love. You ready?'

I stood up, grateful for the subject change. 'I am,' I said.

Alessandro's office was comfortable, made for creativity, with soft chairs and big cushions. It was the opposite of Diana's highly stylish work space and I much preferred Alessandro's relaxed vibe. There was a door in the corner that led to Alessandro's private studio. That was where he did all of his designing and no one, not even Laurie, was allowed in there.

'So, Amber,' Alessandro said, 'I'm very pleased with your work so far. The senior designers have been very impressed by your input into the new range and there are a couple of your own designs I like very much. I think they need some small amendments though. Here, take a look. See what you think.'

I walked around the desk and stood next to Alessandro so that I could see his computer screen. I gasped. My designs looked so . . . professional. Seeing them sitting alongside the rest of what had been confirmed for the line, well, it was what I'd been waiting for.

'I love what you've done to them,' I said excitedly. I pointed at the screen. 'Just straightening that line there makes the skirt look more elegant. And the change in neckline to the dress is genius.'

'Good, I'm glad you approve,' Alessandro said. 'These two pieces are confirmed for the Selfridges range, then.'

'What?' I yelled. I hugged Alessandro. 'Are you serious? I can't believe this!'

'Believe it, bella,' Alessandro said, patting me on the back. 'You're doing great work. I told you you'd have a real say in how this range looked and I meant it.' He clapped his hands excitedly. 'Everything is shaping up nicely. We'll move these pieces on to sample stage now.'

'I've had some ideas about fabrics,' I said. 'Maybe if we—'

'Relax, Amber,' Alessandro said laughing. 'There is time for that. We have that meeting tomorrow afternoon. Come prepared and we'll listen to all ideas then. Right now I wanted to see the new sketches you've been working on. Did you bring them?'

'Yes, here they are.' I handed over my book and felt that familiar pang of nervous excitement as Alessandro started flicking through the pages. His opinion meant everything.

We were launching in the autumn and we'd only signed off half of the designs so far. There was still so much work to do and I wanted at least a few of my designs to be good enough to be included. If I did well, maybe Alessandro would let me take the lead on the next collection. *Easy now, Amber*, I said to myself. *One step at a time.*

'These are good,' Alessandro mused. 'Let me have a closer look and we'll discuss again in a few days. But there are many designs here, bella. You are still making time for fun, yes?'

I blinked, not sure what to say. 'Er, yes.' *What a lie*, I thought. *The odd drink in Jalou doesn't really count and let's face it, the only sausage I've been close to in months is the pepperoni on my weekly pizza binge.*

Alessandro looked at me seriously. 'You have talent, bella, but you are also young. There is time for work and there is time for play.'

'I know that,' I said. 'I'm just making the most of this opportunity.'

'And that is good, but you are also an artist. You need inspiration to make your work stand out. And inspiration comes from the world, from living. You understand what I'm saying to you?'

'I think so. You want me to have fun?'

'I want you to *live*,' Alessandro said. 'Be inspired and be inspiring.'

'OK,' I said. I wasn't entirely sure what Alessandro was getting at but it sounded like he wanted me to drink more and that was something I could easily get on board with.

'Good.' He looked at his watch. 'Oh, I'm late! I need to go. You go too, and put that inspiration to work.'

'Where's he off to?' I asked Laurie as I watched Alessandro hurry down the corridor. Laurie was checking her make-up in her compact.

'He's casting for the new menswear campaign. I have the *terrible* job of sitting next to him while he interviews a bunch of gorgeous male models.' *That explains the make-up check,* I

79

thought. 'I'll save one for you,' Laurie said with a wink before heading off after Alessandro.

I headed towards the lifts and waited for one to take me back down to my floor. The doors opened and to my surprise Jamie stepped out.

'Geordio Armani!' he said, grinning and engulfing me in a bear hug. 'It feels like forever since I've seen that face of yours.'

'Hey J, it's good to see you. What are you doing here?'

'Big casting for Alessandro Rossi.'

'Oh!' I said, the penny dropping. *He really did have a casting,* I thought. *I shouldn't have assumed the worst.* 'If only I'd known you were coming I could have put a good word in.'

'And if I ever saw you these days, I could've asked you for that favour,' he teased.

'I know, I know. I'm always here, but I love it. I'm finally designing and I couldn't be happier, babe.'

'That's good, but we all miss you. *I* miss you.'

I smiled up at him. He sounded sincere. Maybe . . . I gave myself a mental shake. *He's a model. He knows exactly what buttons to push.* 'I bet you don't miss me having a go at you about your bed-hopping and corridor-creeping all the time,' I said.

'I don't take half of what you say seriously, Raey,' Jamie said, a smile playing at his lips. 'It's schoolyard flirting tekkers. I think it's cute.'

'Keep telling yourself that, babe.' I couldn't help but giggle. *When did I get that function? I swear I have never giggled in my life.* 'Well, you never know, maybe we'll get together one day and live happily ever after.'

'I'll hold you to that.'

'Aren't you going to be late for the casting?' I said.

'Yeah, I should go.' He looked nervous.

'You all right, pet?'

'I really want this, Amber,' Jamie said quietly. 'Modelling for Rossi could be a real game-changer for me.'

'Babes, come here,' I said, reaching up and pulling him into a hug. 'Just go in there and do the best you can. Alessandro is a fair man. He's bound to spot your potential when he sees your package in boxers.'

Jamie burst out laughing and wrapped his arms around my waist a little tighter and a shiver ran down my spine. 'I hope so. You always know the right things to say, you little sort,' he whispered.

I pulled away and awkwardly laughed off the moment. Jamie and I didn't do intense. *Best to keep things light*, I thought.

I pressed the lift button again. 'Go and get that job, and then we'll have something to celebrate. Are you coming to Tom's birthday party?'

'Definitely,' he said, clearly deciding to let the moment pass as well. 'You won't be able to resist me in my bedroom attire.'

The lift doors opened and I stepped in. 'What's your bedroom attire, then?' I asked.

'Nothing,' Jamie said as the lift doors closed. 'I sleep naked!'

God help me.

Chapter Nine

'Present time!' Jess and I yelled in unison.

Tom came thundering out of his room, dressed in his Olaf from *Frozen* onesie. *What a knob! I hope he never grows up*, I thought affectionately.

It was eight-thirty on the night of Tom's birthday party. People would be arriving from nine but Jess and I had decided to give Tom his gifts before the party started. The fruit punch – fruit punch Amber-style: Malibu and Archers with a splash of pineapple juice – had been made, the vodka jelly was ready, and we'd bought enough tequila to render a small country sozzled.

'Guys,' he said as he looked at the stack of presents on the coffee table, 'you didn't have to get me anything. But seeing as you did, GIVE ME THE PRESENTS!'

We laughed as Tom began ripping open present after present with the enthusiasm and gusto of an eight-year-old at Christmas. After each one he opened there was a cheer of 'thank you', 'omg you shouldn't have' and 'fuck off! I can't believe you got me this!' It was cute to see him so happy. Jess and I had clubbed together and, thanks to my amazing staff discount, we'd managed to pull in a decent haul. There were a couple of the more casual House of Rossi shirts that were perfect for Tom's laid-back style, and a bottle of Rossi cologne. Then we'd got him some silly stuff too – fake plastic moustaches, an apron with a pair of boobies on, some Haribo (Tangfastics, obvs) and some Disney DVDs. What can I say? He loves a good Disney film. He's a fanny.

'I love everything!' He was wearing a big bushy moustache from the pack, so no one would be able to take him seriously at all. 'I love you guys.' He lunged at us both, plastering us with wet, sloppy kisses.

'Argh, geroff,' Jess said, laughing.

'You melt,' I said, finally escaping from his sloppy, hairy-lipped clutches. We pretended to be annoyed, but Tom was so excitable tonight I knew there'd be no reining him in.

Time to have some of that fun Alessandro was talking about, I thought.

Tom had tried to get Jess and me to wear some sexy lingerie but we weren't having any of it. Jess was in an oversized Topshop nightshirt that read 'hangover daze' across the front and I'd opted for my favourite Victoria's Secret shorts and T-shirt set. They were grey and white, and while I wasn't going to be snapping any necks tonight in the sexy stakes, it was comfy. This evening was about letting my hair down, having a drink and enjoying myself – comfy attire was exactly what I needed.

Tom's party playlist was blasting out from the iPod dock and we'd spent half of the afternoon blowing up balloons. I was certain that none of them would last the night but Tom had insisted, and what the birthday boy wanted the birthday boy got. Having extricated myself from Tom's slobbery grasp I took a sip of my glass of rosé. Jess topped us both up as soon as I'd finished drinking.

'Here's to the best flatmates ever,' Tom said, raising his bottle of Corona.

'Are you including yourself in that?' I teased as we all clinked drinks.

'Naturally,' he said, smiling. Just then, Jess's phone beeped.

'Who's that?' I asked, curious.

'Sam,' she said shyly. 'He's coming later.' Tom looked at Jess in surprise and she blushed slightly.

'He is?' Tom said. 'I thought you weren't going to invite him?'

'Who's Sam?' I asked. I'd been with Jess all day and she hadn't mentioned any lad.

'We've been on a few dates,' she said. 'I invited him when we were out earlier this week. I might have been a bit drunk.'

'Wait,' I said. 'You mean you've been seeing this guy for a while and didn't tell me?' Jess usually told me everything. And I can't remember the last time she'd been on more than two dates with a bloke before she'd decided to move on.

'It's early days,' Jess explained. 'I haven't really seen you apart from that night in Jalou, and I didn't want to make a big deal out of it by WhatsApping you about him. But I think I might really like him.'

'That's great, babes,' I said, trying to ignore the stab of jealousy I felt that Jess had shared something with Tom that she hadn't with me. I pushed the feeling away. *This is not about you,* I told myself. *It's about Jess. Be happy for her.* 'How did you meet him?'

'Tinder,' Jess said shaking her head. 'Can you believe it? It turns out it's not completely full of weirdoes and tossers after all. Anyway, you'll meet him tonight. He's a trainee solicitor too, so we've spent a lot of time bonding over being treated like crap. It's only been a few weeks but it's going well.'

'Have you seen his penis yet?' Tom asked, without any shame.

'Very mature, Tom,' I mock-scolded. 'But seriously, mate, have you?' *I mean, if you can't beat 'em, join 'em, eh?*

'Yes, thanks,' Jess quipped. 'And it was very nice,' she went on, blushing.

Jess was getting serious about someone and they'd already slept together? Was I that far out of the loop that I was starting to miss the important things? Jess must have noticed my expression because she reached over and squeezed my hand.

'I wasn't keeping it from you intentionally. It just worked out that way. He'll be here tonight and I can't wait for you to meet him. I hope you like him.' She looked at me with big, sincere eyes and I felt bad all over again. Jess was so lovely. I needed to pay more attention to what was going on around me.

'I can't wait to meet him,' I said, plastering a smile on my face, 'and tell him all about you.'

'Like the time you got so drunk and still had the key for your ex-boyfriend's house so you went round, let yourself in and got into bed with his dad by mistake,' Tom suggested, a mischievous look on his face.

'Don't you *dare!*' Jess exclaimed.

Ah, bless our little Jess, I thought. *She doesn't get that smashed that often but when she does, it's pretty special.* #dadgate was up there as one of the best things any of us had done while pissed.

*

The party was in full swing. The flat was rammed, drinks were flowing and the atmosphere was buzzing. Sam had arrived about an hour ago and as soon as he had Jess had made a beeline for me so that I would meet him first. He seemed like a nice lad, quite good-looking but a bit on the skinny side for what I go for. He suited Jess though and I noticed how attentive and sweet he was with her, without being too overbearing – she hated that. They teased each other quite a lot, I noted approvingly. And Jess looked happy, which was all I really needed to see. I didn't want to speak too soon and jinx it but it looked likely that Sammy would be getting the coveted Amber Raey, best friend, seal of approval.

Tom was surrounded by women, a fact that always made him very happy. I don't know if it was the onesie, or the plastic moustache he was now wearing, but whatever he had going on for him tonight was working. There were all the usual faces from Jalou around, meaning I'd spent the last couple of hours downing shots and playing drinking games with various people. I was well on my way to getting truly hammered. *Put this in your pipe and smoke it, Alessandro,* I thought to myself as I downed another tequila. I was in the middle of a round of 'I Have Never' with some of Tom's old schoolmates when I heard a voice whisper into my ear.

'I knew I'd get to see you in your PJs one day.'

I turned round and hit Jamie in the arm. 'Do you ever stop?'

'Not when it comes to you, my Geordio Armani,' he said, giving me a hug hello.

'Let's get a drink,' I said. 'I'm dry.'

'Well, there's something I *can* do—'

'Don't,' I said, pushing him into the kitchen. 'Don't you dare finish that sentence.'

I grabbed some more punch for me. I was pretty sure it was entirely Malibu and Archers now – it was practically clear – although I did spot a stray lime wedge in there and for that reason that it could still be classed as 'fruit punch'. That crafty little lime wedge had no idea of its significance, just floating around, minding its own business ... *Christ, Amber, you're pissed. Stop thinking about the lime and get back to being a sociable host.* I snapped out of my drunken reverie and grabbed a beer for Jamie and we found an empty corner to stand in. I took in his Calvin Klein boxers and tight black vest. Even I had to admit he looked fit.

'Did you walk down the street like that?' I asked.

'I wore a big coat,' he said. 'Pretty sure I looked like a flasher.'

'So how was the casting?' I'd asked around at work if they'd picked the new male models yet but they hadn't. I had managed to put in a good word for Jamie to Alessandro, though. Alessandro had remembered Jamie and although he hadn't made any promises, I took that as a good sign. Best not to tell Jamie that, though. I didn't want to raise his hopes just in case it didn't work out.

'OK, I think,' Jamie said. 'Alessandro was great, I really liked him, but you can never tell what people really think about you at these things. I really want this job. It would mean a lot to me.'

I wasn't used to seeing Jamie looking so despondent. Maybe it was the booze, maybe it was the look on his face, but I moved in for a hug. We stood like that for a while and it wasn't until the people around us started cheering at us that

I remembered neither of us was wearing much of anything and I pulled away. *Whoa, slow down,* I told myself. *You're standing in the middle of your kitchen, full of people, wearing practically NOWT and snuggling with the village lothario. Let's take a breath, shall we?*

Jamie grabbed my hand and led me towards the living room. 'Let's go dance.'

And, forgetting all about the cheering, for the next hour that's exactly what I did.

At midnight, Jess and I carried out the boob-shaped cake – it seemed appropriate: Tom is a massive tit – and led a drunken chorus of 'Happy Birthday'. Tom was lapping up the attention, a goofy smile plastered over his face. It took him three attempts to blow out all twenty-six candles and that was only after Jamie helped him out.

'Speech, speech, speech,' everyone yelled.

Tom, more than happy to oblige, climbed on top of the table. He looked quite the sight, dressed in his onesie, icing on his nose and the plastic moustache in his hair.

'I'm so happy you're all here,' he slurred. 'You're the best friends a bloke could ask for. And I have the best flatmates ever. You all look great, I feel great. Happy birthday to me! Now let's get smashed!'

Jamie helped Tom down from the table, someone turned the music back on, and Jess and I started passing around the vodka jelly shots. The party was back under way.

At about two a.m. I decided I was a bit too drunk and I needed a bit of a breather so I grabbed a couple slices of boob cake and slipped away to my room for a few minutes of quiet. I switched on the light and nearly jumped out of my skin when I spotted Silvia sitting on the edge of my bed, crying.

'Bloody hell, pet, you nearly gave us a heart attack.' I sat down next to her and put my arm around her shoulders. 'What's wrong, babe? And what are you doing crying in the dark?' My head was spinning and I desperately wanted to eat my titty cake but I tried hard to concentrate and listen to what she was saying.

Silvia looked at me with bloodshot eyes. She was hammered. 'I'm being silly,' she sniffed.

'Tell me,' I said, giving her a squeeze. 'Tell Auntie Amber what's wrong.' I smiled and tried to lighten the mood but only succeeded in sounding like a twat. *Auntie Amber? Yip, total twat. A very drunk total twat.*

'I tried to crack on with that fit bloke, but he knocked me back. Totally pied me. I feel like an idiot.'

'Which bloke?' I asked.

'Your mate, the one you introduced to me in Jalou the other night.'

'Jamie?' I asked.

Silvia nodded. 'He's so fit, and I thought I saw him checking me out earlier so I tried to flirt with him and it was just embarrassing.'

'Jamie turned you down when you look like that?' I said in disbelief. Silvia was wearing a lacy silk negligée – the kind you only really saw on Victoria's Secret models. She looked drop-dead gorgeous.

'Yeah. I mean, he was really nice about, he just said that he wasn't up for that tonight. He was still talking when I ran away and came in here to hide. I've been sat on your bed for ages. I can't go back out there now.'

I gave Silvia another hug. 'Aw mate, don't be so daft, man! Of course you can. You think you're the first lass to ever cry over a boy? Come on, come with me. I'll take you out there.'

'No way,' Silvia said, wiping away her tears. 'I'm not good enough for someone like Jamie, and now everyone out there knows it. I don't know why I thought that was a good idea! I've totally mugged myself off.'

I liked Silvia, but she needed to man up. There was a whole flat full of people out there. I'm almost certain that most of them were too busy getting smashed or tashing on to notice Silvia getting a cheeky custard pie from Jamie. *I can't say that to her though, could I? No ... No, I can't. Definitely not.*

'Come on, babe,' I said. 'No man is worth your tears.'

'Jamie is,' Silvia wailed as a fresh wave of tears started.

Jesus. *This is getting on me tits now, like.*

I sat like that, my arms wrapped around a sobbing, scantily clad Silvia for ten minutes before Jess came to find me. She took one look at Silvia and even through her own drunken haze she knew what was needed.

'Cab?' she mouthed at me.

I nodded.

Ten minutes later, Jess and I were ushering Silvia and one of her friends into a cab. We gave the driver strict instructions to see the girls to their door and make sure they were safely inside before driving off.

Jess and I rejoined the party and she was quickly lost to Sam's embrace. I spotted Jamie talking to a couple of girls in the corner and I felt irrationally angry. He hadn't done anything wrong with Silvia, I knew that. He'd let her down gently but she'd been too drunk to handle the rejection. This was exactly why I couldn't take his flirting seriously. There were women around him all the time and I knew what male models were like. I may have felt a couple of sparks between us recently but that was just part of his charm. I bet you sparks flew when he talked to any woman. He was a fire hazard, like a human Catherine wheel, that boy. And he was not to be trusted. No, it was best to keep him at a distance and just stay friends. I didn't need that kind of distraction in my life right now. Emboldened by my internal monologue I went in search of more alcohol.

I headed into the kitchen to grab another drink and was pulled into a game of beer pong. *The night is still young*, I thought, *there is still plenty of fun to be had*. I pushed all thoughts of Jamie away.

It was four-thirty a.m. and we'd finally closed the door on the last of the guests. Sam had fallen asleep on the sofa, so Jess and Tom were taking the opportunity to draw willies on his face with her lipstick. *Welcome to the family*, I thought. I decided to head off to bed – the clear-up could wait until the morning – and was just heading towards my room when Jamie emerged from the bathroom. I hadn't realised he was still here.

'What are you still doing here?' I was drunk and that came out sounding sharper than I'd intended.

'Thought I'd help you clear up, didn't I?' he said.

'Right, well we're leaving all that until the morning. Silvia was crying over you earlier,' I added bluntly.

He blinked, clearly too drunk to understand what was happening. 'Silvia? She was crying over me?'

'Yeah, because you turned her down.'

'I tried to let her down gently.' He ran his hand through his hair in frustration.

'You might want to work on your delivery, otherwise you'll have every lass in London in tears.'

God, what's wrong with me?

'For fuck's sake,' Jamie said, sounding cross. 'What do you want from me? One minute you think I'm getting with someone new every night, and the next you're giving me a hard time for saying no to a one-night stand. I can't win with you!'

'Why do you care what I think so much?' I was on dangerous ground, being unfair and hassling him for something that wasn't in any way his fault, but drunk Amber has even less of a filter than sober Amber.

Jamie stared at me and for one silly, drunken moment I thought he might try to kiss me. But instead he just shook his head. He looked genuinely hurt as he looked deeply into my eyes and said, 'You're a piece of work, Amber. Thank you for having me tonight. It was a great party.'

He said a quick goodbye to Tom and Jess and then he was gone.

Well, you've screwed that as well, haven't you? You helmet.

An army of tiny little drummer boys were trapped inside my head, banging their tiny little drums TOO LOUDLY. My throat felt like sandpaper, my mouth tasted like a foot and I was clutching cake breast in my right hand. I felt like a bag of piss but if I just lay still I wouldn't be sick, I was sure of it. *Ugh, how did I get to bed?* I remember going back into the living area after Jamie had left, too annoyed at myself for being drunk and acting like a psycho girlfriend to go to sleep. Tom had decided we should all have a night cap and then ... Nothing. Nada. Zip. Zilch. I couldn't remember a bloody thing. There was a knock on my door.

'Mmrrf,' was all I could manage.

Jess's head popped round the door and she gave me a weary smile. 'Afternoon,' she said.

'Mmrrf,' I repeated.

She came into my room and crawled into bed next me. 'I feel like balls,' she said.

'Where's Sam?' I croaked.

'Still asleep,' she said. 'He drank more than us. Think he was nervous.'

'He didn't need to be. I like him.'

'I like him too.'

'Babe, what happened after Jamie left? I can't remember a thing.'

A grin broke through Jess's hangover. 'You were hilarious. You climbed on the table and started singing. We couldn't figure out what you were signing but we think it was either "Shake It Off" or "Firework". It might have been a mash-up of both. Your wailing even woke Sam up.'

My bedroom door opened again and it took me a while to spot Tom because he was crawling in on his hands and knees.

'Help me,' he wailed. 'I'm dying.'

'Join the club, kid,' I said.

After much huffing and puffing, and possibly a few tears, Tom made it into the bed and squeezed himself in next to Jess.

'Did you enjoy your birthday?' I asked.

'Best birthday ever,' Tom said. 'Can we have another party soon?'

'No!' Jess and I said together. It was going to take me the rest of the year to recover from this one. I may want to party like a rock star, but it seemed that my body couldn't recover like one. *I hope this was enough 'fun' to get Alessandro off my back for a while, because my liver can't cope with any more 'fun'.*

Chapter Ten

'Aw, Mam,' I said. 'I don't know what to say.' I was in my office and had phoned Mam as usual before starting work, but there was nothing usual about our conversation. 'I want to kill her,' I added.

It was Ruby. I knew her behaviour had been difficult lately, and we'd let her get away with a lot because of her age and her grief over Dad, but she was pushing things too far now. She'd told Mam she was going to watch a DVD at her friend Sara's on Sunday night, but hadn't come home – without so much as a text letting Mam know where she was. Mam had been up all night, calling her mobile without getting through, and without Sara's number or details. She was frantic – after what happened with Dad, she'd obviously assumed the worst. And then Ruby had turned up without a care in the world that morning, and made some excuse about falling asleep at Sara's by accident and how her phone had been on silent. Utter bollocks. I didn't believe her and neither did Mam. I was fuming.

'Mam, you should've called me,' I said.

'No, love, I shouldn't have,' Mam said gently. 'I didn't want to worry you until I had all the facts. There's nothing worse than letting your imagination run away with you. It always takes you to the worst-case scenario.'

'And she hasn't gone to school today?'

'No, she said she didn't feel well enough to go. She gone straight to her room.'

'Maybe she's telling the truth,' I said, trying to smooth things over. 'Are you sure she wasn't with Sara?'

'I'm not sure about anything. If she was with Sara then they were drinking. I'm certain I could smell it on her when she came in. Why else would she disappear into her room so quickly? And I know there are boys on the scene, but again she won't talk to me about any of it.'

'You don't think she's taking drugs or anything like that, do you?' If Ruby went down that road, I don't know if I'd be able to cope.

'No, I don't think so, not after everything. But I'm positive she'd had a drink.'

'Do you want me to come home for a few days? Do you think it would help?' I wasn't sure if I'd be able to take the time off work, but if I explained things to Alessandro I'm sure he'd approve it. I didn't like the thought of leaving with the launch fast approaching, but I liked the idea of what was happening to Ruby even less.

'I think if you suddenly appeared, Ruby would withdraw even further. She might feel ganged up on. Give it a couple of weeks and then come home for a visit. She might be easier to talk to then. I've just got no idea what's going on with her.'

Suddenly, I had an idea. 'Why don't you and Rubes come

down to London this weekend or the one after? You can stay at the flat so you won't have to pay out for a hotel.' Jess and Sam had been spending so much time together recently, almost every night in the two weeks since Tom's party, that I was sure she wouldn't mind lending us her room for the weekend.

'You don't mind?' Mam said. 'A change of scenery might be just what we need. Ruby might even be excited about a weekend in the big smoke, and I haven't been down to London since you moved into the flat.'

Mam sounded so relieved I was glad that I'd suggested it. 'We'll have a great time,' I said. 'We can do whatever you want. Visit some of the London landmarks, do some shopping on Oxford Street, see a show. Anything you want.'

Mam laughed. 'It would be nice just to see you and spend some time together. We don't need anything fancy. Are you sure you can spare the time?'

'Yes,' I said determinedly. 'I'll graft my tits off this week so I don't have to work over the weekend and we can spend some quality family time together. I haven't seen you since your birthday and that was months ago. I miss the balls off you both.'

'Amber Raey! What the hell kind of chat is that to have with your mam?' she said. 'I'll wash your bloody mouth out with soap next time I see you!' She tried to scold me but I could hear the laughter in her voice. The idea of the weekend had cheered us both up. Hopefully it would sort Ruby out as well.

Freddie knocked on my door a couple of hours later.

'Hey,' I said. 'What's up?'

'I just wanted to remind you that you have a designers' meeting straight after lunch. All the junior and senior designers have to attend. No one knows what it's about but one of the other assistants told me that some kind of announcement is going to be made. My thinking is that Alessandro has finally seen sense and is getting ready to make me the new face and bod of House of Rossi.'

'But you're too valuable to me in your current role,' I said. 'You can't leave me!'

'That's all I wanted to hear. A man likes to feel needed, you know. Right, and don't forget Alessandro wants to see the rest of your designs on Friday afternoon, so you need to make sure Laurie has them by the end of day, OK?'

I nodded and looked at the pile of sketches strewn across the floor. They were a long way off to being ready to share with Alessandro.

'Jesus, I'm going to be here all bloody week.'

'Can I help?' Freddie asked hopefully. 'Maybe there's something you need a second opinion on?'

'Of course, pet.' I brushed away the bag of Monster Munch that I'd been absentmindedly working my way through and patted the space next to me on the floor. 'Take a seat and tell me what you think of these patterns.'

Freddie and I spent the next hour casting a critical eye over the design that had been causing me the most trouble. It was a jumpsuit, one that that I wanted the wearer to be able to dress down for daytime, but to also dress up for the evening. It needed to be classic and simple, but right now it looked a bit boring. Actually, boring is an understatement. If this jumpsuit were a biscuit it would be a plain digestive. It was painfully average and I knew it. I just couldn't put my finger on what to do to improve it. Freddie and I were in the middle of a debate about whether to give it sleeves when there was a knock at the door.

'Come in,' I called.

Laurie walked into the office and stopped short when she saw the two of us sitting cross-legged on the floor. She shook her head, amused. 'I don't know how you can work in this mess. It's like a teenage girl's bedroom.'

'It looks like a mess to you, but everything is exactly where I need it to be,' I said shoving the half-eaten bag of Monster Munch even further behind my desk. 'What's going on? Is something wrong?'

'No, nothing like that,' Laurie said. 'I've got a bit of news I thought you might be interested in. Your friend Jamie – well, Alessandro has just told him he's going to be new face of Rossi menswear. We're launching him during New York Fashion Week in September.'

'Seriously?' I stood up and threw my arms around Laurie. 'That's amazing news! Thanks so much for letting me know. He'll be made up! This calls for a celebration. Cappuccinos all round!'

'Cappuccinos? Oh, you wild woman! You really are throwing caution to the wind. What would have to happen for you to order espressos?' Freddie teased, and I gave him my best 'I'm your boss so watch it' impression. It was useless, but he humoured me.

'OK, tough crowd. Right, I'll go and get them,' Freddie said. 'My legs are about to seize up anyway. Laurie, you in?'

'Sure,' she said. 'I can always do a celebratory caffeine refresher.'

'Jamie's going to so happy about this,' I said after Freddie had left.

'He should be,' Laurie said. 'He was brilliant in the casting: professional and focused. To be honest, he really stood out from the rest. This could really take him places, you know?'

'I just can't wait to congratulate him. I hadn't even thought about what it would mean for his career if he got this.' The truth was that I hadn't seen Jamie since Tom's party two weeks earlier. I'd WhatsApped him the awkward monkey emoji the next day and said I was sorry for being a bit aggy. I blamed it on the drink and thankfully he seemed keen to forget about it as well. Things seemed to be back to normal but it was never the same as seeing someone face to face. Anyway, this was huge news for him. As his friend, I was thrilled.

'First stop New York, next stop super-stardom,' Laurie said.

New York. Now there's something to aim for. Apparently Alessandro took a team with him to New York each year during Fashion Week, but that team hadn't been confirmed for this year yet. It was still a few months away but I couldn't help but wonder . . .

'Babes, do you think I'll get to the shows?' I asked quietly. I'd love nothing more than to see Alessandro in action.

'Aw mate, I don't think Alessandro has decided yet, but I'm keeping everything crossed for you.'

'I've never been to New York,' I said. 'I think me and New York would get on like a house on fire.'

My phone beeped with an instant voice message on WhatsApp. Jamie. I pressed play.

'Oi, oi, my Geordio Armani. I've only gone and got the job, ain't I? I'm part of your team now, and what a team we would make if only you'd agree. We could rule the fashion world together. I could be the Moss to your Dolce! Bring it on, you sort! Thanks a million! Drinks on me in Jalou next time I see you!'

'I love it,' Laurie said, laughing. 'The Moss to your Dolce!'

I stopped smiling long enough to record a message in response. 'Hi babes, I just heard the news: welcome aboard. I'm so happy for you. And don't thank me – this was all you and those striking features of yours. Let's get Tom and Jess and celebrate. Jalou tonight, man! You deserve this. Not sure about the Moss and Dolce thing though. You might want to rethink that one on account of you not having a vagina . . . See you later, kid. And well done, you!'

I had so much work to do this week but I'd put it aside for one night to celebrate with Jamie. And I'd make sure I'd cleared the decks by the weekend so I could enjoy Mam and Rubes's visit too.

I was floating on cloud nine and flew into Jalou, looking for my friends, with Freddie close on my heels.

'There you are,' I exclaimed excitedly as soon as I spotted Jess, Tom and Jamie. I was buzzing – I couldn't wait to tell them my news.

Freddie rested his head on Jess's shoulder, panting like a dog. 'I've never seen Amber move so fast,' he moaned. 'I'm knackered.'

'What's going on?' Jess asked.

'Tom, Prosecco for everyone!' I said. 'It's on me.'

'Something tells me this isn't just about me,' Jamie said.

'This is definitely for you,' I said, 'I'm so proud of you, J. But I've had some good news too so it's a double celebration.'

'It's great news!' Freddie declared.

'Out with it then you Northern monkey,' Tom laughed as he handed the Prosecco around.

I cleared my throat and lifted my glass. 'First up, huge congrats Jamie on landing this amazing gig. We all knew you could do it and we're all behind you. You're going to be huge and you deserve it, lad.'

'Cheers, mate,' Jamie said, looking embarrassed.

'Jamie's going to be the face of the new menswear range we'll be launching during New York Fashion Week,' I continued, 'and, mate, you're not going on your own. I just found out . . . ' I paused and took a breath. Was this really happening? 'I just found out that Alessandro likes so many of my designs that, rather than wrap them up into the main collection, he wants to launch a small selection of them separately. A spin-off range, if you like.'

'What does that mean?' Jess asked, smiling.

'It means that we'll be launching it as a separate line during New York Fashion Week. I'm going to New York, as the designer of my own collection for House of Rossi!'

Everyone rushed forward to hug me with such force I was nearly launched off my feet. I still couldn't believe it. The meeting that Alessandro had called earlier that afternoon had been to tell the design team of this amendment to the Selfridges launch. For once in my life, I'd been struck dumb, completely speechless. I'd just stood there, mouth open, while everyone around me had offered their congratulations. I'd managed to get the power of speech back now but my mind was still whirling. Me, my own line, New York. It was like something out of a film. I was literally living my dream.

'Well done you,' Tom said ruffling my hair. 'I knew all that doodling would pay off one day.'

'It's more than doodling,' Jess said, giving Tom a shove. She gave me another hug. 'Congrats, babe. New York! You lucky sod! The only place I've ever been for work was Bolton for that training course last year. I'm so jealous.'

'You're a star,' Jamie said. 'We're going to kill it in New York.'

I looked at my friends and their happy faces. Three months ago I was over-worked, tired and miserable about my job. And now Jamie and I would be heading off to New York Fashion Week in a few months and Mam and Rubes were visiting at the weekend so I could celebrate with them as well. I only wished Dad was here too to share in my happiness. I blinked back the tears that were threatening to fall. One glass of Prosecco and I was ready to cry a river. I was such a fanny.

I noticed Jamie giving me a concerned look so I slapped a smile on my face. Still, he quietly said, 'He'd be the proudest one here, your dad.'

I gave him a grateful smile that I didn't have to explain, and just nodded. How did he know what I was thinking? Maybe I wasn't as strong or as mysterious as I thought. But now wasn't the time for a deep and meaningful discussion about my dad. Luckily J got the message and ordered another round of drinks instead. Good lad.

'To Jamie and Amber,' Tom yelled. 'First London, now New York. Next stop world domination!'

I didn't know about world domination, but I did know that all my hard work was paying off. I'd made the right decision to leave Diana and join Alessandro's team, and the only way was up from here. Right now, I was winning at life. I felt like I could take on the world. Come at me, New York Fashion Week! I felt confident and happy, the best I'd felt in years. And that was a feeling I was starting to like very much indeed.

Chapter Eleven

'And this is my office.' It was Sunday morning and I was showing Mam and Ruby around House of Rossi.

'This is lovely, pet,' Mam said.

'It's all right,' Ruby said, shrugging.

Despite Ruby's irritatingly lukewarm reaction, I felt so proud showing her and Mam around. It was important to me that they knew where I worked, that now when I spoke to them when I was at work they could picture exactly where I was. And even though Ruby tried to give off the impression that she wasn't impressed, I think she was really. Her 'trying to be cool' act didn't fool me. I invented that act as a teenager, man!

Mam and Rubes had arrived the previous morning and we'd spent the day exploring London. We'd taken a walk down the South Bank, had a look around the shops and markets in Covent Garden, and because it was almost summer and the weather had actually been nice I'd taken them on river cruise down the Thames. Mam bought us lunch in a

Thai place I loved near Carnaby Street. She'd insisted on paying for everything this time. 'It's a celebration,' she'd said. 'A well done for all you've achieved so far. I'm so bloody proud of you.' We'd been exhausted by the time we got back to the flat so we'd ordered in a Domino's and watched a Jennifer Aniston rom-com. Ruby hadn't exactly been talkative throughout the day, and she'd been on her phone a lot of the time, but she'd done everything without complaint and I'd hoped the change in scenery had done her good. I think I even saw her smile when I got attacked by some rogue pigeons near the South Bank, so that's something.

We'd had a lazy morning, eating toast and drinking tea. Tom had made an appearance before he had to dash out to meet some friends and had left with a promise he'd be back for lunch. Ruby had visibly perked up when he'd walked into the room. Clearly, Tom had a fan in my little sister. And now I was showing Mam and Ruby where I worked before we headed back to the flat for lunch; they had to catch their train back to Newcastle from King's Cross this evening. It was a long way to come for just one night but I was so glad that they had made the trip. After the brilliant week I'd had at work, sharing this time with them was the icing on the cake.

The only issue was that I hadn't had the chance to talk to Ruby about the night she'd gone AWOL. I'd wanted to do it sister to sister, without Mam there, but there hadn't been a good opportunity for me to bring it up when it was just the two of us.

'Rubes,' I said, 'let's leave Mam here to have a proper look around – feel free to tidy up by the way, Mam – and me and you can go and see some of the samples from the collection.'

Mam and I exchanged a look. She knew what I was doing. I grabbed Ruby by the shoulders and marched her out of the office before she could argue. I led her to the room that had the wardrobe we kept the samples in.

'This is top secret,' I told her. 'I shouldn't really be showing you these so no tweeting or Instagramming about it, OK?'

She nodded and then opened her mouth to say something but I cut her off. I knew what was coming.

'No freebies,' I said. Then, as an afterthought, I added, 'Yet.'

I started pulling out my samples and felt surprisingly nervous about showing them to Ruby. She was the first person outside House of Rossi to see the collection. She was a few years younger than our target market but her opinion really mattered to me. What if she hated them? My palms were actually sweating.

'Wow,' Ruby said. 'You really designed these? They're like outfit goals.'

'You really think so?' I asked, chewing my bottom lip nervously. I wasn't exactly down with the way teenagers talked these days but I was pretty sure 'outfit goals' was a good thing.

Ruby nodded enthusiastically and for a minute she was back to her old self. 'I love them. They're as good as anything that's in Topshop, maybe even nicer.'

'Thanks Rubes. That means a lot coming from you.' That was a huge accolade coming from my little sis. Topshop was the height of sophistication to her.

'You really care what I think that much?'

'Of course I do, kiddo – sorry, sorry, I know you hate it when I call you that.' I paused to collect my thoughts. This was the moment I'd been waiting for all weekend. 'You're my sister. Your opinion matters to me. I care what you think and I want you to be proud of me. I know I haven't been able to get home for a while and I'm sorry. I promise I'll try to make more of an effort.'

'It's hard without you at home,' Ruby said quietly, not quite meeting my eye. She fiddled with the hem of her top and I suddenly realised how young she was. Painfully, achingly young. Behind all that teenage sass and attitude she was still just a little girl and right now she looked lost. 'It used to be four of us, and then you went to uni and it was the three of us. And then Dad . . . ' She trailed off. 'And now I suppose it's just me and Mam.'

'It's not just you and Mam,' I insisted. 'I'm here. I'm only ever a phone call away and you can call me any time. Or drop me a text. It's going to take some time before I can take my foot off the pedal but I promise it'll be worth it in the long run.'

'It's not the same, though,' Ruby said. 'Everything's different. I miss you, and I miss . . . I miss Dad.'

'Come here.' I wrapped my arms around her. She was all skin and bones, still a child. 'I miss him too, and so does Mam. Everyone does. We're all still struggling with him not being around any more. But it's OK to talk about him. In fact, you should talk about him all the time. It's good to remember the people you love.'

'I don't know how to,' Ruby said simply.

I pulled back and looked down into her face. 'You walk up to Mam and you say, "I want to talk about Dad." Or you call me and say the same thing. And then we'll talk about him.' I took a breath. I had to say the next thing while I could.

Who knew how long I'd have before Ruby shut down again. 'But, Rubes, you can't bottle stuff up and act out, man. Like the other night. You staying out and then coming home smelling of drink and that. It's not on. Mam was worried sick and she's not stupid. She knew what you were up to. You can't do that to her. It's not fair.'

Ruby pulled away and angrily brushed her tears away. 'None of this is fair! I just wanted to forget about everything for a while. Why can't I do that?'

I grabbed her shoulders and looked her straight in the eye. 'Because if that's the reason, where does it stop? What happens when a bottle of wine isn't enough to make you forget everything? What happens if you need to turn to something else? After Dad . . . ' My voice trailed off. I couldn't verbalise what I wanted to say. I couldn't think about losing Ruby to the same thing we'd lost Dad to.

'I wouldn't do that,' Ruby mumbled.

'Rubes, it's as simple as this: I love you and Mam loves you. We all miss Dad so talk to us. We can help you and you can help us. The answer to your problems is not getting drunk or shutting yourself away. We're here for you, babe.'

Ruby looked away and shrugged. I hoped I had got through to her but I wasn't completely sure. I'd been a stubborn teenager so I couldn't exactly hold it against her if she was showing similar traits. I think she'd heard what I was trying to say and that she'd come to me or Mam the next time she wanted to 'forget'. At least I hoped so.

'Let's clear this lot away and then go find Mam.' I said, changing the subject. 'And I'm starving. Let's head back for some lunch.'

*

We arrived back at the flat to find that Jess had returned from Sam's and was putting the finishing touches to lunch – lasagna, a mountain of garlic bread, and Tom was chopping up a simple salad. That boy continued to surprise me every day – I had no idea he knew what a salad was. We piled our plates up high, settled down at the table and got stuck in.

'Rubes, can I get you a drink?' Tom, always the barman, asked.

'Coke, please,' she said, blushing.

If Tom noticed the effect he was having on Ruby, he didn't let on and for that I was grateful. Things were already sensitive enough without him involuntarily putting his massive feet in it.

'How was your birthday, Tom?' Mam asked. 'Amber tells me you had a party. Did the flat make it through in one piece?'

'The flat was unscarred,' Tom said. 'Can't say the same for us though. I think I've only just about recovered.'

'None of us got out of bed the next day,' Jess admitted. 'We spent most of the Sunday doing rock, paper, scissors to see who had to get up and make the tea or order a takeaway.'

'Oh, to be young again,' Mam said wistfully.

'And your eldest,' Tom said pointing his fork accusingly at me, 'was the life and soul.'

'Oh really?' Mam said. Even Ruby looked interested. 'And how's that?'

'Let's just say that she tried to give Taylor Swift and Ellie Goulding a run for their money, complete with twerking and the running man.' Jess laughed. 'And she failed. Miserably.'

'Oh shut up, you two, will you?' I protested.

'Admit it,' Jess said. 'You can't sing a note in tune to save your life.'

'Was she really that bad?' Ruby asked.

'She was shocking,' Tom said, taking a huge bite out of his garlic bread. 'The neighbours knocked on the door and asked if we were strangling cats in here. Nosey bastards nearly alerted the RSPCA!' Tom pressed on with his piss-taking. 'Your sister might be a great clothes designer but she's a dreadful singer. Stick to the day job, mate. It's safe to say, it was a no from me!' Tom laughed while doing his best Simon Cowell impression.

And as much as I tried to convince everyone that wasn't true, no one would believe me. *With friends and family like these, who needs enemies, eh?* I thought affectionately.

Chapter Twelve

The summer passed by too quickly for my liking. The entire design team had been run off their feet getting everything ready for Fashion Week, and when I wasn't in the office or sketching at home, I was in Jalou trying to let off a bit of steam. I'd also managed to get back to Newcastle for a long weekend. Ruby had still been a little withdrawn but she was more quiet than surly now, so at least that was a step in the right direction.

And then all of a sudden, somehow, the summer is over and here we all are, backstage at New York Fashion Week with me getting ready to unveil my spin-off range to the world. The minute we'd landed at JFK airport I'd immediately felt that NY buzz everyone goes on about. We'd only had a day and a half to ourselves before we had to focus entirely on the shows so Freddie, Jamie and I had packed in as much as we could. We visited Carrie Bradshaw's stoop – Jamie had grumbled the entire time but Freddie and I were too excited to care – we spent a long afternoon in

Bloomingdale's, went up to the Top of the Rock, rowed across the lake in Central Park and then took a trip on the Staten Island Ferry to take in the views: the Statue of Liberty is teeny in real life, man. Freddie said she must have been doing no carbs. There were already Christmas displays up in Hamleys and all along Madison Avenue and Fifth Avenue. Clearly Americans got as excited by the festive season as us Brits. I don't think it's ever too early to start thinking about Christmas – it's my favourite time of the year and was pleased to see that New Yorkers seemed to share my enthusiasm.

And the food! We'd found an incredible Mexican restaurant, and completed the meal with lashings of tequila, and I insisted on going to this lovely little place we'd discovered in Midtown for breakfast every day. But that was only the half of it. Bagels, pizza slices, Carnegie Deli, Hershey's. *I'm going to have to join the Statue of Liberty on her no carbs after this trip if I'm not careful.* It was worth it. I felt so alive – I had fallen completely in love with the Big Apple.

But after a weekend of jetlag and sightseeing, all the clothes we'd had shipped over for the show had arrived and it had been time to get our heads down and work. We had taken over an entire floor in the boutique hotel we were staying in just off Times Square, and set up a work space in two of the suites. As ever, we'd been working against the clock to get everything ready in time. All the clothes had to be perfect, Alessandro had to finalise the look he wanted to accompany each outfit with the hair stylists and make-up artists, there were models' schedules to coordinate, as well as the Fashion Week's production team to liaise with. There was so much to do but we'd managed it and now I was standing –

pinching myself trying to believe it – backstage at New York Fashion Week!

Every now and again I'd experience a moment of doubt and wonder if I was truly up to this. Maybe Alessandro had been crazy to put his trust in me. Had I been kidding myself for the past few months? Every time I mentioned my nervousness Alessandro replied that a true perfectionist is never happy with their work, that they always think they can do better, and if that's how I felt, then I was behaving perfectly normally. I wasn't sure about normal, but if Alessandro thought the doubt and nerves were natural, that was good enough for me.

House of Rossi was presenting a full roster of new lines, of which mine was just one. It had the fewest pieces in it, but it was my name against them all, so any reviews printed in tomorrow's papers would mention me by name. *Balls*, I thought. *I'm going to be reviewed by professional fashion journalists. No hiding behind anyone now. This is all down to me.*

I did a quick sweep, running mentally through my list. I'd triple-checked all of the clothes myself – no frayed hems or nipple-exposing lapels for me, thank you very much – all of the models were either in hair and make-up or waiting for their turn with a stylist. Freddie was running around, and though I wasn't sure what he was doing he looked busy. I trusted him to keep the logistical side of things moving smoothly. I checked my phone. I definitely had time to watch the menswear show from the sidelines. There was no way I was going to miss Jamie's big debut.

I found a secluded spot where I could still see the catwalk and one side of the audience. As the show started I felt a flutter of nerves, not for myself but for Jamie. When he came out, I hardly recognised him at first – he hadn't spotted me – he was in the zone, 100 per cent focused. I held my breath as he walked the catwalk like a pro, owning every inch of the clothes he was wearing. He commanded everyone's full attention and he got it without question. I'd never seen Jamie in work mode before and I was riveted. I knew he was a good-looking lad – I mean, I have eyes – but this was the first time I fully appreciated that he had *something*. I couldn't put my finger on exactly what it was but whatever it was, it was working for him. It was a certain presence that he had, a charisma. Something that made sure every eye, male or female, in that room was transfixed by him. He belonged up there. I'd never had Jamie down as having a serious work ethic before but seeing him move so smoothly – looking so casual yet focused the whole time – it was obvious he'd worked damn hard to get so good at it. I was proud of him. Alessandro had made the right decision; Jamie was the perfect lead model for this collection.

The menswear portion of the show drew to close and the turnaround for the womenswear range began to kick in. Out front the applause continued, while backstage Jamie was surrounded by people congratulating him. I hung back, not wanting to spoil this moment for him. He spotted me and came bounding straight over, like an over-excited Golden Retriever.

'My Geordio Armani! Did you see?' He was almost exploding with joy and had a happy, goofy smile on his face.

I nodded. 'Just amazing,' I said sincerely. 'You had the audience eating out of the palm of your hand. Alessandro could've put you in a bin bag and they still would've loved you.'

Jamie grabbed me and twirled me round, both of us laughing.

'Put me down!'

Eventually he did, but he kept his hands firmly on my waist.

'It's your turn,' he said. 'How you feeling?'

'Ridiculously nervous.' *No point in lying, eh?* 'I'm worried my designs are boring, or they're last season, or that one of the models will fall over, or that I'll get booed and people will throw rotten tomatoes at my collection.'

'Stop being such a twat,' Jamie stated, laughing.

'Nice,' I said. 'It's just this—'

'Babes,' he interrupted. 'You've worked your arse off, you're talented, it's going to be perfect. Now go and enjoy it. You deserve it.'

There wasn't much I could say to that. 'OK.'

Jamie grinned. 'Good.' He kissed the top of my head. 'Enjoy every moment.'

'You'll stay?' I asked. Suddenly, I needed to know that he was backstage.

'Definitely,' he said. 'I'll be right here. Now go.'

I went.

Alessandro was gesturing at his watch, indicating it was almost time. I tried to calm the butterflies in my stomach and leant against the wall, concentrating on taking one steady breath after another. *Come on, lass,* I thought. *Pull yourself together.*

I felt a tap on my shoulder and I turned around expecting to see Alessandro, or even Jamie. I was greeted by a face that was familiar to me but I couldn't immediately place. The

man standing in front of me was tall and kind of scruffy looking, but in that way that had clearly been carefully put
together. He had just-got-out-of-bed stubble, and his dark
floppy hair fell over one of his grey eyes in a way that had to
be intentional. A lazy, sexy smile lit up his handsome face.
*Who is this guy? Is he a model who's taken a wrong turn? Whatever, I
don't have time for this right now.*

'Can I help you?' I asked, trying to keep the irritation out
of my voice.

'Hey,' he said. *Ah, he's American,* I thought. 'I saw you standing here and I just wanted to introduce myself.'

'Are you one of the models?' I asked. *Let's wrap this up.*

'No, I'm actually—'

'Are you with one of the design houses, then?'

'Ah, no, not that either. I'm—'

'Then how did you get back here?' I asked, suddenly angry.
No one except those directly involved with the shows were
meant to be backstage.

He laughed as though I'd said something incredibly sweet.
'I was invited backstage. I like to come back here and wish
everyone luck. You look nervous. Is this your first time walking the catwalk?'

Who is this moron? I thought. I wanted to get into this but
Freddie was waving at me. The models were ready. I didn't
have time for fannying about.

'Listen,' he went on. 'You look beautiful. There's nothing
to be nervous about, I promise.'

'That's sweet and all,' I said, 'but I'm not a model. I'm the
designer and my show's about to start so I better go.'

'What? But I thought—'

'You thought wrong, pet. Anyway, thanks for the support –

120

however misguided,' I called back as I quickly walked away. 'Enjoy the show!'

He looked at me, a perplexed expression on his face, but then I rounded the corner and he was instantly out of sight, out of mind.

'You were great! Keep going, we're almost there. Brilliant, babes. On to the next!'

Platitude after platitude came out of my mouth as model after model came off the runway. I threw words of encouragement at each one of them as they pulled off their shoes and outfits and quickly redressed in their next pieces. Later, when people would ask me what it was like backstage, I'd say the clichéd words I'd heard a million times before but never understood until now: 'It all passed by in a blur. It was over before I knew it had started.' But right now, in the moment, I was buzzing like an old fridge. The adrenalin had kicked in and I was on fire. It was everything I'd ever wanted and I was determined to make sure it all went off without a hitch.

And then, seemingly as soon as it had started, the show was over and it was time for my moment in the spotlight. Freddie thrust a huge bouquet of flowers into my arms, and with Alessandro gripping my hand firmly I walked down the runway with my mentor. Flashbulbs were going off nineteen to the dozen. People in the crowd were on their feet. The applause was rapturous. The cheering was deafening. I spotted one famous face after another and some of those familiar faces were even blowing air kisses in my direction.

Alessandro stepped forward and took his bow. If it was possible, the volume in the room went up a notch. Then he turned to me and beckoned me forward, and suddenly all eyes were on me. I gave a small bow. *I must look like a right knob,* I thought.

'Congratulations, bella,' Alessandro said over the applause, beaming up at me. 'They love you.'

I did another sweep of the room and my gaze landed on the American who'd been backstage. He nodded his head in hello and threw a dazzling smile in my direction. And just as suddenly it was all over and Alessandro was leading me back up the catwalk. I glanced over my shoulder and caught the eye of the American again. *Seriously, who is that man?*

Jamie was waiting for me as soon as I stepped backstage.

'There, right there, *that's* why I call you Geordio Armani. You smashed it, babe!'

I couldn't keep the smile off my face. 'I've never felt like that before. That was the most amazing thing that has ever happened to me. Better than strawberry Pop-Tarts, fruit ciders in beer gardens, Domino's when you're hungover, your mam's Sunday roast. J, it was better than sex!'

'Not so sure about that, mate. I reckon you must doing it wrong,' Jamie said, amused.

'You know what I mean.' I was struggling to find the right words to express everything I was feeling right now. 'It was, just, so, I've never—'

'I get it,' Jamie said. 'I feel it too.'

'I want to do it again!' I shouted. 'Someone get me my sketchbook!'

'Listen to this one,' Freddie said, appearing at my side. 'One successful show and she's ordering everyone around already.'

I threw my arms around him. 'Thank you! I couldn't have done it without you!'

Freddie hugged me back and then pulled away and looked at me critically. 'You're looking a bit sweaty,' he declared. *Cheeky bastard,* I thought. 'Alessandro's going to be back here with some journalists. They'll want to talk to you, so let's get that face fixed. At the moment you look a little bit Ed Sheeran after the Brits.'

I laughed and waved bye to Jamie and then let Freddie propel me towards where I'd left my bag. One look in my compact mirror and I realised Freddie was being kind. 'Sweaty' didn't even begin to cover it. And I think poor Ed Sheeran would have taken offence at the comparison.

'Did you see who was sitting at the end of the Frow?' Freddie asked.

'Who?' I said through pursed lips as I sucked in my cheeks and started sweeping blusher across my cheekbones.

'You didn't see him? I'll give you a clue – he looks like Harry Styles's older brother. Or Adam Levine's younger one,' Freddie said, a faraway look in his eye. 'And I love him.'

'Oh *him.* He was backstage earlier trying to talk to me. He thought I was a model. I recognised him but couldn't think from where. I was pretty short with him.'

Freddie's mouth dropped open. 'Are you kidding?'

'What?' I said. 'I was busy and stressed and he was trying to put a shift in. Who is he? And how'd he get backstage anyway?'

'He can go anywhere he likes,' Freddie exclaimed. 'That's Brandon Bailey!'

My hand stilled, the mascara wand left adrift mid-air. *Balls.*

Double Balls. A hundred thousand balls. 'Brandon Bailey? From The Starks?'

Of course I recognised him, and I was mortified. Until recently, The Starks had been the biggest boyband to come out of the US this century – America's One Direction, but with a rockier edge. All four members of the band were fit but Brandon had been the star. He was the lead singer, played the guitar and it was Brandon who all the girls were mobbing at gigs. He'd recently left the band to go solo and, according to the *Daily Mail* sidebar, was getting ready to release his first single and album later in the year. *How did I not recognise him?* Launching the new line must have distracted me more than I'd thought it had.

'Yep. Brandon Bailey from The Starks,' Freddie said, exasperated. 'A regular *Heat* Torso of the Week was standing right in front of you and you didn't recognise him?!'

'All right, calm down, pet,' I said. 'No need to scream. It was hardly the perfect moment for me to bump into him, was it? I was a bit preoccupied with my *first-ever* catwalk show. It just proves that I really do put work first.'

'That's nothing to be proud of,' Freddie said with a withering look, 'especially if he was trying it on and you turned him down! There must be cobwebs down there by now. You shouldn't be pieing the advances of any young, eligible bachelors, especially not when the specimen in question was this week's *Now* mag's Crush Corner.'

'What the hell? Freddie, do we pay you to read magazines? And never mention my fanny cobwebs again!'

'I think I have walked in at the wrong moment?' Alessandro said from behind us both, looking both amused and perplexed.

Christ, that's it, my boss, one of the most powerful and influential men in fashion, has just heard I have a dusty vagina. Fantastic. As soon as he leaves, I'll kill Freddie!

'Sorry, Alessandro.' I scrambled to regain my composure and stop thinking about any cobwebs. 'Freddie had just got his knickers in a twist over some boyband member trying to graft me—'

'Brandon Bailey is not just "some boyband member", I'll have you know,' Freddie chipped in before I could say anything more. 'And Amber, Alessandro has no idea what you just said because you lost me and English is my first language. Tone down the Northern, woman; you're not in Kansas any more, Toto! Anyway, enough about the beautiful Mr Bailey. You mugged him off before the show even started and I highly doubt he's used to that. You ballsed it right up.'

'What is this "mugged him off"? And "ballsed up"?' Alessandro asked, shaking his head, looking more and more confused by the minute.

'Don't worry,' I said quickly. I shot Freddie a look. Alessandro didn't need to know anything more about my personal life – or lack thereof. 'I was just too busy before the show started to realise who he was. I'll find him later and apologise.'

Alessandro waved his hands dismissively. 'Don't worry about that right now. These pretty boys, you need to be careful. Anyway, there is some press I want you to meet. But first—' he clapped his hands to get everybody's attention. The whole team stopped talking and turned to listen to the boss.

'I am so proud of all of you,' Alessandro said. 'Today couldn't have happened without every single person here. The shows were received well and our two newest stars, bella

125

Amber and Jamie, have made their mark with House of Rossi. We have had a beautiful day and now it's time to celebrate. I'm taking you all out for dinner! Cars will be picking everyone up from the hotel at nine p.m. sharp. So get yourselves looking *bellissimo*. Tonight we drink to House of Rossi!'

I cheered and clapped along with everyone else. Right now I didn't think I needed booze – I already felt drunk: I was drunk on life, the show, my collection, these people. I felt like I was finally getting everything I ever wanted. And I was loving every second of it.

Chapter Thirteen

'So how are you feeling?' Jamie asked.

We were still in the East Village Italian restaurant Alessandro had taken us to, and Jamie and I were sat alone at the table. Most of the others had decided to make a night of it and had disappeared off to a bar nearby. It had been a perfect evening. We'd all been buzzing after the day's events, Alessandro had ordered bottle after bottle of wine and had insisted on making a speech every time a new one was opened. He'd toasted us all individually, he'd toasted the team that was still back in London, he'd toasted his mother. It was only when he started toasting the cutlery and napkins that we realised how pissed he was. After a round of strong coffees he had decided against joining the others in the bar and had gone back to the hotel to sleep it off. I don't think Alessandro drinks that often – he was going to feel like a bag of piss in the morning.

So now it was just me and Jamie. I'd told Freddie we'd

meet them all at the bar but the truth was that I had no intention of going. I was already a bit pissed and I didn't want to get so hammered that I missed the papers hitting the newsstands. I'd asked around and apparently the newspapers containing the reviews of today's shows would be ready by about two a.m. and would be on the stands soon after. I couldn't bear the thought of not being one of the first to read them so I was planning to sneak away, buy a copy of every single one and lock myself away in my hotel room to read each review by myself. *What if they were bad and the shows got completely trashed?* I pushed the thought away and focused on what Jamie was saying.

'I feel happy, and drunk,' I admitted. 'And anxious about the reviews. I have all this nervous energy.'

'I know what you mean,' Jamie said. 'It's like, I was on such a high today, I'd been waiting for a job like this for ages, and now I've done it and it's over, well, I don't know what to do with myself.'

'Exactly,' I said, surprised at Jamie's insightfulness. 'I keep thinking about today, what I could've done better. And then the next minute, I'm wondering what comes next.'

'Anything you want can come next, mate,' Jamie said. 'Let's take it in baby steps. What do you want to do right now? Shall we catch up with everyone else?'

'You know what,' I said slowly, 'I actually just want to wait up for the papers. I don't think I can do anything else until I've read the reviews. I definitely won't be able to sleep. Is that completely sad?'

Jamie shook his head. 'No way, I understand.' He looked at his watch. 'Look, we've got a bit of time before then. Why don't we walk back to the hotel? It's not far, so I'll wait up with you and we can get the papers together.'

I hesitated. I really wanted to read them alone, but then I looked at Jamie's hopeful face and I realised that there would probably be some coverage about the newer models too. *We should do this together, I thought. Let's see it through together.*

'You're on,' I said. 'But don't go galloping off like you usually do. These heels aren't made for running after male models.'

I stood up and Jamie helped me put on my coat. 'My Geordio Armani, I get the feeling most men run after *you*, not the other way round.'

The New York night air was crisp and chilly. I pulled my coat tightly around me and buried my nose in my oversized scarf. Jamie and I walked through Times Square arm in arm and looked around in awe at the flashing lights, the huge screens, the crowds of people. It's true what they say: New York really is the city that never sleeps.

'It's pretty cool, isn't it?' Jamie said.

'I love it here,' I said. 'If I could pick up my whole life and move everyone I love here, I'd stay forever.'

'You're lucky. With what you're doing now, you *could* live here one day,' Jamie said. 'Fashion is a global market. It could take you anywhere.'

'And you,' I said. 'This is the start for you too. Do you know what you've got coming up next?'

'There's a print campaign for Rossi menswear, so I'll be busy with that for a while. My agent doesn't have all the details yet but I'm looking forward to it.'

'If you've got time, you could line up another fungal toenail ad. You know, just to tide you over.'

Jamie groaned. 'Not one of my finest moments. At least it was just my feet that made the posters. No one will ever know that was me.'

'*Almost* no one,' I pointed out.

'And you'll keep my secret, won't you, my Geordio?'

'I'll take it to the grave,' I said. 'So tell me, what's been your worst job so far?'

'The fungus-y toe ad came pretty close.' Jamie thought for a moment. 'The shoot I did for a savings account leaflet was pretty poor. But it's got to be the poster campaign for STD testing. The money was good but my face was in GP's surgeries all over the country. My mum was not pleased and it seriously affected my game with the ladies. I mean, not even these eyes can save you if a girl thinks you've got the clap.'

I started laughing. 'Mate, and I thought I had it bad working for Diana!'

'I wasn't laughing when I had to spend hours trying to convince my whole family I didn't have herpes, let me tell you.' Jamie shuddered at the memory.

'None of that for you now, pet. Not now you're the newest face of House of Rossi.'

'It's just the beginning,' Jamie said. 'There's so much more to come.'

I checked my watch. 'Hey, we've been walking for ages. Do you think the papers will be out yet?'

'Let's find out.'

We quickened our pace, walking up and down street after street until we found an all-night newsstand. And there, freshly printed and waiting for us, were the papers. Jamie and I bought a copy of every single one and a family-sized bag of peanut M&Ms – with our arms full we ran back to the hotel, giggling like children.

We rushed through the lobby, and waiting for the lift seemed to take forever but eventually we made it back to my room and tumbled through the door.

'Which one first?' Jamie said, looking at all the papers we'd thrown over the bed.

'I don't know. You pick one. No, wait. I'll do it. No! You do it.' I covered my face with my hands. 'I can't decide!'

I heard papers rustling and then Jamie's voice as he began to read.

'"House of Rossi's new star, junior designer Amber Raey, wowed audiences yesterday with her debut collection, a small spin-off line to complement Rossi's new range for the young female market. Raey, 24 and from the UK, blew critics and fashionistas away with her fresh cuts and ultra-modern fabric choices. She—'

'Give me that,' I said, snatching the paper from him. That couldn't be right. I quickly scanned through the article. Words kept jumping out at me. *Innovative . . . One to watch . . . Inspired . . . A breath of fresh air.* I picked up another paper, and then another one. And another. Each one was a rave review for House of Rossi, for 'strong and talented' Jamie, for me, for my show.

'Howay, man . . . this can't be happening!' I yelled. I was buzzing, absolutely buzzing.

'Here, listen to this,' Jamie said. 'This one calls you "a new designer for a new generation". Mate, you utter legend!'

He grabbed me, lifted me off the ground and spun me around and around, until I had to tell him to put me down otherwise my lobster fettuccine was going to reappear.

131

'My Geordio Armani,' he said softly. 'You've done good.'

'So have you,' I said quietly.

I sensed the change in mood and knew that I should take a step back and put some physical distance between the two of us, but the truth was that I didn't really want to. I was so glad Jamie was here with me. He was the perfect person to share the moment with and I wanted to find some way to tell him how much his support over the last few days had meant to me. I'd seen a different side to him lately. I'd always had him down as a flirt, a party boy, someone who didn't take life too seriously, but he took his work seriously and I admired that. I admired him. *Chill out, Amber. These thoughts are a bit pashy for you. Let's not go all Bella from* Twilight.

'This all feels unreal,' I went on. 'I'm glad you're here. It means a lot, you sharing this with me.'

'Are you going sentimental on me?' he said, pushing the hair away from my face. Oh no. He's noticed too. *Tone it down, Raey.*

'It must be all the wine,' I said. 'Makes me soppy.'

'I won't tell anyone. And you know what? It means a lot, you being here with me too.'

'You're incredible at what you do,' I said. 'I'm sorry if I misjudged you in the past. I can see now how hard you work.' *Too far! Too much! Abort mission, you complete tampon.*

'I want to be able to look after my mum and dad in the future. Dad can't keep climbing up and down ladders, fixing roofs, and I don't want Mum on her feet all day either, serving lunch to a bunch of pissy teenagers at her school. This job means I'll be able to help them out with bills and stuff. Maybe they can start slowing down and enjoying life soon.'

'I want to do the same for my mam.' I gave a small laugh. 'When did us kids decide to turn into the parents, eh?'

'We're not so different, you and me.'

Jamie tightened his hold of me, pulling me even closer to him. My brain was fuzzy with wine and the excitement of the day so the voice that usually told me to keep my distance from Jamie wasn't quite as loud as usual, or maybe she was drunk too. I didn't have the time for a proper relationship, and Jamie and I were just starting to become real friends. I cared about him and I didn't want to ruin that. I knew all this and yet I still didn't pull away. I could see him bending down, his eyes fixed on my lips. Forgetting any of my usual reservations, I tilted my head back, closed my eyes and waited for—

SHAKE IT OFF! SHAKE IT OFF!

'What is that?' Jamie pulled away, confused as to why Taylor Swift was suddenly blaring out of my handbag.

'Bollocks! That's my phone.' I rummaged in my bag and finally found my iPhone. *Why is it so LOUD!?* Without thinking, I pressed answer, not taking my eyes off Jamie.

'Yes?' I said abruptly. *Go away, go away, go away*, I thought.

'Hey, Amber. Brandon Bailey here. We met earlier, before your show.'

'Er, right, OK. Hello.' *Engage your brain, Amber.*

'I just read the reviews, babe, and I wanted to say congratulations. So—'

My brain finally engaged. 'Wait, how did you get my number?' Jamie was looking at me with a puzzled expression on his face so I turned away and took a couple of steps across the room. I couldn't keep staring at him. He was too . . . distracting.

133

'I asked my assistant to get me it,' Brandon replied simply.

'Seriously?' I risked a glance in Jamie's direction. He was tidying up, shuffling the papers together. He was most definitely not looking at me any more.

'Of course. You intrigued me. I wanted to know more about you, especially after I saw your amazing show. Let me take you out to celebrate.'

'Now? It's the middle of the night.' I needed to get off the phone. I needed to talk to Jamie.

Brandon laughed. 'Not now. Tomorrow. I'll pick you up at your hotel at seven tomorrow night.'

'Brandon, I'm not sure about tomorrow night.' I looked at Jamie again. 'I might be busy.'

'"Might" doesn't mean you are. Come for dinner with me – you won't regret it.'

Get off the phone, Amber! 'Fine,' I agreed quickly. 'I'll see you tomorrow night.'

'Great. See you then, honey.' And then he was gone.

I threw my phone back in my bag and turned to Jamie. 'Jamie—'

'Who was that?' Jamie asked. 'Who's Brandon?'

'Oh.' I paused, wrong-footed. 'Brandon Bailey, the singer from The Starks. I met him backstage before the show.'

'And now you're going out with him tomorrow night?'

'What? Yes, but it's nothing. I don't even know him.' *What is happening?*

'You'll know him after tomorrow.'

'It's not like that. I was just trying to—'

'I get it, Amber. Message received, loud and clear. Look, it's late and I'm tired. I'll see you tomorrow, OK?'

I had to try again. 'Jamie, wait. Let me explain.'

'Goodnight, Amber. Congratulations again.'

He walked out of the room, his step heavier than it had been when we'd walked in. I had no idea what the hell had just happened, but I knew I'd completely screwed this up.

PART THREE

Chapter Fourteen

I gave myself a critical once-over in the full-length mirror. I looked . . . OK. Brandon had WhatsApped to let me know that a car would be picking me up and I had about fifteen minutes before it was due to arrive. I was wearing a black Topshop jumpsuit with a cropped tan leather jacket from All Saints. I'd added a couple of silver necklaces, a statement ring, an obligatory pair of heels and was pleased with what the mirror was reflecting back. I looked was smart without being too try-hard. I'd never been out with someone famous before so I had no idea how dressed up I was supposed to be, but I felt good and comfortable, and that was all that mattered.

I checked my phone and saw that I had one message. Jamie.

Hey. Sorry, I went out early with Freddie. Don't worry about last night. Have a good evening. See you at the airport tomorrow. Jx

I sighed and threw my phone on the bed in frustration. I hadn't liked how things had come to such an abrupt end the previous evening so I'd knocked on Jamie's door earlier to see if we could clear the air. He hadn't answered, so I'd sent him a long message explaining that I'd tried to get Brandon off the phone quickly but there had been too much going on for me to think straight, which is why I'd ended up agreeing to a date. I'd tried to explain that we were too good friends to let a drunken moment come between us – but all I got back from him is a casual handful of words? If that's how he wanted to play it, *fine*. And by 'fine' I mean far from it.

I'd woken up at around midday and immediately I got 'the fear'. I hadn't been that drunk last night, but I had been tipsy enough to feel hungover, and also tipsy enough that some of last night's events were a little hazy. *Had I flirted with Jamie? Who instigated the flirtatious behaviour? Was it me? And then had I upset him? I hadn't meant to be insensitive. Did Jamie hate me now? Was our friendship lost forever? Oh, God.* The thoughts had kept swirling around my head along with a feeling of dread in my stomach. I hate hangover guilt.

When Jamie hadn't been in his room, I'd been 99 per cent sure I was going to cancel on Brandon. It hadn't felt right to go out with someone else when Jamie and I had left things so unfinished. But as hour after hour had passed without any response from Jamie I'd become less anxious and more annoyed. The crafty blue double ticks on WhatsApp let me know he'd read my message, so what was he waiting for? I'd started Googling Brandon while I was moping about, waiting for my fuzzy head to clear, and the deeper I'd got into the stalking – sorry *researching* – the keener I'd become on the idea of going out for dinner. I moved from Google to Brandon's

Twitter then finally to his Instagram, and before I knew it I was on his brother's ex-girlfriend's sister's dog-walker's Instagram and I realised it was time to rein it in. Weirdo. Despite feeling like a stage five clinger before I'd even gone on the date, I was glad that I hadn't cancelled – I'd clearly put a dent in Jamie's male model ego and he didn't know how to handle the idea that I wanted to just remain friends. Why should I give up a potentially nice evening with a famous singer who wanted to spend time with *me* for Jamie, when Jamie couldn't even be bothered to respond to a really long, genuinely heartfelt message properly?

It was probably a good thing that nothing had happened between us – I had been drunk on champagne and light-headed because of the reviews. Jamie had been there for a lot of the important moments yesterday and we got a bit carried away – it had all turned into something more serious than it should have. I blame New York, with its bright lights and intoxicating atmosphere. I knew I could have handled things better, but I was trying. The least Jamie could do is meet me halfway and help make things less awkward. But no, I don't hear from him all day and when I do it's a message that he could've sent to any of his one-night stands.

'Enough,' I said to my reflection. 'Tonight's not about Jamie. It's about Brandon Bailey.'

I swept some more blusher along my cheekbones and felt a fizz of excitement go through me. I hadn't been a date, a proper date, in so long I'd almost forgotten how it felt to get ready to meet someone I was attracted to. Because I *was* attracted to Brandon; any woman would be. True, we'd spoken a sum total of twice, and neither of those incidents were going to give Romeo and Juliet a run for their money, but now we had the whole evening ahead to get to know each other. And I was determined to have fun and put all thoughts of Jamie to the back of my mind.

My phone beeped again. Brandon this time.

Hey babe. The car is just pulling up outside your hotel. Take your time, I'll be waiting for you. Bx

Sweet, I thought and sent a quick reply back, saying I was on my way down. I took one last look in the mirror, grabbed my clutch and headed out of the door.

During the whole journey from my room, to the lift, down to the ground floor, across the lobby and out of the hotel, one thought kept running through my mind: *Don't make a tit out of yourself, Amber. Don't make a tit out of yourself, Amber. Don't make a tit out of yourself, Amber. Don't make a tit out of yourself, Amber.*

I stepped out onto the street and looked up and down the road but I couldn't see a yellow taxi pulled up anywhere. Had Brandon got the wrong hotel? I was about to get my phone out when I heard someone call my name.

'Amber – over here.'

I looked up and spotted an impressive-looking town car. The windows were blacked out but the rear one had been lowered and Brandon's face peered out, a big sexy smile on his face.

It took me a moment to put everything together – town car, no yellow taxi, Brandon, my date, private driver – but I just about managed to style it out. The driver opened the door and I slipped in next to Brandon, trying to look as though handsome, famous singers picked me up in town cars with personal drivers all the time.

'Hey,' I said.

'Hello.' Brandon made no attempt to disguise his stare as it swept up and down my body. 'You look incredible.'

Are all Americans so obvious? I thought. Yet there was something electric about the way he looked at me, and now that I could take a proper look at him I realised he looked pretty incredible too. His tight black shirt had one too many buttons undone and I could see the promise of some very toned pecs underneath. *Steady Amber!* His brown hair was neatly styled, and his matching brown eyes twinkled as he smiled at me – they were the exact colour of Galaxy chocolate. When I saw a couple of dimples appear when he smiled I knew I was done for. Who doesn't love a man with chocolate eyes and dimples?

The car pulled away from the kerb and seamlessly joined the busy New York traffic. Yellow cab after yellow cab filled the roads and sitting back against the plush leather seats, knowing that I could see everyone but no one could look back at me through the blacked-out windows, made me feel impossibly decadent.

I turned to Brandon. 'Thank you for taking me out. I know how busy you are.'

'It's no problem,' he said in his sexy American accent. 'I wanted to do something to celebrate your success. Besides, I was impressed that you didn't lose focus when we met backstage. I like an ambitious woman.'

Better not tell him I didn't recognise him straight away.

'The truth is, pet, that I didn't recognise you immediately.'

Or not . . . IDIOT!

'I was so distracted,' I went on quickly, 'that I couldn't place you. It wasn't until my assistant mentioned it to me that I realised the mistake I'd made.'

Brandon laughed. 'In that case I'm glad I got your number. Now you can make it up to me.' He stared at me so intensely that for a minute I thought I had something on my face. When he didn't break his gaze, I forced myself to look away first. *We haven't even got to the restaurant*, I thought. *Let's bring the intensity down a couple of notches.*

'So where are we going?' I asked.

'It's a surprise,' Brandon said enigmatically. 'Wait and see.'

'No where's the fun in that, pet?' I said. 'Me mam always—'

'What's memam mean?'

'Me mam,' I said slowly.

'That's what I said.' Brandon frowned in confusion. 'What's a memam?'

The penny dropped. 'Oh! Me mam. Mum, mother, woman who gave birth to me.'

Brandon's expression cleared. 'Right. Sorry. Guess it's going to take me a while to understand your accent. Where are you from?'

'That's the Geordie accent for you. I'm from Newcastle.'

'Is that in Scotland?'

'No,' I said. 'It's in England. It's not far from Scotland, though.'

'England and Scotland are close to each other?'

Is this bloke having a laugh? I'd heard that some Americans could be a little bit ignorant where the rest of the world was concerned, but this was ridiculous. 'Some parts, yeah,' I said.

I decided to change the subject. 'What part of America are you from?' Of course, I knew the answer to this already after my extensive stalking sesh, but I thought I would go through the traditional first date motions to be polite. And also so he

144

didn't suss that I was a crazy woman who, thanks to Google, Wikipedia, Twitter, Instagram, MySpace and the *Daily Mail* online, knew more about him than possibly his own mother.

'California,' he said. 'It's beautiful. Maybe I can show you it one day.'

'Steady on there, petal. Let's see how tonight goes,' I said.

'OK, OK,' Brandon said, raising his hands in defeat. 'One step at a time.' That didn't stop him shuffling closer to me, though, and placing his hand on my knee. I should've moved away from him I suppose – he was being a bit keen – but the truth was that I kind of liked the way it felt.

We'd been driving for almost forty-five minutes and chatting easily when the car finally came to a stop.

'We're here,' Brandon said.

I made to open the door but Brandon pulled my hand back. I looked at him in confusion until the driver opened the door. I tried to cover up my embarrassment; I wasn't used to personal drivers and waiting for someone to open the door for me – I was used to the Tube and treating myself to the occasional Uber. I tried to climb out of the car with as much grace as I could muster.

'Thanks,' I said to the driver. Was I supposed to tip him? I had no idea. Brandon took my hand and started walking away from the car. *Looks like it's no to the tipping, then.*

I took in my surroundings. I'd worked out we were headed to Brooklyn because we'd crossed the bridge. I liked the vibe of this part of New York. It was laid-back, pretty, full of boutiques and quaint cafés, somewhere you'd find young families and professionals – I felt that if I really did manage to move here, this is where I'd fit in. My eyes finally came to rest on the restaurant we were standing in front of. The River Café. It was situated right by the water and offered up a breathtaking view of Manhattan. The outside was lit up with strings of lights, the night was still and the entrance looked warm and inviting. I was speechless. I hadn't expected Brandon to bring me somewhere with such presence. I'd imagined he'd take me to some super-trendy sushi place with harsh lighting and intimidating waitresses, and an even more intimidating menu. This was a pleasant surprise.

'This is one of my favourite spots,' Brandon explained as we headed towards the door. 'It's been in a lot of films and famous people come here all the time, but it's incredibly special inside. You'll see why in a minute.'

Brandon held the door opened for me. As I stepped inside I fleetingly wondered if I'd see any famous people, and then I noticed that the place was deserted. *Don't tell me it's closed*, I thought. *I'm starving – I could eat a scabby horse*. I craned my neck to look further inside the restaurant and my eyes settled on the view of the New York skyline that glittered through the huge windows. I forgot about the lack of people and my age and ran like an excited kid on Christmas Eve towards the windows, staring in wonderment at the magnificent view in front of me. The iconic skyline that I'd only ever seen in pictures or on television was right in front of me. I took it in, committing every detail to memory. I was so in awe that I didn't notice Brandon was standing right next to me until he spoke.

'So what do you think?' he asked gently.

'This is the most beautiful place I've ever seen. That view . . . I'll never forget it.' I turned to look at him. 'Thank you for bringing me here. But, hang on,' I said as one crucial detail finally resurfaced in my mind, 'why is it empty? Is it closed?'

'It's closed to everyone except us,' Brandon said, taking my hand and leading me to a table by the window so I could still see the view. He pulled out the chair and I sat down. 'I pulled some strings and got them to shut the place down to everyone else tonight. I wanted you to enjoy the experience without being interrupted by someone wanting an autograph or a picture with me. And I wanted us to have some time alone, so I can really get to know you.'

My head was spinning. *He 'pulled some strings' and now we have the whole place to ourselves?* There was a small contingent of restaurant staff but they kept a discreet distance. It really did feel as though it was just me and Brandon. This kind of thing didn't happen to a lass from Newcastle.

Am I impressed? Or is this outlandishly extravagant and a bit pretentious? Or is it romantic?! Is he a bit of a tosser? Or is this like something out of a Reese Witherspoon film and he is the handsome good guy? Does it matter?! Am I enjoying myself? Yes! So for God's sake, Amber, just relax and let the proper fit international über-celeb wine you and dine you a bit and, for once, get out of your own head and chill out.

'Hey, Amber. I'm over here,' Brandon said, laughing.

'What?' I snapped from my thoughts and tore my eyes from the view.

'New York is hard to compete with,' Brandon said, his eyes twinkling again with amusement.

'I'm sorry,' I said. I forced myself to maintain eye contact and pretended that I'd been mesmerised by the view rather than internally debating if this little stunt made him a bellend or not. 'It's just such a beautiful view. I've seen photos but they don't compare to the real thing.'

'I want you to enjoy tonight. This is a celebration,' Brandon said. He beckoned to the staff and they started moving around with the efficiency of people who knew exactly what to do. 'I hope you don't mind but I've ordered us champagne and oysters to start.'

'That sounds great,' I said. Right now, Brandon could've said we were having blue WKDs and cheesy chips and I wouldn't have complained. The view was all I cared about.

The champagne arrived, the bottle was opened, and our glasses were filled. I took a sip and enjoyed the sensation of the bubbles travelling down my throat. I'd only had one sip of alcohol but I was already feeling light-headed. The effort that Brandon had put into this evening was incredible. No one had ever made me feel this special before. Whether this was a one-off or the start of something else, I knew that whatever happened I'd always remember this evening with fondness.

The oysters arrived at the table. *Hmm, maybe I won't remember these with fondness though* . . . I hate the slippery little suckers. Tom had made me try them once when his parents had been visiting and they'd taken all three of us out. I hadn't enjoyed them then and I doubt I'd enjoy them now, but at least I knew *how* to eat them and I wouldn't look like a total helmet in front of Brandon.

'You know what they say about oysters, don't you?' Brandon said, scooping one into his mouth with ease.

'Yeah, that they turn you into a creepy little sex pest,' I joked.

Brandon looked serious. 'Is that another Geordie saying?'

'No, sorry, pet. Erm, ignore me. Go on, what were you saying?' *Slow your chat down, man. He doesn't understand half of what you're saying.*

'Well,' Brandon continued, 'yes, they do say that oysters are aphrodisiacs. They are one of the most romantic of foods.'

'Cheers, then. Down the hatch.' The morsel of food slid down my throat and it took all of my willpower not to spit it out again. *How on earth is this slippery, slimy thing considered romantic?* I forced a smile onto my face and proceeded to eat another four. I didn't want Brandon to think I was ungrateful, but I was starting to feel ill. I wasn't sure if it was Brandon's predictable chat about aphrodisiacs affecting my gag reflex or the slimy, fishy, gooey chunks I was forcing down my throat in a desperate bid to impress him.

Eventually – thankfully – the evil oysters were cleared away, more champagne was poured and as we waited for the main course to arrive the horror of the starter became a distant memory. Brandon and I chatted casually without any awkward silences or tense moments. I told him about how lucky I felt to be working with Alessandro, we laughed over how dismissive I'd been when we'd first met, and he told me about how difficult it was missing home when they were on the road. A lot of what he said felt loaded with innuendo, but when he talked about his family I caught a glimpse of something softer underneath all the bravado and showmanship. It gave me the courage to bring up his exit from The Starks and ask his real reasons for leaving the band. So much had been reported in the papers but I knew how things could be skewed under the media spotlight.

'The Starks were my life for so long.' He looked out of the window, lost in thought. Our glasses were refilled and the waiter had disappeared before Brandon started speaking again. 'Me and the others, we were friends from school. We didn't go on reality TV, we weren't put together by some faceless record label. We just were four friends from California who practised songs in my garage. We thought we would take over the world, and that as long as we stayed friends nothing could stop us.'

I reached over and took hold of his hand. 'So what happened?' I asked gently.

'The start of it was like a fairytale, or something out of a movie. We were performing at some shitty gig and were spotted by a management company. They signed us up and not long after that they landed us our first record deal. The rest, as they say, is history. We became an overnight success – it all happened so quickly, none of us had the chance to take it in.'

'It is a whirlwind.' I nodded my head, understanding how quickly you can go from nothing to something, because it was exactly how I was feeling right now.

'So there we were, four young guys, suddenly famous, recognised everywhere. We were performing and getting number ones all over the world. It was everything we'd ever wanted.'

'It must've been amazing, to have achieved your dreams and have your best mates by your side, sharing in the moment.'

'That was exactly it,' Brandon said, 'we were having the time of our lives and it all felt so good because we were together. Imagine going on vacation with your best friends. Then imagine that vacation being your life. We were nonstop. After the first album came the second one, and we were touring all the time. Our own gigs, plus festivals. And then there were the girls. Everywhere we went, girls were throwing themselves at us – and we let them. I'm not proud of it, but when you've got pretty girls lining up to tell you how great you are, how much you mean to them, it's hard to say no to it all.'

'I get that,' I said. 'Even the strongest person would have a hard time saying no to that.'

Brandon shook his head. 'I should've been stronger. I got caught up. I was partying too hard, sleeping with a different girl every night. A lot of them sold kiss-and-tells to the press but even then I didn't care. I felt like "the man". But the cracks began to appear in the band.'

'In your friendship or working relationship?'

'Both. One too many nights out, one too many girls, one too many kiss-and-tells. Too many parties, too much alcohol. It all came to a head and I decided that I wanted some time off. I wanted to see my folks and regroup. I didn't know where home was any more – I was moving from hotel room to tour bus to hotel room all the time and I was writing and recording too. It was all getting too much for me, but the others disagreed. They wanted to keep going, keep performing, keep making as much money as possible. When I raised it with our label and suggested we all needed a break from the road for a while I was told that if we did that the band would lose popularity. For the sake of the band we couldn't take our feet off the gas, not for one second.'

'That sounds a bit full on. I work hard but I don't know what I'd do if I couldn't just get on a train and visit me mam every so often, chill out and enjoy a sense of home and normality. I think everyone needs that,' I said.

'The record label didn't see us as human beings, just commodities. I could see that we were losing sight of who we

151

were, and the friendship we'd built everything on wasn't there any more. I wanted to salvage our friendship but in the end the other guys started to value the money and the fame more. I didn't know them by the end, I didn't know who they'd become, but worse than that I didn't know myself either.'

'That sounds so lonely,' I said.

Brandon looked at me for a moment before continuing. 'You know, you're the first person to see it like that, and that's exactly what it was. I was lonely. I was surrounded by people all the time but I was always alone.'

I downed the last of my champagne. This was more emotional than the kind of first date chat I was used to. Normally we talked about childhood pets and where we liked to go on holiday. I needed the social lubrication of the bubbles.

'Sorry,' Brandon said. 'Let's talk about something else. I didn't mean to bring the mood down.'

I felt awful. I hadn't meant to make him feel uncomfortable. 'No, no,' I said. 'You haven't, trust me. Please, keep talking to me. What happened next?'

'I gave them an ultimatum. I told them either we take a break, or I'd quit the band. And suddenly here I am, solo, trying to figure things out for myself. I've signed a deal with a smaller label and we're working on new material, but I'm taking it slowly. I'm not used to doing this on my own and I'm determined to keep my word – I have to slow everything down and not get caught up in that hamster wheel again. It feels strange, but I think I'm doing the right thing.'

'Sounds to me as though you are. Are you still in touch with the rest of the band?'

Brandon shook his head sadly. 'It all got a bit . . . difficult towards the end. There have been a couple of times we've all been at the same awards show or something, though they sit miles away from me so there's no chance of us bumping into each other. I think they probably ask to. It's awkward, I suppose.'

'I know nothing about the music industry apart from what I read online,' I said, 'but I do know that you have to be honest with yourself if what you're putting out there is going to be any good. It's like anything – if you're hoping to produce something creative you have to be in the right frame of mind. And family is important. You need to make time for them, so if leaving the band and slowing things down means you get that balance back then I think that can only be a good thing.'

Brandon picked up my hand and kissed the back of it softly. My skin tingled where his lips had been. *I've either had too much champagne or four oysters is all it takes to turn me on these days*, I thought.

'Beautiful, talented and smart,' Brandon said. 'I feel like the luckiest man in New York right now.'

I was saved from ruining the moment with a classic case of Amber Raey verbal vomit by the waiter bringing us our main course.

I popped the last piece of steak into my mouth. It was the most perfectly cooked steak I'd ever had the pleasure of eating. I sighed.

'I take it you enjoyed that?' Brandon said.

'I did,' I said. 'I think that's the best thing I've had in my mouth for a long time.'

Brandon half-coughed, half-choked on his drink. I felt

153

myself go red as I realised what I'd said. I opened my mouth to try to salvage things but stopped when Brandon held up his hands.

'There's no coming back from that,' he said through his laughter. 'Don't even try!'

I groaned. 'You have to at least let me try to redeem myself.'

'No way. You're just going to have to live with it, baby.'

It had been like this through the whole meal. One minute we were talking about something serious and emotional, and the next I'd say something stupid, or that would need explaining because of my accent, and Brandon would tease me mercilessly. I hadn't had this kind of easy banter with anyone since . . . well, since Jamie, but that didn't count.

I'd told Brandon about Mam and Ruby, and Dad. I didn't find it easy to talk about what had happened to Dad, but after Brandon had opened up about the reasons behind him going solo it had felt natural to open up in return. He'd been kind, attentive, sympathetic, and I'd realised with a start that he was the first person who hadn't known me when Dad was alive that I'd truly talked to about his death.

'Did you ever try to find your real dad?' Brandon had asked at one point.

'No, he left us before I was born and he's never tried to contact me. Sometimes I wonder if he went on to have another family and if I have other siblings but it's never more than that – a fleeting thought. I had the best dad in the world and I don't need to go searching for a dickhead one who abandoned me as a replacement. I just wish my dad was still here.'

'There's a destructive nature to people who do drugs, but

the havoc it wreaks on others is criminal,' Brandon had said seriously.

At last, I'd thought, *we're speaking the same language.*

'I'm stuffed,' I said after the dessert had been cleared away. 'That chocolate thing was bloody lush.'

'Lush?' Brandon asked.

'Oh sorry, erm, delicious? Amazing? A little chocolately taste of heaven?' I laughed.

'I'm going to have to start writing some of these words down,' Brandon said. 'Otherwise I'll never be able to understand what you're saying to me.'

'That sounds to me like you're fishing for a second date, Mr Bailey.'

'Maybe I am, Miss Raey.'

Despite my initial reservations, I'd had a great time with Brandon. The restaurant, the view, the food, the endless supply of champagne, the fact that we'd had the place to ourselves – it had been far more than I'd been expecting. I would've been happy with a pizza in a nice Italian, so this had surpassed all my expectations. And Brandon had been full of surprises too. There had been some issues with understanding each other but we'd laughed over it and to be honest it had all added to the fun of the night. He'd been surprisingly insightful and sensitive, and although he'd come on pretty strong at points I hadn't minded – I suppose that was Americans for you. In all honesty, it had given me a bit of a thrill.

'I'm serious,' Brandon said as he helped me on with my jacket. He turned me round to face him. 'I'd really like to see you again.'

'I'd like that too,' I said. 'But I'm flying back to London tomorrow.'

His hands were on my waist. 'That's no problem. It's only an ocean. I'm coming to London next week for some promo on my new single.'

'You kept that quiet.' I hit him playfully on the arm. 'Why didn't you say anything?'

'I'm saying something now. It's my first single as a solo artist and we're going to be using London as our base for a month or two so I can get to Europe easily. If you're interested, we can spend some time together getting to know one another properly.'

'I'm sure we can arrange something, pet,' I said. I wanted to sound flirtatious but after all that champagne I probably sounded like a horny football hooligan, fifteen pints in and ordering a kebab. I am never the most sexy or discreet of drunks.

Brandon took my hand and led me outside, where the car was waiting. He made a move as if to open the door for me and then he turned back.

'I don't want the night to end but I'm guessing you need to sleep if you're flying back tomorrow.'

'Yeah, I'm afraid so,' I said reluctantly. I wanted the night to go on too but my sensible side kicked in and I knew I should try to get some sleep. We had an early start in the morning and I'd already had so much champagne I knew I was going to be hungover on the flight home.

'You can't blame a guy for asking,' Brandon said, opening the door. 'Let's get you back to your hotel, then, Miss Raey.'

The car began its journey back to the hotel. I rested my head on Brandon's shoulder. He put his arm around me and pulled me in closer. He turned his head and I felt him kiss my forehead. *Mmm, that felt nice.* I lifted my head off his shoulder and looked up at him. His eyes drifted from my eyes down to my lips. I parted them slightly and tilted my head back further. He didn't need any more encouragement.

He pressed his lips on mine and kissed me, gently at first but then with more urgency. I shifted slightly so that I was more upright and could wrap both of my arms around him. He ran his hands up and down my back and pressed me to him more firmly. He was a *good* kisser.

It felt like we'd only been in the car for five minutes when the driver coughed discreetly. I pulled away from Brandon, startled, and realised we were back at my hotel.

I straightened my top and ran a hand through my hair, trying to hide my embarrassment. *Weyaye, what are you playing at, necking on like that in the back of a car? You're not eighteen any more and this is not a taxi back from the diamond strip on a Saturday night, Amber Raey! Hasty exit needed immediately to avoid any more border-line slaggy behaviour.*

Brandon caught my hand, and when I turned to look at his face I saw an expression full of lust. No embarrassment at all. He kissed me gently.

'Until London, Miss Raey.'

'Until London, Mr Bailey.'

Chapter Fifteen

The phone in my room started ringing. My mobile phone started ringing too. There was an incessant banging on the door. I stumbled out of bed, picked up the hotel phone and assured the person on the other end that I was awake. I picked up my phone and silenced it when I saw that it was Freddie. I opened the door. I already knew who was going to be on the other side of it.

'Morning, sleeping beauty,' Freddie chirped, bounding into my room. 'Three alarm calls is all it takes to wake you up, I see.'

I slumped back on the bed. 'Why are you so happy?'

'I'm no happier than usual, babes,' he said. 'This is just what it looks like to get a decent night's sleep. Right, you've got twenty minutes to shower and get dressed, then we're going to get breakfast.'

'You don't have to wait here while I get ready,' I said. Maybe I could squeeze in another ten minutes' sleep if Freddie left.

'I do have to stay,' Freddie insisted. 'Otherwise you'll go back to sleep. Don't think I don't know that's why you're trying to get rid of me. Right, come on.'

Damn, he knows me too well.

Freddie pulled me up and escorted me into the bathroom before leaving me to it. I shook my head to try to wake myself up. Freddie was officially my work Jess … and I couldn't survive without either of them getting on my tits in the morning.

'Ooooof!' I groaned. It had taken both me and Freddie to haul my suitcase upright.

'I feel like I've done ten rounds with Floyd Mayweather,' Freddie said, panting.

'Snap,' I replied. I tried to elaborate but couldn't. I was simply too shattered.

'Oohh, you really are a banter wizard this morning, aren't you?'

I gave Freddie my best withering look. He continued, unperturbed. 'Breakfast?' he said. 'That'll make you feel better.'

Fifteen minutes later and I was tucking into a plate of blueberry pancakes, berries and a healthy splash of maple syrup. I was going to enjoy my last hotel breakfast because soon it would be back to toast and coffee made by Jess's fair hand. God bless Jess for putting up with me, but I'd become used to this sugar-fest every morning. Not that my waistline thanked me for it, mind. My Topshop skinnies were getting tighter by the day.

I spotted Jamie across the room and waved hello. He waved back but didn't come over to sit with me and Freddie, choosing instead to join some of the other models who had been in the show. I tried not to be hurt, and frankly I was too hungover to give it much thought, but I was still feeling stung by his abrupt message yesterday. I hoped we could get past this and go back to being just friends soon.

'Right, missy,' Freddie said, taking a bite out of an omelette oozing chorizo, feta and spinach. 'Tell me about last night.'

I hadn't told many people about my prospective date with Brandon. I'd texted Jess because, well, because she's Jess, and I'd told Freddie so he could cover for me in case anyone was looking for me last night. And then Jamie, of course.

'I had a nice time.'

Freddie stared at me.

'What?' I said.

'Seriously? You went out with Brandon Bailey, and all you're going to say is that you had "a nice time"? Spill the beans you sneaky slag or it's the last time I cover for you.'

'But it's true. I did have a nice time.' I laughed, enjoying winding Freddie up.

'Don't act coy with me, woman. You're about as much use as a chocolate watch. I want details and I want them now, Raey!'

'All right, all right,' I said. 'Let me finish eating first. I need the energy. My hangover is raging.'

'Did he wine and dine you?'

I nodded. 'He wined and dined me like I've never been wined and dined before. I felt like a princess.'

Freddie grinned. 'That's all I need to know. For now,' he added as an afterthought. I knew I wasn't going to get off the hook that easily.

*

It took *forever* to get through airport security. And then it took *forever* for our gate to be called. And then it took *forever* to board the plane. OK, nothing had really taken forever but it had *felt* like it. The breakfast pancakes had done very little to ease the hangover; instead, they were now joining the hangover and I could sense the onset of a carb coma. I was powerless against their combined wrath. *Man down! Save yourselves! Leave me behind! I'm done for!*

OK, a little bit over-dramatic, but feeling like death on top of all the flying home malarkey was the last thing I needed. Freddie had to help me find my seat on the plane, that's how useless I had become. I straight away pulled out my blanket, earplugs and an eyemask. The only way to get through the flight was to sleep through it. I was sitting in a duo seat and hoped that whoever was sitting next to me wasn't a talker, a snorer, a handsy bastard or any combination of the above.

'I'm next to you, Geordio,' Jamie said, slipping into the seat I'd been contemplating. He pulled out his headphones and his iPad.

'Great,' I replied, but because I was tired and hungover and still a bit pissed off it came out sounding sarcastic. Jamie raised an eyebrow but I didn't have it in me to apologise.

There was a minute or two of strained silence. I was thinking that it might be a good time to slip on my eyemask when Jamie asked, 'So, how was last night?'

I bristled. This was not the right time to talk to Jamie about my date with Brandon. I wasn't thinking straight.

'It was fine, thanks,' I replied brusquely.

Jamie waited for me to elaborate. When it was clear I wasn't going to, he said, 'It's OK if you don't want to talk about it.'

'It's not that. I'm just tired.'

'Were you out late, then?'

'Not really. Too much champagne.'

'Right. Champagne.'

'Yes. Champagne. Is that a problem?'

'Did I say it was? Take it easy, Amber. I was only trying to make conversation.'

'So now you're Mr Talkative, eh? Now you have something to say? You sure know how to pick your moments.'

I knew I was being unnecessarily rude, and the hurt in Jamie's eyes took my breath away.

'I'm sorry,' I sighed. 'I'm just knackered and hungover as balls. I need to go to sleep, babe.'

Jamie put his earphones in and turned away from me. 'I won't say another word.'

The pilot's voice announcing our descent into Heathrow woke me from a deep sleep. I rubbed my face, trying to wake up properly. At least the hangover seemed to have disappeared.

'Hi,' I said to Jamie, stretching.

'Hi,' he replied, not exactly warmly. 'Sleep well?'

'Yeah,' I said. 'And the hangover seems to have gone.'

'I'm very happy for you.'

I looked at Jamie to see if he was joking. He wasn't smiling. 'J, I'm sorry I was a bitch earlier. I was just—'

'Hungover. Yeah, you said.'

'Come on, you've never been short with anyone when you've been feeling rough?'

'There's a difference between being short with someone and being rude to them. You were rude.'

'I didn't mean to be. I really am sorry.'

'Don't treat me like a mug, OK? Friends don't do that to each other.'

I blinked. I'd really upset him. 'I don't think you're a mug. I think you're a great lad and a wicked mate. If I said sorry one more time, would it help?' I saw the ghost of a smile on Jamie's lips. 'See! You can't be upset with me for long. Am I forgiven?'

Jamie looked at me long and hard. 'This once, Geordio,' he said slowly. 'Just this once.'

We made our way off the plane, through passport checks and baggage reclaim without incident. There was a flurry of goodbye hugs and kisses as everyone went their separate ways and then suddenly I was in the back of a black cab, hurtling back to my little flat. I looked out at the cold autumnal morning and felt like New York was already a distant memory, but it was good to be back.

I was going through my messages, responding to the ones from Mam, Ruby, Jess and Tom, when my phone beeped with a new message.

Hope you got home safe, angel. Can't wait to see you in London. I haven't stopped thinking about you. Bx

I sat back in my seat smiled all the way home.

I'd spent most of the day asleep – my jetlag would not thank me for that over the next few days but, whatever, I was sleepy – and now I was curled up on the sofa under a blanket, curtains drawn against the darkening sky, when the door opened and Jess bounded in.

'You're back!' she said, jumping on me.

I hugged her back. 'Did you miss me, then? I haven't been gone for that long.'

'It feels like *forever*. We've all missed you.'

'You in tonight?' I asked.

Jess nodded. 'Yep. Let me change and then we're not moving from the sofa until you've told me all about New York.'

Jess and I spent an enjoyable few hours munching our way through a large pepperoni pizza, potato wedges and nachos. She told me how well things were going with Sam and in return I told her every detail about the show, and we pored over the online reviews together. Eventually she asked about Brandon.

'It took you long enough!' I said, laughing. 'I thought that would be the first thing you'd want to know about.'

'I've been dying to ask you,' Jess said. 'But I wanted to hear about the show as well. You have too much news!'

'That's what Mam said.'

'So she knows about Brandon Bailey?'

'Yep, I told her. I'm going to leave it to her to tell Rubes, though.'

I smiled as I remembered the conversation I'd had with Mam earlier today. She'd been so excited to hear from me. I was going to Newcastle in the morning to spend a long weekend with her and Ruby before work became insane all over again, but even so we'd still been on the phone for over an hour, catching up.

'So tell me all about your date with Brandon Bailey,' Jess went on.

'I will, but only on one condition.'

'What's that?'

'That you stop calling him Brandon Bailey. Don't double-name him. It's weird.'

Jess laughed. 'OK, sorry. Go on then. Tell me all the saucy details.'

I did my best to explain how much I'd enjoyed myself on the date but I'm not sure I did it justice. Jess looked suitably impressed when I told her how Brandon had booked out the whole of the River Café and she grimaced along with me when I told her about the oysters, so I couldn't have done too bad a job. I decided to leave out the part about how we'd barely come up for air on the drive back to the hotel. I was still feeling mildly embarrassed and that I'd acted like an over-excited teenager, but couldn't help but let slip that we'd kissed.

When I'd finished, Jess said, 'It sounds amazing and like he really pulled out all the stops. But . . . ' She hesitated.

'What is it?' I asked.

'It's just, well, his reputation. You're not interested in Jamie because of his reputation, but isn't Brandon's even worse? Sorry,' she quickly added, seeing the expression on my face. 'It's just Jamie's our mate so it's different – we know him. All I know about Brandon is what I've read and it hasn't all been good.'

'You're right,' I said. 'He does have a bit of a rep, but he spoke to me about it and there's so much more to him than what's been in the press. He got caught up with everything when he was in the band, but now he's slowing things down. We've all done stuff we regret, after all. Remember the time you shagged that ginger bloke from your office who still lived with his mam and smelled like egg sandwiches? I mean, how would you feel if no one let you forget that?' *Did I sound defensive?* I smiled so Jess would know I wasn't mad. I knew she was only being a good friend.

'As long as you're sure,' Jess said. 'You know him better than I do. Just take it slowly, OK? Get to know him away from all the fancy restaurants and champagne. But enjoy yourself too!'

'For God's sake, woman,' I said, hitting her over the head with a cushion. 'You're worse than me mam. But I get what you're saying. I'll be careful.'

'Good.' She grinned at me. 'So, when do I get to meet him?'

'Let's wait and see if I see him again,' I said wryly. 'He might not even call.'

'But you've already heard from him?' Jess asked.

I nodded.

'Then stop being so paranoid, and just enjoy it.'

'Fine.' I tried to stifle a yawn. 'I can't be tired: I've been asleep most of the day! Jetlag's a punch in the dick.'

'Go on and get some sleep. I'll clear up,' Jess said.

'But I wanted to wait up for Tom,' I said.

'He'll be hours yet,' Jess said. 'I'll tell him you love him, don't worry.'

'Promise?' I said sleepily.

'Cross my heart. And we can have a flat dinner when you're back on Sunday,' Jess said. 'Now go to bed before I change my mind about clearing up.'

I disappeared pretty quickly – Jess didn't really need to offer twice – and I was asleep before my head hit the pillow.

Chapter Sixteen

I opened the door, fully expecting the empty house that greeted me. Mam was working and Ruby had stayed over at Maisie's the night before so she would be home later too. I sank down onto the sofa, enjoying the peace and quiet. I was still shattered. How long would this jetlag last? *I'll close my eyes for a minute*, I thought. *I'll be awake before Mam and Rubes get home. I need—*

'Amber,' Ruby's voice cut across my sleep and I sat bolt upright.

I'd only just got home. Had Ruby been in the house after all? I checked my watch. Nope, I'd been here for two hours already. 'I must have nodded off,' I said, stretching.

'Yeah, you were snoring so loud I thought someone was mowing the carpet in the front room,' Ruby said.

'Give us a cuddle then you cheeky little madam,' I said. I hadn't expected her to give me one so willingly but she did, and it was a good one too. I looked down into her face. She looked different, a bit happier. Less surly round the edges. 'You OK?'

'Yeah,' Ruby said, sitting down on the sofa. I sat down next to her. 'Thanks for sending all the photos when you were in New York. Everyone at school was so jealous. Especially of that one of the Kardashians in the audience.'

'I'm glad they were useful! It was amazing, Rubes. I fell in love with New York.'

'It got me thinking,' Ruby said, 'about how much is out there. If I work hard, I could go to New York too. Or anywhere really.'

'Keep your head down and your nose clean and the entire world is yours for the taking.'

Ruby was silent so I snuck a look at her. She appeared lost in thought so I took advantage of her preoccupation and watched her for a second longer. She looked so much like Dad it was painful to look at her sometimes. I didn't know what was going on in that head of hers but it sounded like she was thinking about her future and I took that as a good sign. Maybe she'd finally turned a corner.

'That's what every mother likes to see. Her two favourite girls huddled up on the sofa,' Mam said. I jumped up and gave her a hug – and was happy to see that Ruby did the same.

'What's for tea, Mam?' Ruby asked, and I laughed.

'She's only just got in from work. How about we get a take-away? My treat,' I suggested.

'Sounds good to me,' Mam said, taking off her shoes and rubbing her feet. 'The last thing I want to do is stand in that kitchen.'

'I could murder a chicken korma,' Ruby said.

'Indian works for me,' I said.

'Me too. Rubes, would you grab the menu from the kitchen please?' Mam asked.

When Ruby had left the room, I turned to Mam. 'OK, who is she and what have you done with my moody little sister?' I whispered.

'I know! I'm not sure what the hell has changed but,' Mam smiled as she whispered back, 'she's been happier since we came back from visiting you, and things have been easier. She still has her moments, but no more staying out all night and she's brought your dad up a couple of times. I don't know what you said to her but it seems to have worked.'

'I guess sometimes things just need a bit of a big sister touch, Mam.'

Mam spotted the door opening a second before I did and quickly changed the subject just before Ruby could catch us talking about her.

'So how does it feel to be a famous designer?' Mam teased.

'I wouldn't go that far,' I laughed, 'but the feeling I got before the show, and then the reviews – honestly, I was buzzing, Mam. I can't wait to get back to work and get started on the next project.'

'Can I get any free clothes now?' Ruby cut in.

I exchanged a look with Mam and then we both burst out laughing. 'Weyaye! She certainly is your daughter, isn't she?' I teased.

'Listen, I brought you's both up the same. Shy bairns get nowt!' Mam answered, smiling.

'Well said, Mam!' I agreed. 'But we'll have to wait and see what the sales are like before I can start giving things away. OK?'

'S'pose,' Ruby said grumpily. She may have turned a corner but she was still fourteen and that came with a whole set of other challenges. Like twisting her face when she didn't get her own way.

'Let's order,' Mam said, taking charge. 'And then you can tell us all about this famous singer boyfriend of yours.'

'He's not my boyfriend,' I protested. 'It was one date!'

'I'm so jel,' Ruby said. 'I can't believe you even met Brandon Bailey, let alone went on a date with him. What's he like?'

'Scran first,' I said. 'Boys second.'

'Can I ask you girls something?' Mam said. We'd just finished clearing up the remnants of our takeaway feast, and we were settled on the sofa, with wine for me and Mam, and a hot chocolate for Ruby.

'Go for it,' I said to Mam.

'I'd like to visit your dad's memorial tomorrow. It feels good to go there when things are going well, and we have some good news after Amber's show. Will you both come with me?' Mam fiddled with the stem of her wine glass.

Dad had been cremated and we'd scattered his ashes in the Garden of Remembrance at the crematorium. We always visited him together on his birthday and on the anniversary of his death. I knew Mam went there all the time on her own, and I did too when I was home, but I didn't know how often Ruby visited. She didn't like to talk about it.

'Of course,' I said straight away – as if I would say no. 'Ruby?' I looked at her pointedly.

'Sure, I'll come,' Ruby said quietly.

The three of us sat in silence, each thinking about the most important man in our lives. He'd meant everything to us and life would always be a little emptier without him. I tried not to feel sad every time I thought about him because he'd brought so much good into the world, but it was different for Ruby. She was still so young, and every little girl needs her father. I wished that I could do something about it, but this wasn't something any of us could fix. We just had to stand strong together, Dad's girls.

Ruby and I were in the kitchen the next morning, drying the breakfast dishes. Mam was upstairs. We were planning to leave for the crematorium in a few minutes.

'Amber?'

'Yes, babes?' I said.

'I was thinking, do you reckon, erm . . . Do you think I have what it takes to be a model?'

I looked at her sharply. Where had *that* come from? Ruby was beautiful, stunning, and yes, she probably did have what it took to be a model – she was as striking as any of the models I'd seen in New York – but my sister a model? My *little* sister a model? I really wasn't sure about this. I couldn't say that to her, though. I didn't want this to turn into a fight right before we went to visit Dad.

'Maybe,' I said carefully, 'but you're still growing and you're far too young, Rubes.'

'Girls my age model, though,' she pointed out.

'That's true, but we only used over-eighteens for our shows in New York and my collection was one of the few ranges aimed at a really young market. You definitely have the potential, but I think you should focus on school right now. Pass your exams, have something to fall back on. It's an unpredictable business.' I knew I sounded like a responsible, boring old sod but modelling could be brutal and if Ruby was serious, then I wanted her to be armed with as much fire-power as possible before she entered the lion's den.

'You sound like Mam! Come on, man. Right, I'll make a deal with you. If I work hard and pass my GCSEs, will you help me break into modelling?'

Were we really having this conversation? 'I'm not sure. It's not really up to me. Have you spoken to Mam?'

'A bit.' Ruby shrugged. 'She said the same as you – I need to finish school before we can talk about it seriously.'

'There you go then. Finish school, pass your exams and then we'll see where we're at. You might have changed your mind by then.'

'I doubt it. You didn't. You've always known what you wanted to be.'

That threw me. Rubes had really thought it all through. 'This is something you really want?'

Ruby nodded enthusiastically. 'I really do.'

'Fine. Here's the deal then – work hard, finish your GCSEs *and* stay out of trouble in the meantime. If you still want to model after all of that, then I'll help you. You know it's not all glamorous shoots and exotic locations, right? You'll have to deal with some pretty crap jobs before you get a good one.'

'That's OK. I don't mind sticking it out. It worked for you.'

Well would you look at that? My kid sister has been paying attention after all.

'What are you two talking about?' Mam said, walking into the kitchen.

'Ruby's dream to become Newcastle's answer to Gigi Hadid,' I told her.

'Both my girls in fashion? I'm not sure I can cope. But Rubes, we've talked about this. You know you need to—'

'Finish school. Yeah, I know. And Amber has given me the same lecture. I'll get my GCSEs and then I'm going to become Amber Raey's favourite model.'

'You already are,' I said, ruffling her hair. She hated having her hair ruffled but if this wasn't an appropriate hair-ruffling moment I didn't know what was.

I furiously wiped the tears off my cheeks. The minute I saw the rose bush and the small plaque with Dad's name, I always started crying. Tears were rolling down Mam's cheeks too. Ruby's face was tearless. She stood, biting her lip, her hands curled into fists, just like she used to when she was little and she was upset about something but didn't know how to deal with it. We'd spent the last hour talking to Dad, telling him all of our news, and now we had to say goodbye. It was stupid: he wasn't here any more, it shouldn't be this hard to walk away from his place at the crematorium. But every time felt like the first time; it never got any easier.

Mam pulled me and Rubes close and the three of us stood together, looking at Dad's plaque.

'I miss him all the time,' I said.

'I do too, pet.' Mam kissed my forehead and then Ruby's.

'Life is so fucking unfair,' Ruby said quietly.

'I couldn't agree more, love,' Mam said. She didn't even tell Ruby off for swearing.

The rest of the day went by in a subdued blur. The three of us stuck close to home and to each other. We didn't talk about Dad for the rest of the day, or our trip to the crematorium, but we all knew what the others were feeling and simply knowing that we all understood each other was enough. We didn't need to say the words; some things are better left unspoken.

There really is no place like home, I thought.

Chapter Seventeen

I let myself into the flat and was greeted by the delicious smell of roast chicken. It had been a wrench leaving Mam and Rubes after the emotional time we'd spent together. The only thing that had made coming back to London bearable was that Jess and Tom would be waiting for me at the flat. I'd WhatsApped them on our group, The Tinder Towers Threesome – I know, I know, so bad, but Tom wouldn't let us change it – with my ETA and Jess, domestic goddess that she was, had clearly timed having dinner ready to the second I walked through the door.

'Hey, honeys, I'm home,' I shouted. Tom came jumping into the hallway like a kid at Christmas and picked me up.

'I've missed you, mate. You're never allowed to leave me again.'

'How many times did you wake up in my room while I was gone?'

Tom put me down and looked at my sheepishly. 'Three.'

'Three!' I hit him on the arm.

'I changed your sheets,' he protested. 'That's something.'

That was something. I can't remember the last time Tom changed his own sheets. They probably had chlamydia by now.

'It's everything,' I said, giving him a hug. 'Where's the wifey?'

'Slaving over a hot stove. She's making the Jess spesh.'

'Roast chicken with slightly burnt Yorkshires and all the trimmings?' My mouth was already watering.

'That's right. Come on, it's nearly ready.'

I threw my bag in my room and followed Tom into the kitchen.

'Hey, lovely lass of mine,' I said to Jess as I took in her frilly apron. 'You look like the perfect 1950s housewife.'

'It's a one night only special,' Jess said, handing me a much-needed glass of rosé. 'Don't get too used to it.'

'Too late,' said Tom, downing half a bottle of Corona in one swig. 'I expect this treatment every day, woman.'

'Call me woman again and it won't just be the Yorkshires that are burning. I'll set you on fire as well,' Jess said, pointing a very sharp-looking knife in his direction.

'Tom, don't make the crazy knife lady angry,' I said.

I'd spoken to Jess yesterday, after we'd got back from the crematorium, and she'd obviously mentioned something to Tom because the two of them were going out of their way to distract me and make me laugh. *It's good to be back*, I thought. *If I have to leave Mam and Rubes for anyone, I'm glad it's these two bellends.*

Over roast chicken, roast potatoes, crispy vegetables, a sea of gravy and the world-famous Cajun (burnt) Yorkshires, I caught up with all of Tom's news, and for what felt like the hundredth time I recounted my date with Brandon for his pervy ears. I was helping Jess load the dishwasher when Tom declared that we were all going to Jalou for a drink.

'Mate, it's Sunday and I'm knackered,' I moaned. 'One sniff of a G&T and I'll be asleep.'

'No arguments, you're coming. Besides, you just polished off most of that bottle of rosé – I think you'll be fine,' Tom said, handing me my jacket. 'And when you go back to work tomorrow we probably won't see you again until Christmas.'

'That's an exaggeration, and Jess helped with the rosé!' I protested.

'Yes, it is,' Jess said, gently steering me out of the door and closing it firmly behind us. 'But just in case it isn't, let's make the most of tonight. It's been ages since the three of us were together like this.'

'OK, I surrender, but if I get mortal and can't hold my pencil straight tomorrow, you can explain to Alessandro why I'm shaking like a shitting dog and why my sketches look like they were drawn by a five-year-old.' *God, I'm easily convinced when alcohol is concerned.*

Tom, Jess and I pushed our way through the crowd at Jalou. Even on a Sunday night the place was packed. Jess spotted Sam and we made our way over to him. He'd managed to nab a table and for that, me and my aching limbs thanked him. After all the travelling I'd done in the last couple days I felt like I'd been beaten up. I wasn't in the mood to stand around and get jostled. The bar could be like a sale in Primark, everyone pushing and shoving. Sam grinned at Jess as we approached and as soon as he could get to her he grabbed her and kissed her hello. Tom made gagging noises while I busied myself making sure we had enough chairs. I was happy for Jess and Sam but I didn't need to see *that*. Suddenly, an image of me and Brandon kissing in the back of the car flashed into my head and I blushed. He'd be in London soon and I realised I couldn't wait to see him.

'I'll get the drinks,' Tom said. 'G&T or wine, girls?'

'G&T,' Jess and I said together.

'I'll give you a hand, mate,' Sam said. He gave Jess another quick kiss and then followed Tom to the bar.

Jess gave me a nudge. 'Maybe you'll bring Brandon here one day,' she teased.

'Let's not get ahead of ourselves,' I said. 'We haven't even had a second date yet. He might change his mind about me before the plane lands.'

'Don't be stupid. He's set the bar pretty high with the first date. He's probably wondering how he's going to beat that.'

'It's not realistic though, is it? All the glitz and glamour was fun on the first date but he can't keep doing that. Honestly, babes, I'll be happy with some decent fish and chips, a bottle of Echo Falls, a *Sons of Anarchy* box set and some good conversation.'

'You're so easily pleased,' Jess said. 'How are you still single?'

'It's probably because I'm a borderline alcoholic Geordie nutcase who works eighty-five-hour weeks and cares more about my flatmates than any man I've ever known, meaning my longest relationship has been with a pair of bunny slippers me mam bought me for Christmas six years ago.'

Jess burst out laughing. 'After all that information, I only love you more! I will repeat my question – how are you still single?'

Laughing along her, I gave my usual clichéd but honest

answer. 'I'm just waiting for the right man, I suppose. And I'm *not* saying that's Brandon,' I said quickly, before Jess could get the wrong idea, 'but he has made an impression and I'd like to spend some more time with him. He's so different to anyone else—'

'Ladies,' Jamie's voice interrupted. I turned to see him with Tom and Sam, laden with a tray full of drinks. Jamie quickly kissed Jess and me on each cheek, and as he did I felt him squeeze my arm slightly.

Good, we're friends again.

'How's the jetlag?' I asked.

'Don't believe in it,' he replied.

Typical J.

'Really? I'm almost OK now but I struggled for the first couple of days.'

'To be honest, I took a sleeping pill and slept for about thirty-six hours after we got back,' Jamie grinned. 'I've been fine ever since.'

'Clever bastard,' I replied.

'J, do you know where your campaign is being shot yet?' Jess asked.

Jamie nodded. 'London and New York. I'm going to be travelling a lot between now and Christmas.'

'Christmas,' I said. 'I can't believe it's only a couple of months away. Where has this year gone?'

'I love Christmas!' Tom yelled.

'We know, mate,' Jamie said, slapping Tom on the back. 'Any excuse for a party.'

'Nah, mate,' Tom said. 'There's mistletoe all over the place! The ladies can't escape my Christmas cheer with those crafty little leaves hanging everywhere.'

Tom and Jamie were having a very heated debate about whether standing under mistletoe or dressing up as Santa had more luck with the ladies when my phone beeped. My stomach flipped. It was a message from Brandon.

Hey beautiful. What are you up to? Bx

Sunday night drinking with some friends. I'm so tired! Ax

Lol. You need to slow down! Which bar are you in? Bx

It's called Jalou. My flatmate works here. It is literally our second home! Ax

Haha, looks like my scene! Where is it? Bx

London. I got in from Newcastle a few hours ago. Ax

Where in London? Bx

Puzzled, I sent him the details.

I looked up and caught Jamie's eye. 'Is that lover boy?' he asked, but not unkindly.

'Yeah, he just wanted to know what I was up to,' I replied.

'He's keeping tabs on your already,' Tom joked.

I rolled my eyes at him, and then tapped my empty glass.

'OK, OK, I'm on my way,' he said standing up.

Jess was in the middle of telling us how Tom had made her pretend to be his girlfriend last weekend so that he could let the poor lass he'd necked on with the previous evening down easily when there was a commotion at the entrance to Jalou. Two burly men started parting the crowd, asking people to move back.

'What's going on?' I asked.

Tom shrugged, and Jamie stood up trying to see what was going on. I peered around the groups standing near our table but I couldn't see anything except a sea of people's backs. There was an excited hum in the air. *It must be someone famous*, I thought. *But who would come to Jalou?* Something struck me. *He wouldn't . . . He wouldn't just turn up. He's not meant to be here until the middle of next week.*

And then there he was, standing in front of me in all his beautiful glory.

Oh my a million balls. OK. Be cool.

I stood up and threw my arms around him.

Perfect level of coolness. You twat.

'Brandon!' I said. 'What are you doing here?' I was only partially aware that everyone in the bar was staring at us.

'I wanted to see you,' he said simply, 'so I came over early.' He pulled me towards him again and kissed me in a way that made Jess and Sam's earlier greeting seem like the peck you get off your grannie at Christmas. I heard someone clear their throat – Jess, I *think* – and I pulled away.

'Everyone,' I said turning back to my friends. 'This is Brandon Bailey. Brandon, these are my friends.'

Like a pro, Brandon made sure he said hello to everyone around the table and then settled down in the seat next to me.

Brandon Bailey was sitting next to me in Jalou.

What do we do now?!

Chapter Eighteen

I ducked into my office, late for the first time in ages.

'Freddie, can you come in here, quick?' I said breathlessly.

'My God, babes, what happened to you? You look like Lindsay Lohan circa 2009.'

'I'm hungover as balls, man. Just as I'd recovered from New York, I go and do something stupid and set myself right back again.'

We had gone back to the flat after Jalou had closed and Brandon had insisted on joining us. He'd somehow convinced the bar to let him buy a few unopened bottles of champagne to take home as well. I don't know how he managed it, but Brandon wasn't someone who was used to being told no, that much was clear. Jamie had gone straight home from Jalou, claiming he had to be up early, but everyone else had staggered back to our flat – including a couple of hangers-on I only really knew by sight. We'd ended up drinking until way past three a.m., at which point Jess had seen sense and decided that the party was over. Brandon had wanted to stay the night but even in my champagne-fuelled 'I could quite possibly be dating a bonafide celeb' euphoria I knew that I wasn't ready for that so he'd gone back to the apartment he was renting. I'd had barely four hours' sleep. The whole thing was ridiculous and I felt like I'd been run over by a bus.

I gingerly sat down behind my desk and closed my eyes, just for a second.

'Amber, listen to me,' Freddie said, jolting me awake. 'Don't fall asleep! Anyone could walk in. You need to keep busy. If Britney can get through 2007, you can get through today. What's the plan of attack? Should I run interference if I spot any bigwigs? Or just keep tabs on Laurie? Or draw the blinds, lock the door and help you build a desk fort until this hangover goes away?'

'I need coffee before I do anything,' I said weakly, but with a smile on my face. *God, I love Freddie. And building forts actually— AMBER! Focus!*

'Would you be a love and get me the strongest latte you can, please? If I don't get some caffeine soon I'm worried about what I will do.'

'No problem.' Freddie looked amused at my pitiful state. 'Anything else, Brittaz?'

'Yes. Don't call me that, you knob. Please tell me that I don't have any meetings today.'

'Your calendar is clear, thankfully,' Freddie confirmed. 'Alessandro is still in Italy visiting his mum so it looks as though this little misdemeanour may go completely unnoticed. But remember that you have a meeting with him *next* Monday to start planning next season's range for Selfridges.'

'Right, yes, got it. Freddie, coffee. Please. And something

greasy. And don't say my hair. I can't deal with your sass today, pet. Not on this über-bitch of all hangovers.'

'You know me too well, missus,' Freddie chuckled and walked out. 'I'll be quick, but when I get back how about we start brainstorming for next week?'

'Freddie, man, when in the hell did you become such a workaholic?' I said. 'I swear when I met you, you were a whimsical work-shy wassick. I loved those times.'

'I learnt from the best, didn't I? Your vibe attracts your tribe and all that. I couldn't be working for the hardest graft-ing woman in fashion and not develop some sort of work ethic. You're your own worst enemy, Amber Raey.'

'Balls. So you're saying I created this slave-driving monster?'

'You certainly did, sugar tits. Now hide under your desk 'til I'm back with supplies. And a hairbrush – you look a show.' And with that he flounced out the door and I looked in the mirror on my desk. He was right. I did look a show. *Double balls.*

It felt like Freddie was gone for ages. During that time, I managed to get it together enough to reply to the message Brandon had sent earlier that morning. That kicked off a WhatsApp conversation, meaning I did nothing constructive work-wise while I waited for Freddie to come back. Brandon was certainly attentive. He had the next few days off and he wanted me to spend them with him. I explained that I had to work and I couldn't just drop everything. He kept trying though – *persistence is key*, he wrote in one message – so in the end I had to agree to have dinner with him later to get him to back off a little. All I wanted was an early night but I had a feeling that Brandon wouldn't accept any excuses. Or now that he knew our address he'd turn up unannounced . . .

Eventually, Freddie returned and I launched myself at him and grabbed my latte and Sausage & Egg McMuffin. I loved Freddie more than I loved my mam at that particular moment in time. After half an hour or so more of feeling sorry for myself, Freddie made me focus and we started throwing around ideas for my meeting with Alessandro next week. I wanted to bring something different to the range for the next season, but I wasn't sure what, so we figured that visiting some of my favourite buildings in London to see if they inspired anything in me would be a good starting point. I loved the V&A, St Paul's and Big Ben in particular, and at this time of year, when the nights were drawing in and winter was approaching, there was something beautiful about walking along the South Bank, with it lit up with lights and buzzing with people. Maybe I could take Brandon – I could show him around some of my favourite places while working. Brandon appeared keen to keep seeing me and I wanted to make the time for him while he was in London. After all, he was a long way from home and he'd pulled out all the stops to play tour guide for me in the States. I could already tell that juggling him and my work commitments was going to take some doing but I was determined to make it happen, and putting the two things together would be a good idea. There was something about Brandon. He made me feel special, like he only had eyes for me when we all knew he was in a room full of women who were mentally undressing him, and the rest. Alessandro had told me to live to be inspired. Maybe Brandon would provide that inspiration for me. Maybe he'd be my muse.

Whatever happened with Brandon, I had to make sure I didn't let my work suffer. Like today. I knew I wasn't performing to the best of my abilities and that didn't sit well with me. If this was to continue into something I had to find a better balance. I knew would, it was only that the whole thing was new to me. I just had to find my stride. And get through this hangover.

Miraculously, I somehow made it to the end of the day. Well, there was no miracle. It was through coffee, Freddie, more Sausage & Egg McMuffins, half a pack of paracetamol, a Ginsters Cornish pasty and a family-sized bag of pickled onion Monster Munch. As Brandon was picking me up from the office to take me to dinner I didn't have time to go home to change, so Freddie and I raided the samples wardrobe. We picked out a pair of leather trousers and a loose-fitting white linen shirt, showing just a hint of my black lacy bra, finished with a bold yellow colour-block suit jacket. We accessorised with lots of delicate gold necklaces and bracelets. I topped up my make-up, at which point Freddie declared that I could finally pass for a human being. He made a great personal stylist. I had wanted to slip away quietly but Freddie wasn't having any of it. He wanted to meet Brandon so he insisted on walking me downstairs.

We walked out of the building and I immediately spotted the car – the blacked-out windows were a dead giveaway. The driver held open the door for me but before I could get inside, Freddie pushed me out of the way and poked his head in like a nosey little weasel.

'Brandon, hi. I'm Freddie, I work with Amber,' he gushed. 'I'm a huge fan. If you need anything while you're in London, just shout. I'm your man.' Freddie shoved his hand out and Brandon, looking amused, shook it.

'Nice to meet you,' Brandon said. 'And thanks for that. I might just take you up on your offer.'

'Freddie,' I said. 'Can I get in now please?'

'Sure, sure.' Freddie ducked back out and moved to the side. He gave me a double thumbs-up as I climbed into the car and mouthed 'FIT!'

I waved at him and the driver closed the door behind me. I turned to Brandon.

'Sorry about that,' I said. 'He wanted to meet you and I couldn't—'

Brandon's mouth was on mine before I could finish the sentence. I was slightly taken aback and tried to place a little distance between us. Brandon just pulled me in closer and eventually I gave in. He really was a good kisser.

'Where are we going?' I asked when we finally broke apart.

'Wherever you like,' Brandon said. 'Dinner, drinks, cocktails. Your choice. What would you like to do?'

'Do you know what I want more than anything right now?'

'Tell me.'

'My PJs, a box set and a massive pizza.'

Brandon laughed. 'How about a night in at my apartment then?'

'That—' I kissed him quickly, 'sounds like heaven.'

Brandon's Kensington apartment was immense. It had three huge bedrooms, two bathrooms, an open-plan living area and kitchen and plush cream carpets throughout the rooms. It was at least three times the size of my flat, and there were three of us in there. Brandon had this place all to himself. I was a little intimidated as he showed me around, but he was so sweet that eventually I relaxed. At one point he disappeared to order the food and when the doorbell rang forty-five minutes later I was expecting him to come in bearing Domino's. I should've known better. He's ordered from some small and hideously exclusive Italian restaurant in North London. They'd even sent proper metal cutlery over with it. And it wasn't just pizza that Brandon had ordered, of course. There was bruschetta and calamari to start, seafood tagliatelle and tiramisu for dessert.

'So, what are your plans while you're here?' I asked, taking a bite of the most delicious roasted red pepper, smoked chorizo and goat's cheese pizza I'd ever had – it was the only one I'd ever had, mind you, but I guarantee I'll never taste a better one. I had wondered if I could save some for Tom but it was too late – as quickly as the thought appeared in my head, the pizza was gone. It was too nice. *No savesies unfortunately, Tom lad.*

'I've got loads of interviews and PR lined up, plus a couple of trips to Europe. It won't be completely full-on, though, so I intend to see a lot more of you too.'

'Good to know,' I said. 'I can't take time off work right now, but I should be pretty free in the evenings and at weekends.'

'I can work with that.' He leant across the table and kissed me, hard.

I pulled back, breathless. 'I should go home soon,' I said. 'It's getting late and I'm shattered.'

'But we haven't even had dessert yet,' Brandon whispered into my ear. He softly kissed my neck. I had a feeling he wasn't talking about the tiramisu.

'I really need an early night,' I protested weakly.

'Then let's go to bed.'

Just like that, he put it out there. I couldn't accuse him of playing games, that's for sure.

'I really should—'

He silenced me with a kiss and all of my excuses fell away. This felt so *good*. We clumsily made our way to the master bedroom, kissing the entire time, and when he stared into my eyes and threw me onto the bed I forgot all about the tiramisu. I wasn't going anywhere tonight.

Chapter Nineteen

I ran out of work, pulling my Lulu Guinness suitcase behind me. Brandon's now-familiar driver was already waiting for me and I clambered into the back seat while he hoisted my case into the boot. Brandon wasn't there but I hadn't been expecting him to be. He'd said that he'd meet me at the other end of the car ride – wherever that was. Brandon had just told me to pack for a weekend away.

In the weeks since Brandon had arrived in London I'd been out with him almost every night. The nights we spent apart were usually because he wasn't in London. My life was turning into a constant cycle of work during the day and going from restaurant to bar to party at night. I hadn't seen Jess and Tom for more than a few minutes in several weeks and the chances of popping into Jalou for a quick drink were slim to none these days. Brandon liked to do things in style and I had quickly become used to being picked up from work and then being whisked off to somewhere glamorous, which wasn't always in London. There had been the weekend he'd surprised me with a trip to Edinburgh, where we'd stayed in this secluded luxury castle and had spent half our time between the Egyptian cotton sheets and the other half eating shortbread. At one point I'd suggested that we should go out and do a little exploring, but Brandon had been keener on exploring me so I'd lost that battle very quickly, though I'd insisted on introducing him to Irn-Bru. He was not a fan.

Brandon was sweet and attentive but he also lived life to extremes. We did everything to excess. Why take the train when he had his own private driver at his disposal? No need to bother with an easyJet flight when he could charter a private plane to take us to Scotland as easily as clicking his fingers. It had made me uncomfortable initially, it felt like such a waste, but I had to admit that there was a part of me that enjoyed the luxury of it all.

The one thing that I still wasn't used to, though, was the press attention that came with going out with someone with Brandon's profile. The first time I'd seen my picture in the papers I'd been mortified. It was a snap of the two of us coming out of Nobu and I hadn't even spotted the photographer. Seeing our relationship plastered all over the paper had been a shock to the system. I'd tried to talk to Brandon about how uncomfortable it made me feel but he'd shrugged and said that I'd get used to it soon. It came with the territory. I wanted to say that this was his territory, not mine. But I'd let it go. I was having such a nice time with him, the last thing I wanted to do was kick up a huge fuss over some daft picture of us holding hands in the tabloids.

It wasn't just the cars, and the wining, and the dining, and the press. Brandon was insatiable in bed as well. If I'm being honest, before now I'd never really understood what all the fuss was about when it came to sex. Sure, I'd had good sex and I enjoyed a good neck on as much as the next lass, but I never really understood how it could make you feel. Until Brandon. And he wasn't shy about trying new things either. I blushed as I thought about the previous night. We'd both been a bit drunk, which just made us more adventurous; I'd had no idea I could even bend that way.

The car came to a stop and I was shaken out of my reverie. I looked out of the window. We were parked up near what looked like a private hangar at City airport. He can't be serious, I thought. What are we doing here?

I spotted Brandon standing nearby in a Burberry trench coat that was keeping off the light autumn drizzle. I jumped out and ran to him. I was always so excited to see him.

'Hey, baby,' he said, kissing me.

'Hey,' I said. I gestured towards the runway and the small plane waiting at the end of it. 'What's going on here, then?'

'I'm taking you to Paris,' Brandon announced.

'Eh?'

'Me and you and Paris, baby. What do you say?'

'But . . . I can't just go to Paris! I have to work on Monday and I don't have my passport. And me mam—'

'Sweetie, I've got your passport.' He pulled it out of his pocket and waved it in front of my face. 'Jess helped me get hold of it, and we're coming back on Sunday night so no need to worry about work.'

'Jess helped you?'

He kissed me gently. 'I've sorted everything. All you have to do is get your ass on the plane.'

I think I could manage that.

*

'This is overwhelming,' I said.

'In a good way or a bad way?' Brandon asked, running his hand up my leg.

We were sat in the back of the private plane, sipping champagne. The seats were covered in soft leather and, despite us having quite a large sofa to spread across, Brandon was pressed up against my side.

'A good way,' I said, smiling at him. 'I've never done anything like this before. It's like a dream. Paris. The fashion capital of the world.'

'That's what I thought. And it's also one of the most romantic cities in the world. What better way to get inspired for your work than to surround yourself with fashion and romance?' Brandon's hand moved further up and I gasped softly. 'So you're enjoying yourself?'

'Hmmm,' was all I could manage now that his hand had started moving again.

'Come on, Miss Raey,' Brandon said in a low voice. 'Show me how much you're enjoying yourself.'

And that's exactly what I did.

A limo picked us up from the airstrip when we landed and dropped us off at the Four Seasons Hotel George V, just off the Champs-Élysées. It was like something straight out of a Hollywood film, from the spacious lobby decorated with ornate chandeliers and intricate mosaics, to the lavish cream and gold luxury suite Brandon had booked for us. Everything was new and exciting, over-the-top decadent and I loved it.

It didn't take us long to christen the bed. Afterwards, we ordered up some strawberries and champagne from room service. Clichéd, but who bloody cared.

I propped myself up on one elbow and looked down at Brandon's handsome face. I stroked his cheek, pushing his hair to one side. 'How are you feeling about the single?' I asked. Brandon's debut single 'Wrecked' was due for release imminently and I knew he was nervous about it. It was the first thing he'd put out since leaving the band and all eyes were on him. I wanted him to know that I was there for him with whatever support he needed.

'I'm feeling good,' Brandon said. 'It's been a long time coming. I just want to get it out there now. You know that once the single drops I'm going to be busier? I might not be around as much. That's why I wanted to take you away this weekend, so that we could spend some time alone.'

'I know, but we'll still be able to spend some time together, won't we?' *Chill out, man! What happened to treat them mean to keep them keen? You're acting like such a melt.* I hated how needy I sounded, but Brandon had become such a huge part of my life very quickly and the thought of that changing was unpleasant to say the least.

'Definitely. It's just that life will get busier for both of us once the single is out. But at least we'll always have Paris.'

'Ah, *Casablanca*,' I sighed. It was one of my favourite films – such a classic.

'No, honey, we're in Paris,' Brandon said, frowning.

I sighed and made a mental note to educate Brandon in the ways of Humphrey Bogart and Ingrid Bergman when we got back to London. *It's a good thing you're fit as fuck, son.*

I kicked off my shoes and sighed as I settled into the back of another limo. It was Saturday evening, I was shattered and my feet were killing me, but I was so happy. Brandon and I had spent the day visiting some of Paris's most famous land-marks, including the Place de la Concorde, Notre-Dame Cathedral and the Arc de Triomphe. Brandon had also taken me to Chanel, where he'd insisted on buying me the most beautiful couture dress. I'd tried to convince him that he didn't need to buy me anything, that he'd already done enough, and I'd never have the chance to wear a dress like that anyway, but he'd gone ahead and handed the sales girls his card over my protests.

Now we'd just finished having dinner at Le Jules Verne, one of the restaurants in the Eiffel Tower, and were heading back to the hotel. It had been a beautiful, exhausting, roman-tic and stimulating day – one that I'd always remember.

'I can't wait to get back to the hotel,' I said, snuggling in next to Brandon. 'I'm shattered.'

'Ah, baby, didn't I tell you? We're not going back to the hotel. There's a party I have to go to.'

I sat upright. 'A party? But it's almost one a.m. We've been on the go all day and I'm shattered.'

'It's a work thing, I have to go. Sorry, I thought I'd men-tioned it.'

'Can't you get out of it?'

'I'm under strict orders from management to go. There's a new DJ playing, apparently he's the next Calvin Harris, so I really need to show my face. I can drop you at the hotel if you want. But I'd prefer you to stay with me.'

'I don't know, Brandon,' I said. 'I'm dead on my feet right now.'

'Please,' he said, rubbing the back of my hand with his thumb. 'These things are so boring. It won't be any fun with-out you.'

I looked at his face and I knew that I couldn't say no to him. 'OK,' I conceded. 'An hour, tops. And then we leave.'

Brandon's face lit up with a smile. 'That's my girl.'

The party was in a huge mansion on the outskirts of Paris. It had taken us ages to get there and it was now nearly two a.m. I really wasn't in the mood for this and the car ride hadn't done anything to put me in the party mood. It was late, I was tired and I was turning into a petulant brat. The house was full of people, every room was rammed with bodies, and no one was showing any signs of slowing down. Where did they get their energy from? After Brandon and I arrived, we did a quick circuit of the place and the answer to that question became startlingly clear.

Everywhere I turned people were downing champagne and expensive vodka, but what was most alarming was that people were blatantly and unashamedly popping pills and snorting from the many mounds of white powder around. I stiffened and turned to Brandon. I needed to get out of here; I couldn't be anywhere near this shit.

'I want to go,' I yelled over the music.

Brandon frowned in confusion. He couldn't hear me.

I leaned in closer and tried again. 'I need to leave. Now.' I gestured to everyone around me, hoping that he'd under-stand what I was trying to say.

He kissed me quickly on the lips and shouted, 'One hour, baby. You promised.' Before I could respond, he grabbed my hand and pulled me towards a room that had been cordoned off by a thick red velvet rope. The bouncer on the door nodded at Brandon and he let us in without question. This room was quieter than the rest of the party, and had clearly

199

been earmarked for VIPs only. I recognised many of the faces from the fashion magazines I read and I was stunned to see professionals I respected taking drugs so openly back here as well.

'Brandon,' I said. 'I'm not feeling well. Please, I want to go back to the hotel.'

Brandon looked at me sharply. 'I told you this was for work. I brought you to Paris. Can't you give me just one hour? Is that too much to ask?'

I was taken aback. Brandon had never spoken to me with such hostility before. Immediately his face softened when he saw the shock on my face. He kissed my cheek.

'Sorry, baby. I didn't mean to snap. We won't stay for long. I just need to talk to a couple of people, OK?'

I nodded and let him lead me to a table full of people whose faces I knew from the papers. If the situation had been different I would've been in my element, getting to know these celebs and trying to find out any gossip I could relay to Freddie when I got back to work. But the horrible feeling I always got when I was anywhere near drugs wouldn't leave me. And for the first time since Dad died, I just sat there in silence and didn't do anything to get away from them.

Chapter Twenty

As I slowly woke up I fleetingly wondered where I was. As I gradually became used to my surroundings I remembered that I was at Brandon's place. It was Saturday morning, and we'd been back from Paris for almost a week. I'd spent every night since our return here, only nipping back to my flat for clean clothes and underwear, but I still sometimes woke up disorientated and confused about where I was. If it were possible, Brandon had been even more attentive since Paris. I think he realised how upset I'd been after the party he'd dragged me to. We hadn't really talked about it the next day. He had apologised for putting me in a situation that I was uncomfortable with, and even though I'd accepted his apology I couldn't help but be a little distant towards him for a couple of days afterwards. I didn't feel comfortable in those situations, and if Brandon did were we really compatible as I thought?

A couple of evenings ago – it had been a Wednesday, for God's sake! – Brandon had told me that he was meant to be going to a party, some exclusive bar opening, and had asked me to go with him. My heart had sunk. I wanted to spend the evening with him but I didn't want a repeat performance of our night in Paris. I'd squashed those feelings of unease, though, and we'd gone to the party together, which had been as awful as I was worried it would be.

I was getting used to flashbulbs going off all the time, but I still didn't like the party scene Brandon's management wanted him to be a part of. I knew it was important for Brandon to keep his profile up, though, so despite the fact that I didn't like a lot of the people I was introduced to, I didn't like the seedy turn the evenings took, and I didn't like the amount of drug-taking I was surrounded by, I went along with him. I wasn't proud of myself, but the only way I could cope was to turn a blind eye to it all; I'd have got angry, kicked off and made a huge scene otherwise. I had been planning to talk to Brandon about my unease when we were alone, but the moment had never seemed right and I didn't want to rock the boat unnecessarily. I kept reminding myself that I was only there to support him – and he was only there to promote his first solo single. All the other stuff was peripheral and nothing to do with us.

I reached across the bed for him, only to be greeted by an empty space. *Ah, that's right, he had to leave for Manchester early this morning for some radio interviews.* He must be shattered, bless him. I didn't know how he managed it – he was go, go, go the entire time and it was only going to get more manic when his single was released. I admired his enthusiasm and drive. I'd always thought I was ambitious but Brandon's energy and hunger for it was next level. I'd told him to wake me up before he'd left but either he'd decided against it or he hadn't been able to rouse me. I was going for option number two. I could sleep on a washing line in a thunder storm. I checked the time. Ten a.m. I was tempted to go back to sleep for another hour or so but I wanted to take advantage of the alone time and work on some new sketches so I forced myself to get up. I stretched, preparing myself for the torture of leaving a warm bed, when I spotted something on Brandon's pillow. It was a small blue box. Yes, *that* kind of blue box. The turquoise kind from Tiffany's. The kind from films. The kind that Geordie girls from council estates who drink too much gin and eat too many pepperoni passion pizzas never expect to see in real life. I reached for it and opened it, my heart thumping in my chest. Nestled inside was a delicate chain with a beautiful diamond-encrusted heart pendant. The note inside read, *Something to remind you that you have my heart. Bx*

I stared at the gorgeous necklace for a moment, a grin spreading slowly across my face. I loved it. Brandon had given me a lot over the last few weeks but this was the first thing that truly symbolised how he felt about me. I couldn't deny it any longer – I was falling for Mr Bailey, hard. And it looked like the feeling was mutual. I was on cloud nine. Actually, I was on cloud ten. Cloud nine was reserved for job promotions and great nights out with the lassies. Falling in love with international superstars and finding out they love you back is cloud ten status, defo.

I threw my pencil down in frustration. I'd been sketching for hours but it just wasn't flowing as naturally as it usually did. I'd finished a couple of designs, which Alessandro had liked for the new collection, but a couple wasn't enough. Not at this stage of the game. I should be much further along by now. I scrolled through the photos on my phone of Paris and the last week, hoping something in them would inspire me. Nothing. What was wrong with me?

I knew what was wrong with me: I was tired. It was as simple as that. Burning the candle at both ends was fun for a while, sure, but it wasn't sustainable and now the late nights, the partying, the booze – it was all starting to take its toll. We needed the final collection ready for the end of January. It was almost the end of October now. Three months wasn't a lot of time, especially with Christmas in the middle, so I needed to focus. At least I had a theme for what I wanted the collection to represent: romance. That had been the easy part. With all the time Brandon and I were spending together, and all of his romantic gestures, it had been a no-brainer. But still, when Brandon got back from Manchester on Monday I was going to talk to him about slowing down the going out for a while. He needed to concentrate on his single launch, anyway, so it would benefit both of us.

I rubbed my face. Sitting in front of another blank page wasn't getting me anywhere. I needed a change of scenery. Maybe a bit of fresh air and then locking myself away in my own bedroom in my own flat would have the desired effect. It had worked for me last time; maybe it would work the same magic again.

I threw my things into my bag and left Brandon's apartment, locking the door behind me with my keys. That's right, Brandon had given me my own set of keys to his place. I'd felt like such a grown up when he'd handed them over. Things were definitely serious between us. If it all kept moving at this pace, I'd have to think about introducing him to Mam and Rubes, and soon.

I mentally ran through my sketches on the way home to see if anything I had already done would spark off a different idea. Still nothing. By the time I was unlocking my own front door I was feeling pretty disheartened. I walked into the lounge and found Tom and Jamie on the sofa, the PlayStation loaded up and half-empty family-sized packets of Doritos and McCoy's surrounding them. Tom glanced up and when he saw it was me he screamed.

'Who are you? Get out of here, stranger! Thief! Intruder!'

'Shut up, you,' I replied good-naturedly.

'All right, Geordio?' Jamie said, smiling at me.

'Hi Jamie,' I said, pointedly ignoring Tom. 'Where's Jess?'

'She's at Sammy-boy's. So we're having a lads' day,' Tom explained. 'Didn't think we'd see you this weekend.'

'Don't worry,' I replied. 'I need to get my head down and work anyway so I won't disturb this impressive display of masculinity.'

'Join us,' Jamie said. 'It would be nice to catch up.'

'Yeah,' Tom said. 'You're practically one of the lads anyway. Apart from the lack of knob part.'

'Er, thanks, Tom. I think there's a compliment in there somewhere,' I laughed. 'You know I'd love to, but I've really got to get ahead with these sketches. Sorry, lads. I've really gotta work.'

Later that afternoon, after a few hours of not-very-inspiring sketching, my phone rang. Brandon.

'Hey you,' I said, happy that he was returning my call. I'd

tried to phone him earlier to thank him for the necklace but his phone had been switched off.

'Hey baby,' he said, speaking quickly. 'I'm missing you so much.'

'Already?' I teased. 'It hasn't been that long.'

'It's been long enough. I should've insisted that you come to Manchester with me.'

'Next time,' I said. 'Hey, thank you for the necklace. It's beautiful.'

'So you like it?'

'I love it. You shouldn't have, though. It's too much. I would have been happy with something from Argos!' I joked.

'Argos? Is that a designer?' Oh dear, there's that cheeky little culture divide again. Or was he just a bit thick? *No, Amber, he's American. It's not his fault. Stop getting precious because he didn't get your wank joke.*

'No, babe, never mind. It's just so extravagant. You didn't have to.'

'Only the best is good enough for my girl.'

'Is that what I am, then – your girl?'

'If you need to ask, then I haven't been doing my job properly.'

My stomach somersaulted. He always knew the right thing to say.

'How's Manchester?' I asked, moving the conversation on to less emotionally important territory.

'Full on,' Brandon replied. 'Listen, do you have plans for Halloween yet?'

'Halloween? No, not really. It's too far away to think about just yet.'

Brandon laughed. 'It's next weekend, honey. What planet are you on?'

'Really? I don't know where my head's at these days. But the answer is still the same – I have no plans yet.'

'Good, because I'm taking you out.'

'Where are you whisking me off to this time, Mr Bailey?'

'Oscar Haverstock is having a huge Halloween ball near Hyde Park. And you're my date.'

'*The* Oscar Haverstock?' I asked, incredulous.

'The one and only.'

Oscar Haverstock was a young British actor who was giving Benedict Cumberbatch a run for his money for the position of the nation's favourite actor.

'I'm in,' I said excitedly. 'Is it fancy dress?' I loved fancy dress, especially for Halloween. And I could make our costumes! Suddenly, partying hard didn't seem like such a chore.

'Sure, honey. Let's talk about costumes when I'm back in London after the weekend.'

We chatted for a bit longer, until Brandon was called away for another round of press interviews. After I had hung up I flipped my sketchbook to a fresh page and started doodling ideas for our Halloween costumes. The collection could wait a couple of hours.

Chapter Twenty-one

'I feel like a right tit,' I declared, looking at my reflection.

'You look cute,' Brandon said. 'In that outfit, I'm going to find it hard to resist you.'

'You're not helping,' I snapped.

I was not happy. I had come up with great ideas for our Halloween costumes – a zombie marriage, his-and-hers Dracula-inspired costumes, sexy ghosts – but no, Brandon had refused to contemplate any of them. And now, instead, we were dressed as the captain of a high school American football team and a cheerleader. I mean . . . what the hell?

'You do know Halloween is meant to be scary?' I said, as I already had a thousand times.

'It's just a costume party in the States. I'm not wearing fake blood, fangs or pretend intestines on the outside of my body. I have a reputation,' he replied, which had been his argument the whole time.

Brandon pulled the 'it's for my career' card during every row we had lately. And every time, I gave in to him. Although being dressed as an American cheerleader, complete with my hair in bunches, wasn't exactly going to do wonders for my image within the fashion industry. To be fair to Brandon, I hadn't exactly given in to him on this one. Despite coming up with some rough sketches for costumes, I hadn't had the time to fully develop any of them, so eventually Brandon had said he'd arrange the outfits because I was so busy and he didn't want me stressing out about it. He'd promised to order something scary for me and something more fun for him. So when the football captain and cheerleader combo had turned up this morning, and my 'scary' outfit had gone AWOL, I couldn't help but suspect Brandon had been less than honest.

'You only ordered one costume, didn't you?' I accused him as I looked at myself in the mirror again. My heart sank. I looked like a twat.

'I told you,' Brandon snapped, 'I ordered two. I don't know where the other one is.' He looked at me with cold, hard eyes. 'Just get over it, OK? We need to go. Tonight is fucking important to me. Don't keep whining at me like a little kid because you'll screw it up.' And with that, he turned on his heel and stalked out of the bedroom, leaving me speechless and his words ringing in my ears.

'Don't screw it up'? Since when does he speak to me like that? I'm not his personal assistant to order around. I have never been spoken to like that by a lad and I don't intend to start now. I don't care he's got Taylor Swift's number in his contact list and he owns an apartment in the same building as Jay-Z in New York. I am not a fucking mug and I won't be treated like one. I was fuming.

But hang on . . . I heard the front door open and I realised he was getting ready to leave. Without me. Suddenly panic knocked the anger out of me and I grabbed my bag and pompoms – for God's sake, that's a sentence I never thought I'd say – and managed to make it to the front door just before it closed behind Brandon.

We made our way downstairs in silence. We climbed into the back of the car in silence. The car began its drive to Hyde Park and, still, we sat in silence. Brandon and I had been bickering a lot recently. Given the amount of time we spent together it was probably inevitable, and most of the time it didn't turn into anything serious. But this felt different. He was under a lot of pressure, and so was I, though I was doing my best to support him. I knew that the late nights were taking their toll on the both of us, and though I was trying to hide my discomfort at all the drugs, perhaps my disapproval was more obvious than I thought. Brandon's single was about to be released and his future as a singer hinged on it being a success. I probably needed to try harder to keep my feelings in check and support him at the moment.

'Hey,' I said, sliding over and closing the gap between us. 'I'm sorry. I didn't mean to be such a diva. Look, let's just have fun tonight and try to relax.' I stroked his arm.

'That's all I want to do, Amber: relax. And perhaps if you could try not to be so judgmental about my friends tonight that might help.'

I felt like I'd been slapped. OK, so I wasn't hiding my feelings very well on the drug-taking front, then? Shit. We didn't speak for the rest of the journey.

Brandon's bad mood disappeared as soon as we walked into the ball. He switched on a smile that was brighter than the Oxford Street Christmas lights and grabbed my hand. I knew we needed to talk, but that was going to have to wait – this really wasn't the time or place – so I decided to just go with Brandon's change of mood. The place was packed, full to the brim with celebs and their entourages. As I'd anticipated, everyone was wearing a gory costume and we looked completely out of place – not that Brandon seemed to notice. There were fake cobwebs artistically strewn throughout the entire mansion, the pumpkins had clearly been expertly carved and dim lighting added to the atmosphere. Someone handed us each a glass of champagne and we immediately made our way to the rooftop swimming pool. Brandon spotted some of his usual crowd as soon as we reached the pool and I was saved from going over with him when I spotted Portia by the bar. I couldn't believe I hadn't seen her since London Fashion Week, back in the dark days with Diana. I told Brandon I'd be back in a minute and quickly made my over to her before he could protest.

'Hello stranger,' I said, giving her a kiss on the cheek. 'Nice costume.' She was dressed as a black cat, all slinky and sexy. I started to feel a tiny bit better about my ridiculous cheerleader get-up.

'Thanks, dahling. You look . . . ' Her voice trailed off.

'Like a cock?' I finished for her.

'I wouldn't put it quite like that. But it's . . . an unusual choice for a Halloween costume.'

'Brandon, my new boyfriend, chose our outfits. Being American, I don't think he really understood how we celebrate Halloween here in the UK,' I told her.

'Never mind, no one here is sober enough to even notice. And the pompoms might come in handy,' she joked.

'What do you mean?' I asked.

'There are plenty of wandering hands around tonight. I'd keep anything you can use as a weapon close by.'

'Thanks for the warning,' I laughed. 'Have you been here long?'

'About an hour,' Portia sighed. 'I was with some other models but I've lost track of them, so am just bar-hanging. Have you had a look around yet?'

I shook my head. 'We just got here. I've only seen downstairs briefly, and we came up here straight away.'

Portia grabbed my hand. 'In that case, let me show you around and you can tell me all about this Brandon. The house is huge, and some of the rooms have their own themes. I want to go and explore, please!'

'OK,' I said. 'Let me just let Brandon know where I'm going.'

I turned to find him. He was in the middle of a crowd of people who were hanging on his every word. I caught his eye and gestured that I was going with Portia. He barely nodded and then turned his attention back to his adoring public.

Twat.

Two hours went by and I didn't see Brandon at all during that time. I checked my phone a few times but there were no messages and no missed calls. He clearly didn't want to spend the night with me, so instead of moping around I decided to have a good time under my own steam. Portia and I had bumped into a fashion crowd, and by the time midnight rolled around I was well and truly buzzing from all the champagne. If truth be told, I was smashed – but not throw up in your handbag smashed, just dance the night away and tell everyone you love them smashed. Portia was right, though –

so many people here appeared to be off their faces, and once again, not just from the booze, none more so than the host, Oscar. He was being flanked by two bodyguards at all times, but right now they were spending most of their time holding him upright rather than protecting him.

'He's too young for this, you know,' Portia said to me.

'What, this party?' I asked.

'No, dahling. For this life, for the fame. He's barely out of his teens, and suddenly he has everyone telling him how wonderful he is, he's getting paid obscene amounts of money and it's all going to his head.'

'Do you know him well?' I asked.

'Yah, our parents are old friends. Take my word for it — Oscar will be in rehab before he hits thirty. We used to go horse-riding together, but now when I see him all he talks about is riding Victoria's Secret models and how much coke he's snorting. He was like a little brother to me, and now I have nothing to say to him. And no one around him is going to tell him to get his act together. The fame game isn't all it's cracked up to be.'

'Yeah, but we don't have to worry about that, not in our business,' I said. I thought for a moment. 'Actually, as a model, it might be something you do have to think about.'

'That's why I keep myself to myself. No falling out of clubs, and I try to stay clear-headed whenever there are paps around. You can never be too careful. And I'd never date anyone famous.'

'But what if you fall for them? You can't help how you feel about someone.'

'Like Brandon?'

I nodded. 'I never expected to fall for someone like him.

You know, it never even entered my head that I'd end up going out with someone people consider a "celebrity". I'm not a fan of this scene either, but if I want it to work between us I have to accept that it's a part of Brandon's life. And when it's the two of us, it's amazing. It makes it all worth it.'

Portia opened her mouth to respond but was interrupted by the arrival of Jamie.

'Portia, babes, so sorry I'm late,' he said, leaning down to kiss Portia's cheek. He was dressed as a zombie, and even when his face was covered with white face paint and bloody gashes he still looked fit.

'Er, hello? What about me?' I prompted.

Jamie looked at me and his eyes widened. He burst out laughing. 'Unbelievable. I didn't recognise you, Geordio. What the hell are you wearing?!' he said, unable to keep the grin off his face as he kissed my cheek.

'You're very late,' Portia said, pouting.

'Sorry, gorgeous,' Jamie said, treating her to his sexiest smile. 'I've been trying on outfits all day for House of Rossi and we ran over. They've only just let me out, and I had to get myself into character, didn't I?!' He stopped the flirting to do an almost-convincing zombie impression.

'Hmm,' Portia said, still pouting, but more jokily now. 'I guess I can understand that. You're forgiven. Just this once.'

I looked between them. Had I missed something? Since when did Jamie and Portia make plans with one another? Was there something going on here? We carried on chatting easily for a few minutes and I took the opportunity to assess the two of them together. They weren't exactly all over each other but they were comfortable together. Jamie was laughing at something Portia was saying and she had her hand on his arm. *Am I so out of touch with my friends that no one thought to tell me when two of them got together?* I tried to ignore the surprising stab of jealousy that went through me. I had Brandon. Jamie could do what he wanted.

'Right, ladies, I'll go and get us some drinks,' Jamie said. 'Champagne?' Portia and I nodded and Jamie disappeared into the crowd. I fleetingly wondered what my boyfriend was doing and checked my phone again. Still nothing.

Portia and I talked about the new collection and the next job she had lined up before we started wondering where Jamie had got to. He'd been gone for ages. We were discussing sending out a search party of monsters and ghosts when he finally appeared, looking slightly dishevelled and more than a little harassed. Portia didn't seem to notice and quickly ran off to the ladies. She must've been holding it in the entire time Jamie had been gone.

'Are you OK?' I asked Jamie when we were alone.

'Not really,' Jamie said, running a hand absently through his hair. He looked around us.

'What's wrong? Has something happened?'

'Yeah, sort of.' Jamie looked at me and then led me to a quieter corner. 'Sorry, I didn't want anyone to overhear us.'

'Jamie, talk to me.' Whatever had happened in the last half an hour couldn't be that bad.

Jamie took a deep breath. 'Amber, do you know where your boyfriend is?'

My eyebrows shot up in surprise. This was about Brandon? 'Not right now, no,' I said slowly. 'I haven't seen him for a couple of hours. Why?'

'I just bumped into him when I went to the toilet before getting the drinks.'

'OK,' I said slowly. 'And?'

Jamie chewed his bottom lip, clearly struggling with what he was going to say next. 'Is everything OK between the two of you?' he said eventually. 'You know, if you're having any issues, you can talk to me.'

'Just the usual bickering that happens between couples. It's normal. Everything's fine.'

I couldn't understand why Jamie was digging into my relationship right now. He was just looking at me without saying anything.

I threw my hands up in exasperation. 'Jamie, you clearly have something you want to say. So just spit it out, man, will you?'

'Amber,' Jamie said gently. 'Does Brandon have a problem with drugs?'

'What? No way! He doesn't touch them.'

'You're sure?'

'Of *course* I am!' I cried. Even though something really worrying was stirring in the back of my mind.

'Babes, I'm sorry – when I say I bumped into Brandon, I mean that I walked in on him snorting lines of gear. I'm so sorry.'

I stared at Jamie, open-mouthed. *What the hell is he talking about?*

'It couldn't have been him,' I said. 'You must've got it wrong.'

'No, hun, I haven't. He was so off his face on a mixture of whatever the fuck he's been taking that I had to help him to the nearest bedroom and get him to lie down. He couldn't stand up without leaning on my arm. But he wouldn't stay there – I think he went back up to the roof. He looks a state.'

'Nah,' I said stubbornly. 'You're wrong.'

'I wish I was, but I'm not. Has he ever done anything like this before?'

I didn't respond immediately and Jamie narrowed his eyes, sensing my hesitation.

'You know what, Amber, you don't actually seem that shocked.' he said.

'It's not that,' I said quickly. I didn't want Jamie to get the wrong impression. 'He's exposed to drugs quite a lot. His management make him go to these parties and there's always loads going on there, but didn't think . . . ' I trailed off. Why hadn't I thought? Or had I already known but just didn't want to accept it?'

'What?' Jamie looked angry. I suddenly realised I'd never seen Jamie properly angry before. 'What didn't you think? That your heartthrob, millionaire boyfriend drags you to all these parties with drugs everywhere and he's politely declining every night? You aren't that naive, Amber. You hate all this shit. How can you be OK with this?'

'It's what he needs to do for his career. I'm just trying—'

'Would you listen to yourself? Since when do you make excuses for this kind of behaviour? This isn't you, Amber. Well, it's not the Amber I knew anyway.'

'Don't you *dare* judge me,' I said, matching his anger. 'You couldn't possibly understand the kind of pressure Brandon is under. And I don't even know it was him that you saw.'

'I didn't just see him. I spoke to him, I carried him and I put him in the recovery position so he didn't choke on his tongue. And then I argued with him when he refused to stay in the room. You might be confused right now, but you know that I would never lie to you.'

He was right. Jamie was a lot of things, but a liar wasn't one of them. 'I know you wouldn't,' I admitted sadly. I felt deflated. 'So what do I do now?'

'You need to get him out of here and away from all the gossips. Don't worry,' he said, probably seeing how lost I was feeling, 'I'll help you.'

'What about Portia? You can't leave her on her own.'

'We could use her help too, I think. We'll just tell her Brandon's had too much to drink and you need our help getting him home.'

'OK,' I said quietly.

'Babes,' Jamie said, pulling me into a hug. 'Get through tonight and then talk to Brandon properly. But if this really is the world he's living in, then as your friend, I want you as far away from it as possible from now on.'

'It's a one-off,' I said desperately. 'It has to be. He was forced into it. I bet with all the pressure he's under about the single he felt so stressed and vulnerable and someone has just preyed on that. Someone must have made him do it.'

'Everyone has pressure in their lives,' Jamie said through gritted teeth. I could see his patience was beginning to wear thin with my pitiful excuses for Brandon. 'This isn't the way to deal with it. And you know what? This isn't pressure and being forced into anything. I think he wanted to do it. I think he's fallen for the rock 'n' roll lifestyle and he enjoys the debauchery. I just never thought you'd fall for it too.'

'I haven't,' I protested. 'But I've fallen for him. I think I love him.'

Jamie gave me a hard look. 'Does he know about your dad? Does he know how you feel about drugs?'

I nodded.

'And even after you told him all of that, he still does something like this? Insensitive tosser. Literally, what a bellend. Brandon fucking bellend.' There wasn't even a hint of a smile on Jamie's face. All the anger from a few minutes ago had come back.

'Shut the fuck up, Jamie! Don't call him that! I'll talk to him about all this in the morning, but he's been with me most nights he's been in London so there's no way he could've taken anything during that time without me knowing about it. Tonight has to have been the first time. So, please, just back off.'

'Would you listen to yourself? I never thought I'd see the day you'd stand back and let yourself get mugged off like this. You're deluded. You're like some sort of weird groupie, Stepford Wife – validating his fucked up behaviour.'

'What's going on?' Portia asked, suddenly reappearing. 'You two look serious.'

'It's nothing,' Jamie said, not taking his eyes off me. 'Brandon's had a bit too much to drink so Amber needs our help getting him home. Isn't that right, Amber?'

I didn't trust myself to speak so I just nodded.

The cold hit me as soon as we stepped onto the rooftop. At any other time I would've been in awe of the stunning view of London at night, all lit up against the pitch-black sky. But now wasn't the time for appreciating my surroundings. The deck was still full of people but it didn't take me long to find Brandon. He was lying on the sun lounger closest to the door, and next to him was Oscar. The phrase 'looking a bit worse for wear' didn't even begin to cover it.

'It's time to go, babes,' I said to Brandon. I wanted to get him out of here with as little fuss as possible.

'But I'm having fun,' Brandon slurred. I could barely bring myself to look at him.

'Come on, mate. Party's over,' Jamie said jovially, pulling him up and encountering barely any resistance. I was shocked at how out of it Brandon clearly was.

'Is my party over already?' Oscar asked, and then promptly fell off his sun lounger. His bouncers lifted him back up and we managed to escape unnoticed during the commotion.

It took all three of us to get Brandon into the lift – he was a dead weight. None of us spoke as we descended to the ground floor and I made a point of avoiding any kind of eye contact with Jamie. The two of us stood on either side of Brandon and half-dragged, half-carried him out to street level, with Portia holding the doors open for us. As soon as we hit the street a cascade of flashbulbs went off but there was nothing I could do to get us away from them. The image of us putting Brandon into the back of his car would be every-where by the morning.

And I was with him. Dressed as a cheerleader. Double balls.

Chapter Twenty-two

The next morning I got out of bed early and left Brandon snoring away. I'd barely slept a wink – I kept replaying the events of the night in my head. I'd been so relieved to get Brandon into the car and away from the paps, and an increasingly angry Jamie, that I hadn't thought about how I was going to get him up to his apartment on my own. It had taken the combined efforts of me, his driver and the night doorman to get him upstairs. I had no idea if we could trust the doorman, but at that point I didn't have a choice and really didn't care. Though I'd been exhausted, as soon as I got into bed sleep had proved elusive. If I wasn't thinking about the fight with Jamie, I was thinking about the state Brandon had got himself into. And then I'd start thinking about the blogs, papers and mags that might be printing photos of me and Jamie practically dragging Brandon out of the party at that moment. Neither me nor Jamie should be appearing in photos like that – it wasn't going to reflect well on either of us, or on House of Rossi.

There wasn't any point in delaying the inevitable so I grabbed my iPad and pulled up CelebSpot the most popular celeb blog in the UK. And, predictably, there they were – picture after picture of me hauling Brandon out of the party. Thankfully they'd cut Jamie out of the picture so it looked like I was carrying Brandon on my own. At least I didn't have to feel guilty about ruining Jamie's reputation as well.

I scanned the web to see if anyone else had picked up on it. I was horrified. The pictures were everywhere Brandon's single was due for release next week and had been used as a not-so-clever pun in headlines like, *'WRECKED' SINGER LIVES UP TO HIS NEW SINGLE* and *BAILEY GETS 'WRECKED'!* It was bad enough that I looked like a poor Britney Spears impersonator in the cheerleader outfit, but because of the way I was holding Brandon it looked as though we were holding each other up and I was as smashed as he was. We were hardly love's young dream.

I began reading the copy that accompanied the photos and my heart sank even further. All the stories were pretty much the same – that 'a close personal friend' had confirmed Brandon had been snorting coke at the party because the 'pressure of his forthcoming single release was too much for him'. Most of the pieces also mentioned me by name and confirmed that I was a junior designer at House of Rossi. When I read that I'd apparently been as high as Brandon and we'd been snorting coke together, I couldn't hold back the tears.

I'd been avoiding my phone but decided to rip that plaster off as well. I had messages from everyone – Mam, Ruby, Jess, Tom and Jamie. I sent quick replies saying I was OK, that I hadn't been wasted but that I couldn't talk today, which was true – I literally didn't know what to say. But there was one phone call I had to make straight away. I just hoped Alessandro was awake.

'Alessandro, it's Amber,' I said quickly when he picked up after a couple of rings.

'Amber, bella, I was just about to call you. About the story in the papers—'

'It's all bollocks,' I cut in. 'It's not true.'

'Slow down,' Alessandro said. 'Tell me what happened, from the beginning. Leave nothing out.'

As quickly and as succinctly as I could, I told Alessandro everything that had happened the previous evening. When I'd finished, there was a silence at the end of the line.

'Alessandro? Are you still there?'

'I am, bella.' He sounded tired. 'Amber, this Brandon, does he always do the drugs?'

'No, no.' I paused. Was that true? If last night was anything to go by, he probably was more at home with them than I wanted to admit. 'But he's under a lot of pressure for his single to do well. It must all have become too much for him. Not that I'm making excuses.' But I was making excuses, the same ones I'd been making over and over again.

'OK, bella. I trust you know him better than the papers but I am not happy with House of Rossi being associated with all of this. Our press office will have to work on damage control so, bella, please, stay out of trouble from now on. The market for your designs is young and, like it or not, some responsibility comes with that.'

'I know. I'm so sorry, Alessandro. Nothing like this will ever happen again.'

'And one more thing.'

'Yes?'

'Please never dress up as a cheerleader again. That hurt more than the drugs.'

'Never again, Al. Soz about that.'

One apology down, about 5,768,339 to go.

It was almost three p.m. before Brandon emerged. I'd spent most of the morning on the phone to Mam, Rubes and Jess. I should've known that none of them would've been happy with just a single text message. I'd had to repeat the story another three times, reassure each of them that I hadn't taken anything and that the papers had got it wrong about me. I couldn't, however, say the same about Brandon. Rubes and Jess were no longer part of the Brandon Bailey fanclub and Mam had had some strong words of her own to say about him. I felt like a sack of shite. I was drained.

I looked at him and felt a wave of disgust. He looked like hell but that wasn't what disgusted me. I was disgusted with myself for letting things get like this. I should've spoken up sooner and all of this could've been avoided.

'So, I'm guessing last night wasn't really a success,' Brandon said, trying and failing to make me smile.

'Is that really all you can say? Have you been online? Have you seen the photos? Read the stories?'

He nodded and couldn't meet my eyes.

'You know what the worst thing is? It isn't even that I've been named as your partner in crime, or that I look as bad as you in the photos. It's that you *did* take drugs, you *did* do this. And you did it after I told you about what happened to my dad, you selfish dick.'

'I know it looks bad—'

'Looks bad? It doesn't just look bad, it *is* bad, pet. You made it seem like you didn't touch drugs, that you might be surrounded by them but that you stayed away from them. You lied to me. You tricked me. All those parties we went to and I turned a blind eye to what was going on because you said it was for your career and that I was being judgemental of your friends. You made me out to be some sort of uptight bore who wasn't supportive of you. But tell me how all of this is helping your career right now?'

'Baby, listen to me. It was a lapse. I admit that when I was in the band things could get . . . a bit out of hand. That's one of the reasons I left. And I've been clean ever since, but last night, I don't know what happened. I was tense, I'm nervous about my single and we haven't been getting on so well lately – I felt insecure. I just wanted to forget about everything for a while and it went too far.'

'None of that is an excuse,' I said. 'If this is part of your life I can't be with you. I mean it, Brandon. It's a dealbreaker and there's nothing you can say to change my mind.'

Brandon took a step closer and grabbed my hands. 'Please don't leave me. I promise it won't happen again. I'll do anything, I need you.'

I looked into his eyes. He looked so sincere and panicked at the thought that I might walk out on him. Had I meant what I said? I felt my resolve weaken. We were all human and even superstars made mistakes. But Brandon was only allowed to make one in this vein. He wasn't getting another chance.

'Say something,' Brandon implored. 'Tell me this is all going to be OK. Tell me we can work it out.'

'If I so much as suspect you're even *thinking* about taking *anything* again, I'm gone. Understand?'

'I get it. I understand. You don't have to worry, it's not going to happen again. It's not worth it if it means losing you.' He pulled me into a hug and I rested my head on his chest.

'Listen,' I said eventually. 'I think I should go home for a bit. I need some space.'

'I thought we were OK?' Brandon said, a note of panic in his voice.

'We are.' I gave him a small smile. 'But I need some time on my own. I need to try to do some work today and get some proper sleep.'

'I don't want you to go.'

'I don't want to go either but I think it would do us both good to spend a night apart and get some rest. I'll see you after the weekend, OK? On Monday night.'

'You promise?'

'I promise.'

It would've been easy to stay but I knew I had to go. Right now, I needed to be by myself.

Chapter Twenty-three

'Freddie, is it important?' I snapped. 'Sorry, but I haven't had a moment today. If it's not urgent, can it wait?'

I rubbed my head. I was having the day from hell. It seemed that now the world knew I was Brandon Bailey's girl-friend, the world also wanted to know about me. House of Rossi's press office had been inundated with requests for interviews. It wasn't the kind of thing they were used to deal-ing with and it was taking some time to sort through everything. Not all of the requests appeared to be coming from legitimate publications. Alessandro and I had agreed that it would help House of Rossi's image – and mine – if we agreed to one interview with a reputable journalist so that we could lay all the negative headlines to rest. So now, as well as trying to finish the new collection, I also had to fit in this inter-view *and* deal with my incredibly contrite and needy boyfriend.

Brandon had not stopped sending me gifts. Flowers cov-ered every available surface, boxes of chocolates and cupcakes were stacked in a corner and there was even a new pair of Louboutins under my desk. Freddie had spent most of the day running up and down to reception to collect yet another parcel. He found it amusing, but even though I was flattered, it was starting to become too much.

'Er, there's someone to see you in reception,' Freddie said tentatively.

'If it's a fucking singing telegram you can tell him to do one.'

'No, nothing like that. This isn't from Brandon.'

'Then who is it?' I asked.

Freddie looked uncomfortable. 'Amber, he says he's your dad.'

I didn't move. The world went very still.

'Amber?' I could barely hear Freddie's voice. The blood pounding in my ears was deafening. 'Amber, are you OK?'

I stared at Freddie and snapped myself out of it. 'What did you just say?'

'There's a man in reception, and he says he's your dad.'

'Is this some kind of sick joke? You know my dad's dead.'

'I know. I'm sorry. Reception just called me. I wasn't sure what to do. I can—'

'No, you're all right. I'll call down.' I picked up the phone and dialled reception. 'Hiya, it's Amber,' I said when they picked up.

'Hey, Amber, it's Tiffany. I have your dad here. Do you want to speak to him?'

'Tiff, can you do me a favour? Would you ask the man what his name is please?'

'You want me to ask your dad what his name is?' she repeated.

'Yes, that's right.'

'Er, OK. Hang on a second.'

Tiffany put me on hold and those few moments were the longest of my life.

'Amber,' Tiffany said, coming back on the phone. 'He says his name is Karl Simpson. But your surname is Raey, right?'

'Tiff, would you please tell him that I'm busy and I can't see him.'

'Are you sure? He must—'

'Please, just get rid of him,' I said forcefully.

'Right, of course. I'll do that for you. I mean, he's obviously not your dad is he? Although he has the exact same colour eyes as you.'

I slammed the phone down without saying bye and fell into my chair. Freddie was looking at me with concern. 'His name is Karl,' I said quietly. 'He says he's my dad and Tiff says he has eyes like mine.'

'Amber, babes, is this what I think it is? I mean, could he be your father?' Freddie asked gently.

'I don't know. Maybe. Mam always told me my biological dad's name was Karl but I don't know much else about him. After Mam married Dad I rarely thought about him. And whenever I did, I bit back any of my curiosity. It seemed disloyal to want to know about him. He walked out on Mam when she was pregnant with me and he's never tried to get in touch. Until now. How did he even know where to find me?'

'Maybe it was seeing you in the paper?' Freddie offered. 'Most of the stories did mention that you worked here. Sorry, I know you're trying to put all that behind you, but it's the only reason I can think of.'

'Well whatever it was he can crawl back under whatever rock he came from.'

'Aren't you curious?' Freddie asked.

231

'No. I have no desire to see that man. Now or ever. He's a scumbag who abandoned his family and the only dad I've ever known is dead. That's the end of it.'

I tried to settle back down to work but the day was totally shot to pieces. I couldn't stop thinking about the fact that Karl had been here.

Why now, after all this time? Freddie was probably right, that he'd seen the papers and found out this is where I worked. *Should I tell Mam?* No. I couldn't. What would be the point? It would only upset her and I hadn't even seen him or spoken to him. There was nothing to tell, not really. And Mam was already upset about all the Brandon chaos. She hadn't even *met* him yet, and already she thought he was a bad influence on me. *Mam is worried enough as it is – she doesn't need anything else on her plate right now.*

I finally gave up trying to do anything constructive and left the office at six. As promised, I was going round to Brandon's. Maybe if I saw him he'd stop sending gifts to the office. It was starting to get embarrassing. I made my way down to the lobby and onto the street. I was about to head for the Tube when I heard someone call my name.

'Amber, is that you?'

I turned and saw a man who looked to be in his early forties. He was taller than me and dressed in a business suit, with thinning black hair that was turning grey at the temples. And his eyes were just like mine.

I was rooted to the spot, unable to speak.

'Look, pet, I know this is a shock but I had to see you.'

'What are you doing here?' I whispered. My voice didn't sound like my own.

'I told you, I had to see you.'

'Why? Why now?'

'It's complicated, love.' He reached out and touched my arm. I snatched it away and took a step back. This level of familiarity was absurd. I didn't know this man.

'Complicated doesn't even begin to cover it. I don't know why you're here, but I don't want you here. I don't know how you have the balls to track me down just because I was in the papers.'

'I already knew your name, I've always known it, but when I saw that you worked for House of Rossi I couldn't resist coming down to see you. I've wanted to see you for so long.'

'So why didn't you then?'

'Because—'

I cut him off. I didn't need to hear his answer. 'Because you're a snake and a coward who walked away from me and Mam. I've never needed you before, and I don't need you now.' I took one final look at those eyes and then turned on my heel and ran away from him as fast as I could.

I didn't cry until I was safely inside a cab; I was worried Karl would have caught me up at the Tube. I had been wound up as tight as a coil all day and then seeing his eyes had triggered something in me. Growing up, I'd always been the spitting image of Mam, but the only feature we didn't share was my eyes. Now I knew where I got them from. And that one small thing, that tiny detail, meant I had something in common with that man. We would always be linked. Every time I looked in the mirror and saw my eyes, I would be looking at his eyes too. And I hated the fact that I'd felt a pull towards him when that realisation had hit. I needed to put as much distance as possible between me and Karl Simpson. I needed to forget I'd ever met him.

I walked into Brandon's apartment and found him on the sofa idly watching Netflix. Things were still strained between us but right now I really needed a hug. Wordlessly, I climbed onto his lap, wrapped my arms around him and buried my face in his neck. He pulled me in closer.

'Hey,' he said eventually. 'What's going on?'

'It's been a rough day,' I mumbled into the side of his neck.

Brandon stroked my hair. 'I'm sorry if I've made things hard for you at work. Is there anything I can do? I could talk to Alessandro.'

'It's not that,' I said. I lifted my head up to look at him.

'You've been crying,' Brandon said, frowning. 'What's happened? Tell me.'

I started to tell him what had happened with Karl and a fresh wave of tears hit. It took a while to get the story out, but eventually I told him everything.

'So this guy is your real dad?' Brandon asked.

'He's my biological father,' I corrected.

'Woah, that's huge. We have to go out to celebrate.'

'Eh?' Was he for real? Had he listened to anything I'd just said? Was he aware of what happened last time we went out – or had it already slipped his mind?

'Yeah, we should celebrate that your dad got in touch. It's awesome,' Brandon continued. It was like we were on completely different planets.

Has he not just seen me crying about what had happened?

'Are you mad? This is not "awesome".' I used the air quotes. The last thing I needed now was a dose of Brandon

234

Bailey's misguided American positivity. 'This man left me mam before I was even born. He's a scumbag. I want nothing to do with him.'

'Oh,' Brandon replied. 'I hadn't thought about it like that. Sorry, baby. But listen, I do have to go out tonight with a bunch of radio DJs. I have to keep them sweet if I want them to play the single.'

I looked at him in disbelief. 'Seriously? I've just told you my biological father has turned up out of the blue, and we've be talking about toning down the partying anyway after what happened over the weekend, and you're still telling me you want to go out on the lash tonight with a bunch of knobby radio DJs you don't even know, rather than comfort your distressed girlfriend?'

'It's work, Amber,' he stated as though that was enough to justify his behaviour. I didn't have the strength to argue with him.

'You know what, Brandon? Do whatever you want. I'm not coming with you, though. I'll go home.' I expected Brandon to beg me to go with him, or at least to argue, but he didn't.

'That's cool. We'll drop you off on the way.'

Helmet.

The flat was in darkness when I let myself in. Tom was working and Jess was staying at Sam's tonight. I was slightly relieved to have the place to myself. I needed to think. Questions were going around in my head but I couldn't concentrate on a single one for more than a minute. *Why had Brandon been so keen to go out alone tonight? Why had he insisted on going out at all? Would Karl leave me alone now? What would I do if he turned up again? And finally – when had my life become so complicated?*

Chapter Twenty-four

'Thank you for agreeing to meet me,' Karl said. We were sitting opposite each other in a small Thai café. I'd ordered a
large glass of Pinot, but refused to order any food. I wasn't
planning on staying long.

'You didn't give me much choice, did you?' I replied.

Over the past two weeks Karl had been waiting for me
outside the office every night. It didn't matter whether I left
at six p.m. or ten p.m., he was always there. I'd refused to
even talk to him at first, and had just walked away – but the
anxiety over whether he'd be waiting for me yet again had
proven too much. I had agreed to meet him for half an
hour, for one drink, and to listen to what he had to say. And
if I still didn't want to see him, he had agreed to leave me
alone. That was the deal we'd made. I only hoped he'd stick
to it.

Brandon had had a tough couple of weeks too.
'Wrecked' had failed to make any kind of significant
impression on the charts and, despite his nights out with

DJs, radio stations were barely playing it. It looked like 'Wrecked' was going to sink without a trace and Brandon wasn't coping with failure well. Instead of staying true to his word and slowing down on the partying, he'd been out every night. He kept saying it was for his 'career' but I didn't believe him any more. I suspected he was too busy drowning his sorrows to do anything as constructive as networking. I wanted to support him and help him through the tough time he was having, but he wasn't opening up to me so I felt that I couldn't share how I was feeling about Karl with him. We weren't communicating well, and where we should have been talking about each other's lives, opening up and discussing the problems we were both going through, we were arguing instead. I was preoccupied with the Karl situation, he was preoccupied with his music and we were clashing about it all. In a nutshell, our relationship was a bag of dicks.

More than anything I wanted to talk to Mam, but I couldn't bring myself to tell her about Karl. She would be so hurt that I'd kept it from her before, and hopefully after tonight I'd be able to close the book on that chapter of my life for good. With no Brandon to talk to, and not feeling like I could bring it up with Mam, I'd turned to Tom and Jess for their advice. They had been supportive about my meeting Karl but had also urged caution.

'Get it over and done with, hun,' Jess had said, 'but don't let him push you into talking about anything you don't want to share with him.'

'And meet him in a public place,' had been Tom's helpful suggestion. 'Just in case he turns out to be some kind of psycho killer.'

Great, I thought to myself as I took another sip of wine and remembering their advice. *Now I'm terrified Karl is going to drag me outside and slit my throat and use my skin to make some sort of weird Amber coat. Thanks, Tom. Helpful as ever.*

'I thought you might be curious about me.' Karl's voice cut into my thoughts and brought me back to the present.

'Don't flatter yourself. I've hardly thought about you at all over the years.'

'I know and that hurts. I was young and foolish when I walked away from your mam. I've regretted it ever since.'

'Have you?' I didn't believe a word that was coming out of his mouth.

Karl nodded. 'Of course. You don't believe me.' It was a statement, not a question.

'To be honest, I'm having a hard time believing you, yes. You were eighteen, I get that you were young and scared. Most people would have been. What I don't get is why you waited this long to get in touch if you've always had these regrets. That's the bit that's puzzling me.'

Karl looked lost in thought for a while.

'When your mam married and David wanted to adopt you, they had to get my permission,' he said at last. 'Your mam tracked me down. I was living in London by then. I had a good job and was still single. When she turned up I thought she might want to get back together, and I would have, but then she told me about David and it became clear to me that I'd missed my chance. You already had a dad. It hit me then, what I'd lost, but I thought if there's one thing I ever do for you I could make sure you had the father you deserved. So I signed away my rights to you and didn't stand in David's way.'

I'd never heard this before. I was intrigued but still wary. 'What do you want now?' I asked.

'I want to get to know you. That's all. I know I have no rights as a father any more but I'd still like to spend some time with you as a person. What do you think?'

Was this something I wanted? I had no idea.

'This is all too much.' I stood up. 'I have to go. I can't think about this right now.'

'Can I see you again?' Karl asked quickly, standing up too. 'No pressure. Maybe just coffee. Or lunch. Or dinner. Whatever you're comfortable with.'

I knew nothing about this man. I didn't know if he was married, if he had kids, where he lived. I wasn't ready to know those things. Not yet. But maybe I would be ready one day, so I nodded.

The café wasn't far from Brandon's place, so after I left Karl I walked back to his, hoping the crisp night air would clear my head. It didn't. Brandon had said he'd take me out for dinner after I'd seen Karl but what I really wanted was to curl up on the sofa and watch something mindless on TV. Maybe I could convince him to order a takeaway instead. Feeling buoyed up at the thought of a cosy night in with my man, I let myself into the apartment only for my heart to sink. There were at least half a dozen men in the living area. The coffee table was strewn with beer bottles and empty food containers.

'Hey, baby,' Brandon said when he saw me. He stood, walked over and planted a wet kiss on my mouth. He tasted of stale beer and cigarettes.

'What's going on?' I asked quietly.

'We're hanging out. You know, beer, pizza, fun. Remember fun?' he sneered.

'You know I just saw Karl, right? You do remember saying that we'd have dinner together afterwards, don't you?'

The lads in the room had stopped talking and now they were all staring at me. I suddenly felt very uneasy. I didn't want to be here.

'Come with me,' Brandon said, pulling me towards the bedroom.

The lads started cheering Brandon on. If he thought I was having sex with him while they all sat there and listened, he had another thing coming. Brandon shut the door behind us and one look at his face told me that sex was the last thing on his mind. He looked pissed off.

'Look, Amber, those guys out there are huge influences in the music business. Don't embarrass me in front of them,' he said.

'Really? They look like a bunch of pissy tramps to me.'

'Amber, seriously,' he hissed. 'I need you to be supportive. It's make or break time for me. Why are you always so difficult about these things?'

I was taken aback. 'I'm not making things difficult for you. I have stuff going on too. I need support as well. You haven't even asked me about Karl, you know.'

A dark look crossed Brandon's face but it was gone so quickly I wondered if I'd imagined it.

'You're right,' Brandon said, kissing my forehead. 'I'm sorry. Why don't we have dinner tomorrow night instead? You can go home and get some sleep – I won't be so distracted then either.'

'OK,' I said, although I couldn't help but feel disappointed. What I really wanted was for Brandon to kick everyone else out and spend the night with me. But that wasn't going to happen, and I didn't want another row so I decided to let it go. I seemed to be doing that a lot lately. Maybe I was just overthinking it.

The following Monday, I found myself having lunch with Karl. I had hoped our first meeting would have made him back off but it had had the opposite effect. He'd been even more persistent, and so I'd agreed to have lunch just to get him away from the office.

'So how are things with you and Brandon?' Karl asked.

'That's not a question I'm going to answer,' I said. 'Look, I don't know anything about you, not really. This isn't some father–daughter bonding lunch, and don't for one second think I want you or *need* you in my life in any kind of father role. That's not going to happen. This is just lunch. The minute you try to probe into my life too deeply, I'm out of here, mate.'

Karl put his hands up. 'Fine, I get it. I'm just concerned about your relationship, that's all. It's a natural instinct but I understand you don't want to talk to me about it. What would you like to talk about then?'

'Why you left Mam,' I said immediately.

'I already told you,' Karl said and I thought I caught a flash of impatience cross his face.

'So tell me again, but with the details this time.'

'OK,' Karl sighed. 'I had just turned eighteen and your mam was a real stunner. Every boy was after her but she chose me. I felt like the luckiest man in the world. So we started going out and everything was going great. I hadn't expected it to last as long as it did, and while I didn't want it to end I was thinking about the plans I'd been making for my future.'

'What kind of plans?'

'I'd always dreamed of moving down south. I have family in London, my uncle offered me a place to live, so the plan was that as soon as I finished school I'd be off. I did care about your mam in my own way but I was selfish, young and daft. So when she said she was pregnant I was totally devastated.'

'Go on.'

'I'm not proud of any of this, Amber, but I owe you the truth. I offered Ange money to take care of things.'

'You mean abort me?'

He nodded. 'But she wouldn't. She said that she was keeping you and that was the end of it. At first I said I'd stand by her but I soon realised that I wasn't ready to be tied down with a child. I tried, but the more Ange got excited about the baby, about you, the more I felt like I was drowning. One night I took off. I just took off. I made my parents promise not to tell anyone where I'd gone, especially Ange. I came to London, moved in with my uncle and I didn't look back.'

'And that was it, until Mam got in touch about the adoption?'

'That's right. I don't know if she'd tried to get in touch before, but the next time I saw her was when she turned up to talk about David adopting you. I wanted to see you, to see if you took after me in any way, but I knew I needed to leave you alone.'

I felt hate welling up inside me. *How dare he try to abort me? To get rid of me? How dare he call Mam 'Ange' like they were old pals? How dare he just leave Mam like that?*

'You know, you might have given me your eyes but that's it. I'm nothing like you. I stick by the people I care about.'

'Amber, listen. Let me try to—'

'I don't want to listen any more. I've heard enough.'

243

I walked away from the table, ignoring Karl's shouts behind me, asking me to stay. I really had heard enough.

Someone was shaking me awake. It took a while for my eyes to adjust to the darkness but I eventually made out Brandon's form. I'd come to Brandon's after storming away from Karl. I knew Brandon wouldn't be here, that he was working late in the studio, but I wanted to feel close to him. I hated how things were between us right now. His single had officially bombed and he was on a downward spiral. I knew he was hurting, but so was I, and after the latest confrontation with Karl I'd decided I needed to put things straight. I needed one relationship in my life to work and I wanted it to be the one with Brandon.

'Hey,' I said sleepily.

'Baby, I'm so glad you're here. It's a sign. I wanted to tell you about the song I wrote tonight. My manager thinks it's good enough to release as my next single. We're going to forget what happened with "Wrecked" and start over with this new song. And guess what? It's about you. You're my inspiration.'

'You wrote a song about me?'

'Yeah, it's called "My Geordie Girl". It's about how we fell in love.'

'Er, that's great,' I said weakly. *'My Geordie Girl'? Was that the best he could come up with? It sounds awful.*

'Wait until you hear it. You're going to freak.'

I'd freak, all right, but maybe not in the way he was hoping. Still, he seemed happy and more like the positive person I'd fallen for. If writing dodgy-sounding songs about me helped him sleep at night then I was in full support of that.

Please God, let it be a good 'un. It's not going to be, is it. It's going to be shite. Christ on a cracker.

Chapter Twenty-five

'You seem more like your old self,' Freddie said. We'd gone for a cheeky end of the week drink at Jalou. It was nice to spend some time with him outside the office, and Tom and Jess had joined us.

'Yeah, welcome back, babes,' Jess said, winking.

'I haven't been *that* bad, have I?' I asked.

'Hmm, a little,' Tom said. 'But you've been busy, and in *luuuuuurve*.' I gave him a shove. 'I'm joking!' he protested, rubbing his arm. 'You've had a lot on, we know that. Every-thing OK with Crazy Karl?'

'Nice, Tom. As always, very witty and mature.' He did a little bow at my remark and I carried on, 'I think so, you know, he's given me some space over the last few days. He's stopped just turning up unannounced, which is a relief.'

'And how's Brandon?' Jess asked.

'Better,' I said. 'He's been in the studio a lot and that's put him in a good mood. He's still upset about "Wrecked" but he's putting a brave face on it.'

That wasn't exactly true. He had been spending a lot of time in the studio, yes, but he'd also been out almost every night. Without me. It had got to the stage where he wasn't even bothering to respond to my messages any more. He would stumble through the door in the early hours of the morning and climb into bed, then wake me up and drunkenly apologise for being a knob. I was almost certain that he was just drunk – he was never in a bad enough state for me to suspect he was high – but I worried he was just one step away from going down that road again. He'd mentioned that he was going to go straight home after he'd finished in the studio today so I was planning on setting up a romantic evening in to help him relax. I wanted to show him that I was there for him whenever he was ready to let me in. I couldn't talk to my friends about any of this, though. They weren't exactly over the moon about Brandon's recent behaviour and I didn't have the energy to defend him yet again.

'I'm glad he's coming out the other side,' Jess said. 'Just remember that you don't have to put up with his shite.'

'OK, OK,' I said, giving Jess a smile. 'But right now it's my turn to be supportive, which is why I'm going to have to love you and leave you in a bit. I'm going to surprise him tonight when he gets home from the studio.'

'Oh yeah?' Tom wiggled his eyebrows suggestively. 'How's that then?'

'As if I'd tell you!'

'Have another drink with us first,' Freddie said.

'All right, pet. But just a quick one. I want to get back to the apartment before Brandon does.'

Out of the corner of my eye I saw Jamie approaching and my heart started beating a little faster. I hadn't seen him since

Halloween, and although we'd exchanged a few WhatsApp messages I knew I owed him a proper apology. I couldn't do it here, though, not with everyone around. I'd just be normal for now and make it up to him later.

'Hey,' I said to him. 'You all right?'

He looked at me steadily. 'Yeah, Geordio. I'm just fine. You?'

'Better,' I said. 'Things are starting to calm down.'

'That's good.'

Tom and Jess exchanged a glance and I knew exactly why; it wasn't like me and Jamie to be so stilted with each other.

'Mate, let me get you a drink,' Tom said, slapping Jamie on the back.

'You know what,' I said, 'I really should get off.'

Jamie shot me a look but didn't say anything.

'If you're sure?' Jess said hesitantly.

'Yeah, babes. I'll see you all later. Have a good night.'

I left Jalou as quickly as I could, suddenly desperate to get away from my friends. It wasn't right, it wasn't OK, but I did it anyway.

I hummed to myself as I let myself into Brandon's apartment. I'd stopped off at his favourite sushi place and picked up a selection of things I knew he liked. I had felt bad about the way I'd practically run out of Jalou but the thought of the night ahead had put me in a happier mood. This was exactly what Brandon and I needed – some time alone without everyone else's opinions or agendas getting in the way. I was going to make a real effort. I'd set up dinner so it was ready for when he walked in and we'd have an easy-going evening. Perhaps if he didn't feel as though I was having a go at him he might relax enough to open up and talk to me. *Yes, this is going to be a good night.*

The apartment was silent. Good: that meant he wasn't home yet. The lights were on though, which was strange. Brandon was anal about making sure everything was turned off before leaving. He must be distracted if he left without doing his usual round of all the lights. I walked into the kitchen and started pulling plates out of the cupboard.

I began arranging the sushi as artfully as I could manage when I heard a noise coming from the bedroom. It sounded like laughter. *Has he left the television on as well?* I could definitely hear voices. A banging started up. Hang on – that didn't sound like TV noises. It sounded like ... No, it couldn't be. My heart started hammerng loudly in my chest as I made my way to the bedroom door. The noises got louder with every step and I could hear a very distinctive moaning sound. No ... No fucking way.

I pushed open the bedroom door and my whole world came crashing down in an instant.

I took in everything:

The empty champagne bottles littering the floor.

The remnants of a bag of white powder coating the bedside table in a fine dust.

The clothes and underwear thrown in ecstatic abandon around the room.

And Brandon. Naked. On the bed.

With two girls I'd never seen before.

At first I didn't say anything. I just watched the three naked, writhing bodies. Was this really happening? I couldn't have been standing there for more than a few seconds but it felt like an eternity before Brandon noticed me.

248

'Amber!'

He disentangled himself from the two girls and leapt off the bed. The girls looked straight through me, too smashed to care. They flopped back on the bed like they didn't have a care in the world. I wrenched my gaze away from them and looked at Brandon walking towards me, completely naked, his eyes wide and wild. He was completely off his face.

I snapped.

'What the fuck are you doing?!' I screamed.

Brandon froze in his tracks.

'Don't just *stand* there! Answer me!' I yelled.

'Baby,' he slurred, 'it's not what it looks like.'

'It *looks* like you're taking part in a human jigsaw!'

'Baby ...' His voice trailed off. There was nothing he could say.

I looked down at my hands. I was carrying a plate of sushi. I couldn't remember bringing it with me. Tears spilled down my cheeks. I was crying for the lost potential of the night, for the time I had wasted on such a knob, for the stark realisation that I had changed so much of myself for him. And for what?

'I brought you sushi!'

Brandon blinked.

Sushi? Amber, seriously, that's what you're thinking about right now?

'I wanted to cheer you up. To support you. I wanted to have a romantic night with you!'

'I didn't mean for it to happen. I'm just so stressed—'

'Shut up!' I was screaming at banshee level now. 'You don't have a drug-fuelled orgy because you're stressed, you fuck-boy.'

'It was a threesome not an orgy.'

A threesome not an orgy? Oh. My. God. Was this complete and utter knob prince really going to stand here and debate the particulars of the correct terminology for which compromising sexual situation I'd found him in? Yes, yes he fucking was. And that was it, my mind went blank and I switched to autopilot. Before I knew what I was doing, I threw the plate of sushi straight at him. It hit him square on the shoulder. Maki rolls littered the floor. One of the female orgy-partakers took a California roll to the eye and as I took one last fleeting glance at Brandon, the last thing I saw before I ran out of the apartment was salmon sashimi sliding down his schlong.

The cab pulled up outside my flat. I stumbled out, blinded by tears, ignoring the driver's look of concern. I was sobbing so much I could barely walk straight. I made it to the door of my building but my hands were shaking too hard and I couldn't get the key in the lock. I felt a pair of strong arms around me, comforting not threatening. I looked up and pulled away immediately.

Karl.

'What are you doing here?' I asked between sobs.

'I wanted to see you. I know you don't like me turning up unannounced but now I'm glad I did. What's wrong?'

'I don't want to talk to you about it.'

'Fine. But I'm not leaving you in this state.'

'Please, just go.'

'No.'

He pulled me into another hug and even though I knew I should push him away, go inside and close the door on him, I didn't. I needed comfort and he was here providing it. It felt so good to just be held, to not have to be the strong one all the time. After a while, I pulled away.

'Let's get you inside,' Karl said.

I handed him my keys without a word. Once we were in I let him guide me to the sofa and I sat there while he went to put the kettle on. He returned a few minutes later with two mugs of steaming hot tea. We sat in silence, sipping our tea. I was still sniffling and he kept throwing looks at me.

Eventually he broke the silence to say: 'Tell me what happened.'

It wasn't a question, but it wasn't an order either. He wanted to know why I was upset; he wanted to help. After the betrayal I'd just faced, I needed someone on my side. I needed someone to look out for me for a change.

So I told him everything.

It took a good hour to explain it all to Karl. It wasn't just about what happened tonight – it was the sweeping me off my feet, the parties, the drinking, the drugs. It all came out, and by the time I had finished I was utterly drained. I had nothing left – I was all cried out. I was a shell, an Amber-shaped husk.

'Jamie had the right idea,' Karl said. 'Brandon fucking bellend.'

I tried to laugh but it came out more like a bark. Nothing was funny any more.

'You've had a lucky escape, pet,' Karl went on. 'Just imagine if you'd—'

The lounge door burst open and a drunk Jess bounded in, followed by an equally drunk Tom. They both stopped in their tracks when they saw me and Karl.

'Amber,' Jess hiccupped. 'You OK, hun?'

'Have you been crying?' Tom said, squinting at me.

'She's had a rough night,' Karl said. 'Maybe we can leave the questions until the morning?'

'Who the hell are you?' Jess said, pointing an accusing finger at him.

'Um, this is Karl,' I said quietly. 'My, er ... well, this is Karl.'

Jess's eyes widened. Tom puffed his cheeks out in surprise.

'What's going on?' Jess said. 'Why is he here?'

'Sit down,' I said wearily. 'It's going to be a long night.'

Over toast and another round of tea and the majority of a pack of Tunnock's caramel wafers I found in the back of the cupboard, I told Jess and Tom what had happened after I left Jalou. They quickly sobered up and threw around their own names for Brandon. I don't think I'd ever heard such obscenities come out of Jess's mouth. Hearing myself recount the story for a second time made me feel devastated all over again. Is love really that blind? I'd been so taken in by all of Brandon's grand gestures that I'd talked myself into believing he was a good person underneath all of his vices, but he wasn't. He didn't care about me – he couldn't if he was able to do what he had. I wasn't interested in how smashed or high he was. There was no excuse for it. Had he been acting the whole time? Maybe I'd never know.

'I've got so much stuff at his place,' I said through a fresh wave of tears. 'I don't want to see him right now but I left some of my sketches there. I need them for work.'

'I'll pick up your things,' Karl offered. 'Will you let me do that for you?'

'I guess,' I said. 'You don't mind?'

'Of course not. You shouldn't have to face Brandon again until you're ready.'

I rummaged around in my bag and pulled out my set of keys to Brandon's place. 'Here, these are keys to his apartment.' I pulled out my phone, and even though I hadn't really been expecting anything from Brandon I still felt sad that he hadn't even tried to get in touch with me. I tapped out a quick message to him.

Someone will be round tomorrow to collect my things. Pls have them ready.

'It's late,' Jess said, yawning. 'You should try to get some rest.'

'I don't think I'll be able to sleep.'

'Come on,' Tom said, pulling me to standing. 'I bet you crash out straight away.'

He was right. I was asleep as soon as my head hit the pillow. But all night I dreamt about giant sushi pieces attacking the city of London, and while I struggled to escape them I was caught up in a torrential blizzard. I didn't need a dream analyst to help me work out what that one meant.

The next morning I woke up and for a few seconds I thought it was a normal day. Then the memories of the previous night came flooding back and it was like someone had punched me in the stomach. I gathered up enough willpower to get up out of bed and walk into the kitchen. Tom and Jess were already in there, but when I spotted Karl leaning on the counter I stopped. What was he doing here?

'Hey you,' Tom said kindly.

'Morning, babe,' Jess said, giving me a big hug. 'Do you want some breakfast?'

'I'm not hungry.' I looked at Karl, the obvious question in my eyes.

'I crashed on the sofa,' Karl said. 'I was too worried to leave. You should eat something, pet. How about some scrambled eggs?'

'I'm not sure that I can eat anything,' I said, feeling queasy. 'Has anyone seen my phone? It wasn't in my room.'

'Sorry, I haven't seen it,' Jess said. Tom shook his head.

'Amber, I'm going to go and collect your stuff now,' Karl said, putting his mug in the sink. 'I'll bring it round later tonight and then I'm going to take you out for dinner. No arguments.'

I just nodded. I didn't have the energy to argue anyway.

I spent most of the day on the sofa, staring at the TV but not really watching anything. Jess, Tom and I had searched the flat from top to bottom but we hadn't found my phone. I knew I had it last night. What the hell had I done with it? It didn't matter anyway – there was no one I wanted to speak to. Jess and Tom barely left my side all day. I was grateful for their support but I really just wanted to be alone, so when Tom had to leave for work I packed Jess off to see Sam. She was reluctant at first, but when I told her I was only going to sleep she finally agreed to go out.

I didn't sleep, though. Instead I paced around the flat and I worried. I worried about all the time and attention I'd wasted on a man who didn't even have the decency to come after me now. I worried about all the time and attention I hadn't paid to work in I don't know how long. I'd lost my focus somewhere along the way and I didn't know how to get it back. Not now that my head was all over the place. The theme of the new collection was romance, for crying out loud. The last thing I wanted to think about right now was romance.

At around eight p.m. the buzzer went and I hated myself for hoping for a split second that it was Brandon. *You twat, Amber. You complete and utter twat.*

It was Karl. When he walked through the door he was carrying a large box full to the brim of my belongings.

'Where shall I put these, love?' he asked.

'Just dump them in my room. Did you see him?' I asked when he came back. I couldn't help myself – I needed to know.

'No, the place was deserted. He'd piled your stuff up in the living room and had left a note asking me to leave the key. I think he's shipped out.'

'Right. Well that's a bit of a punch in the dick, isn't it?' was all I could say.

'Come on,' Karl said. 'Dinner. I bet you haven't eaten all day.'

When I got home later that night I felt marginally better. Dinner had been surprisingly nice. Karl was good company when you got him talking. He was full of stories and funny anecdotes, and he was a good listener. Despite everything that was going on, I'd enjoyed myself. For the first time since he'd turned up at House of Rossi I was seriously considering the possibility of having some kind of relationship with him. Karl would never replace Dad but that didn't mean I couldn't let him into my life in some small way. Maybe there was hope for us after all.

I switched on the light in my bedroom and spotted my phone on my bedside table.

That's odd, I thought. *I'm sure it wasn't there before.*

Later, I'd kick myself for not putting two and two together, but in all honesty there was no way I could've stopped what was about to happen. The damage had already been done.

Chapter Twenty-six

I stared at the tabloid article in front of me. Weyaye. This couldn't be happening.

STAR BRANDON BAILEY DRUGS AND ORGY SHAME

Caught Red-Handed by Girlfriend Amber Raey
Father's Guilt at Screwed-Up Daughter

Amber Raey went to her boyfriend's apartment like any normal girlfriend would do, but when she arrived she discovered him in bed with two naked lingerie models.

'Amber was beside herself,' Karl Simpson, her father, 43, said. 'She came straight to me, distraught, and I just held her like any father would.'

Brandon Bailey has a history of sex and drug issues but Amber was oblivious to all of it, according to her father.

'She loved him and she believed his lies. She was naive but I know she's a good girl and she doesn't condone drug use. He pulled the wool over her eyes. He probably cheated on her all the time they were together – the world saw how wasted he was after Oscar Haverstock's party.' Karl is referring to the infamous Halloween party his daughter and Brandon attended where he was photographed just before his single 'Wrecked' was released. Amber was holding him up but she maintains she wasn't using drugs that night and evidence supports her claims.

'Her stepdad died in a car accident that was caused by a drug user, so she never touches drugs,' Karl explained emphatically, defending his daughter.

Karl wasn't in Amber's life until recently. Although Amber is now an accomplished fashion designer, Karl hasn't been in contact with his daughter for very long. He says he regrets his decision to leave her mum before Amber was born, but he was only 18 at the time and he believes that Amber's mum got pregnant on purpose to trap him. He tried to be part of Amber's life but her mum, angry at his refusal to marry her, forced him to let her new husband, David Raey, adopt Amber instead. Karl looked tearful as he recounts how Amber's mother used emotional blackmail to ensure he gave up any rights to the daughter he longed to get to know.

'Signing those papers was the hardest thing I've ever done, but I thought it would give Amber a more stable life. I did it for her. I thought I was putting her first, but now I realise my mistake. If I had been in her life before maybe she wouldn't have made so many bad choices with men. Perhaps she would have seen through Brandon and not tried to be part of his sordid world. I blame myself,' Simpson says.

Because it's clear that Brandon Bailey's world is sordid. Not only does he have a penchant for orgies, he was kicked out of his band, The Starks, when his drug habit started to affect his singing voice. Although his new management claim that Brandon left because of 'creative differences', the fact that his first solo single was a flop suggests that the band carried him, rather than the other way round.

'Amber was quite simply blinded by him. He took her to the River Café in Brooklyn on their first date and he'd hired the whole restaurant for her. It sounds like any young woman's fantasy but I was concerned so I did some digging. Amber met Brandon backstage before her first fashion show during New York Fashion Week, when he mistook her for a model. I have since found out that he's a regular at fashion shows, hanging round backstage and picking up models – that's his MO. But Amber is so naive she didn't even question why he was there. I feel responsible for this whole mess,' Simpson explains. 'If only I'd been there for her, perhaps she wouldn't have been so easily led by him.'

Many young ladies would have fallen for Bailey's charms. He whisked Miss Raey away to Paris on a private plane, bought her jewellery from Tiffany and took her to every A-list party in London. But Miss Raey claims to be a sensible girl from Newcastle with a successful career, so why was she so blind when it came to Mr Bailey?

'It's my fault,' Simpson reiterates. 'I wasn't there for her and although David came into her life, it could never be the same as having your real father around. Blood is thicker than water and I should have known that. I made a huge mistake and I've been paying for it ever since. The worst thing is that now my daughter is also paying the price and I'm not sure she'll ever be able to have a functional relationship with a man. I feel as though I've screwed up her life and I want nothing more than to put things right between us. I think Brandon Bailey could sense her vulnerability and he preyed on her weaknesses. I want to make sure no man ever does that to my beautiful daughter again.'

It is a sad fact that women find power and fame attractive, but hopefully Amber has had a lucky escape. Brandon has returned to the States, his career in tatters and his reputation ruined. Rumour has it that he has checked into a rehab facility but as yet we have been unable to confirm this. Amber Raey is currently working on her second collection for House of Rossi. The first was a huge hit and she was being touted as 'one to watch' in the fashion world. But where does this leave her career?

'I intend to keep a closer eye on her,' Simpson says. 'Obviously her mother tried to do her best but she needs real guidance now and I'm here to provide it. I'm going to encourage her to focus on her career. She's young, there's plenty of time for romance. And I can teach her about me now so hopefully she won't make this kind of mistake again.'

Karl Simpson is a father. One whose only wish is to reach out to his wayward daughter.

'I hope this article will help,' Karl said. 'From now on, Amber is my priority. It's about time she had some stability in her life.'

Photos of me and Brandon covered a double-page spread. Photos that Karl could only have got from my phone.

How am I going to come back from this?

I put my head in my hands just as the phone started ringing.

PART FOUR

Chapter Twenty-seven

I was huddled in the doorway outside a building near the office. It was bitterly cold – a vicious, icy wind blew all around me and rain was lashing down. December had well and truly arrived. There was a phone call I knew I had to make but I didn't want to do it in the office. Too many people might overhear and I didn't know who I could trust any more.

I'd read the article a dozen times, each time hoping it would be different to the last. It wasn't. Each and every word remained the same. I'd felt betrayed by Brandon, but Karl had left me feeling utterly violated. The memory of his 'support' while secretly he was stealing my phone and talking to reporters behind my back left a bitter taste in my mouth. I'd started to believe that his attempts at building a relationship with me were genuine. I should've trusted my first instinct about him. He'd taken me for a mug. And me mam. My lovely, caring, wonderful mother. Karl had made her sound like a manipulative, small-minded, cruel woman – that was the furthest thing from the truth. I'd had a text from Rubes, simply asking

How cd you?

I'd replied, telling her I had no idea what Karl was up to, that I felt deceived too, but she hadn't responded. The silence hurt more than anything she could've said to me.

I pulled up Mam's number and pressed dial. She answered almost immediately.

'Amber.' She sounded weary, hurt, tired and angry all at once. I wasn't aware a person could be all those things at one particular moment.

'Mam,' I said, my voice thick with tears. 'I'm so sorry. I don't know where to start. It's all—'

'You might want to start by telling me when he got in touch and why the hell you didn't tell me.'

I'd been so consumed with the article that it hadn't crossed my mind that I hadn't even told Mam that Karl had turned up in my life. I took a deep breath. It was time to come clean. I told Mam everything, from the first time he'd turned up to all the times I'd walked away from him. I told her how I'd only agreed to meet him that first time so he'd leave me alone. I tried to explain how I hadn't meant to let him in at all, so I'd thought there was no point in telling her he'd shown up – it would only have upset her. I left nothing out when I explained what had happened with Brandon and how Karl had just been in the right place at the right time, how I knew now that I'd been stupid to trust him for even a second. And during all of that, Mam didn't say a word. I knew she was still there because I could hear her breathing, but she didn't interrupt, she didn't ask any questions. She just let me talk.

'Mam?' I said when I'd got to the end of the entire horrible story and she was still silent. 'Say something.'

'What is there to say, Amber? Let's forget about that ex of yours for a while and just consider the fact that the man who walked away from you before you were even born turned up and you thought it would be best not to tell me. What were you thinking? Were you thinking at all?'

'I just told you,' I sobbed, 'he wouldn't leave me alone. I thought the best way to get rid of him was to hear him out. I didn't want to hurt you for no reason and I thought he'd be gone soon enough so there didn't seem any point in telling you. I was trying to protect you.'

'And when he came back again? And again? Why didn't you tell me then?'

'I didn't know what was happening. It was too confusing and I was angry with him myself. I just wanted him to go away. And then after Brandon . . . Karl was just there. It felt OK. It felt nice,' I admitted.

'*Nice?*' Mam practically spat the word down the phone. 'There is nothing nice about that man. You should've come to me the second he turned up. You didn't think it was odd that the first time he shows an interest in you was after you were papped with Brandon? The first time he gets in touch is after you're splashed all over the national press with that Yankee twat and you didn't think there was anything wrong with that? Nothing suspicious?'

'He said he didn't know where I was. It was the first time he knew how to find me. He—'

'He's always known where you were living!' Mam exploded. 'After he signed the adoption papers your dad told him that he could be part of your life if he wanted.'

'Dad told him that?' I was stunned. Karl had never mentioned that he'd met Dad.

'Yes. Your dad was adamant that he wouldn't stand in the way if Karl wanted a relationship with you. But he didn't.' Mam paused and I could hear she was crying. 'I'm sorry, love, I never wanted to tell you that he left you a second time. But he did.'

I was heaving with sobs now. 'I feel like such a fool.'

'If you'd told me about any of this I could've saved you from this heartache. I would've made sure he never got close enough to hurt you.'

'I got it all wrong. About Karl, about Brandon. I'm sorry. I got caught up and everything happened so fast. What's wrong with me? Why am I such a bad judge of character? Everything's falling apart, Mam.'

'What about everything you've worked so hard for? Where did that fit in to all of this?'

'After New York I was distracted by Brandon,' I admitted. 'I wasn't feeling inspired.'

'Oh, love. What's happened to you? Your work was everything to you.'

'I don't know,' I said quietly. 'Everything's a mess.'

'Do you know what the worst thing is?' Mam said sadly. 'It's not that you kept something so important from me. It's not that you felt you couldn't tell me what was really going on between you and Brandon. It's that that article was so dismissive of your dad. They treated David like nothing more than a footnote.' Mam's voice cracked. 'And he was more than that. He was everything.'

We were both sobbing now.

'You've been drifting away for a long time and I let you have your space because you're young and I thought you were happy and falling in love. It hurts that you stopped making the time for us but it hurts even more that you shared so much with a man who didn't deserve it.'

'I've said I'm sorry. I don't know what else to say. Tell me what to do to make this better.'

'It's not going to be that easy. One phone call isn't going to make this right. We're hurt, Amber. It feels like you betrayed us.'

'Us?'

'Ruby hasn't said a word since she read the paper. She refused to go to school today. She's locked herself in her room and she won't come out. Imagine what this is like for her. She's just a teenager – and you know how teenagers can be cruel to each other.'

'I'll call her. I'll explain, tell her everything.'

'Don't. She won't understand.'

'But, Mam—'

'No, Amber. I don't really understand you *myself* right now. Let her cool down and I'll speak to her first. Then you can talk to her. Ruby's not much more than a child, for God's sake. She shouldn't have to deal with this on top of everything she's been through.'

'I'm still me, you know, Mam,' I said, my voice small.

'Are you? Really? I'm not sure you know *who* you are any more. And you can't fix this until you figure that out.'

When I got back to the office I locked myself in the disabled toilets and called Jess. She'd called me twice while I'd been on

269

the phone with Mam. I couldn't stand out in the rain any longer but I wasn't ready to go back to Freddie, the other designers and all the whispering either.

'Are you OK?' she asked as soon as she answered.

'Not really. I've destroyed everything. Mam is mad at me and Rubes won't even respond to my WhatsApp.'

'Where are you right now?'

'At work. Hiding in the disabled toilet.'

'I'm on my way.'

'But don't you have to work as well?' I protested.

'Work can survive without me for once.'

Freddie had brought my lunch to my office and he and Jess were trying to get me to eat something.

'I'm not hungry,' I said, pushing the limp-looking chicken salad around on my plate. 'I haven't faced Alessandro yet. I'll probably lose my job.'

'It'll be OK,' Jess said. 'He sounds like a reasonable man.'

'He is,' I said. 'That's why I feel so bad. He's been so good to me and the press office has already had to deal with stories about me once. I can't believe all this shit has happened again.'

'Alessandro will know this isn't your fault,' Freddie said.

'Yeah but he'll hate having House of Rossi associated with bad press again. He told me to stay out of trouble.' I put my head in my hands. I couldn't lose my job, not on top of everything else.

'You're the victim here,' Jess said. 'That's clear to everyone. Brandon, Karl – they're the ones in the wrong.'

'Have you looked at the online comments?' I asked.

'Don't do it,' Freddie warned but I didn't listen.

Almost every gossip blog had picked up on the story and there were hundreds of comments underneath all of them. Most people said they felt sorry for me, but that was because they believed what Karl had said.

No wonder the girl has such bad luck with men.
She's never had a strong male role model in her life.

Others were calling Karl out on his behaviour:

What kind of dad sells a story about his own
daughter? Tosser.

But then there were the ones that were downright cruel:

Wow big news, stupid fame-hungry airhead falls for
rich famous man then complains when he turns out
to be a perv. Use your brain, love, rather than
spreading your legs.

'That's enough,' Freddie said, turning my screen off. 'Stop reading. It won't do you any good. These people are all fat, ugly weirdos with social disorders anyway. Fuck them.'

'Do you think I've been a knob?'

'I think you've been tricked,' Jess said. 'Not by one, but by two men. You're not the first girl it's happened to, and you won't be the last.'

'What's that saying? "Fool me once, shame on you; fool me twice, shame on me"? This is on me now. I have to stop trusting all these dickhead blokes. What's wrong with me?'

I fleetingly thought of Jamie. He'd tried to warn me about Brandon at Halloween and I'd repaid him by pretty much avoiding him ever since. I had so many bridges to build that I didn't know where to start. I looked to Jess and Freddie – even my most loyal supporters were lost for words. I'd disappointed everyone I loved and cared about in favour of people who'd used me and mugged me off. I couldn't stand the thought of my mam being hurt by my careless mistakes.

'Your mum will calm down,' Jess said, reading my mind. 'Just give it time.'

'Are you sure there's nothing I can do about this?' I asked desperately.

After Jess had arrived she'd made a few phone calls to see if there was anything I could do legally, but in the end it just came down to my word against Karl's. The actual events in the piece had happened – I couldn't dispute that. And I couldn't even prove that he'd taken my phone without my permission.

'I'm sorry, babes. It's probably best to just ride it out.'

'Who's going riding?' Alessandro asked, walking in.

I sat up straight. I hadn't expected him to turn up unannounced.

'Er, Alessandro, this is my friend Jess,' I said quickly.

'Pleasure to meet you,' Alessandro said warmly, shaking Jess's hand.

'You too. I've heard so much about you.'

'And one day I shall hear about all the tales you have heard about me. But now,' Alessandro looked at me, 'would you mind giving me a moment alone with Amber?'

'Of course.' Jess quickly grabbed her things. She gave me a hug and a kiss on the cheek. 'I'll see you at home later.'

'Come,' Alessandro said when we were alone. 'Sit. We have much to talk about.'

'I'm sorry, Alessandro. I know you told me to stay out of trouble. I didn't mean for this to happen.'

'Bella, only the weakest of men would do to this to their own flesh and blood. I know this is not your fault. I'm not angry, I'm concerned about you.'

That did it. I burst into tears. Anger I could cope with, pity made me come undone.

Alessandro put an arm around my shoulders. 'Do not cry. These men do not deserve your tears.'

'I know this will mean more bad press for House of Rossi. I've let you down.'

'This is, what do you call it, an alarm call?'

'A wake-up call?' I offered.

'*Esattamente!*' Alessandro said. 'A wake-up call. That's right.'

'What do you mean?' I asked, wiping my tears away.

Alessandro paused, collecting his thoughts. 'You are a real talent, bella, one of the most promising designers I've had the pleasure of working with. The reaction you got in New York – it was wonderful. I was so proud of you.'

'But now?' I was dreading his response.

'I still believe in you, but you have been distracted recently. This new line is not coming together as easily as your last one. Have you lost your passion for this?'

'No,' I said forcefully. Of that I was certain. 'Definitely not.'

'Then where have you been?' Alessandro asked.

I was confused. 'I've been here, every day.'

'Have you really?' Alessandro said gently. 'Have we been getting your full attention when you're here?'

Well, now what am I supposed to do with that?

'I have been, er, preoccupied lately, I guess. But I thought Brandon was helping me. You don't think so?'

'I think he confused you.' Alessandro patted my hand. 'Listen, bella, you have a gift. Please don't waste it. I once told you to live life in order to be inspired, but you have to make sure you're living your life, not someone else's.'

Right. Now I'm even more confused. What is he talking about?

Alessandro saw my confusion and smiled. 'You need to remember what makes you truly happy. Only then will that fire come back to you. Take some time, think about things and let's take a look at your sketches together at the end of the week. OK?'

'OK,' I said. I still had no idea what Alessandro was getting at, but perhaps focusing on work was exactly the distraction I needed right now. 'I'll do you proud, Alessandro. I promise.'

Chapter Twenty-eight

It had been ten awful days since the article had first appeared. There had been another tense phone call with Mam; Ruby was still ignoring me; I hadn't heard a thing from Brandon. Karl, on the other hand, wouldn't go away. He'd turned up at the office but security had sent him packing, and the one time he'd come by the flat Tom had told him in no uncertain terms to, and I quote, 'Fuck the fucking fuck off.' He hadn't been back since. Jamie had been out of town working but he'd sent me some nice messages, telling me to keep my chin up and that things would get better soon. But I'd also been getting a fair amount of abuse from so-called friends. I was seriously considering getting rid of my phone altogether. Even work was difficult. Despite Alessandro's peptalk and encouragement I couldn't seem to pull any designs together. Nothing felt normal or natural any more. I was lost.

The only silver lining was how Jess and Tom had rallied around me. I knew how lucky I was to have them – I'd been pretty absent from both of their lives for months now and yet when things got real, there they were. Which was why I hadn't felt that I could say no when Tom had suggested the three of us go to Jalou for a drink. I'd been on lockdown for almost two weeks and I was very happy to keep it that way permanently, but Jess and Tom weren't having any of it. 'You need to start living like a normal person again,' Jess had said, hands on hips. 'Spend some time in the real world and get things back on track. So get changed. We're leaving in twenty minutes.' There was no point in arguing with her when she was like this so I'd done as I was told and now the three of us were sitting in one of the more secluded corners in Jalou.

'Everyone's staring at me.' I shifted uncomfortably in my chair, acutely aware of all the furtive glances and whispering going on around us.

'Let them,' Jess said dismissively. 'They've got nothing going on in their lives so they have to get their fun from somewhere.'

'Hey,' Tom called out, standing up. 'Why don't you take a picture? It'll last longer you nosey twats.'

'Sit down,' I hissed, tugging at his T-shirt. I was embarrassed by Tom's outburst but there was also a small part of me that was incredibly touched. I had no idea he had such a protective side.

My phone beeped. It was Karl.

You have to reply to me sometime. I am your father and we need to talk. You can't keep ignoring me.

Why couldn't he leave me alone? Seeing the expression on my face, Jess took my phone from me and she and Tom read the message.

'Tosser,' Jess said under her breath.

'Can I reply?' Tom didn't wait for me to respond. He started tapping away, his face set in stone. 'Here,' he said after he'd pressed send. 'Now block his number.'

You don't know what it means to be a decent human let alone a parent. I wish I'd never met you. Fuck off out my life. PS You're a helmet

I smiled. God I loved Tom and Jess. Hopefully those would be the last words I ever exchanged with Karl – Tom had summed up my feelings pretty succinctly. I felt a sudden pang as I thought of Brandon. It kept happening. I hated him for what he'd done to me, to us, and I knew I was better off without him but he hadn't even tried to get in touch. No explanation, no apology, nothing. One minute he was my entire world, and the next he was just gone. There had been reports that he'd checked into a rehab facility in Los Angeles and I hoped that was true. He had an addiction and he needed help. Maybe one day he'd re-emerge and try to make amends for what he'd done, but I knew the chances were slim to none. Underneath it all, he was a coward. I understood that now and the knowledge that I'd let someone so unworthy into my life made me feel utterly stupid.

'Hey, squad.'

I looked up, startled. I'd been so lost in thought that I hadn't noticed Jamie approach.

'Hey, man,' Tom said. 'I didn't realise you were back. How'd the shoot go?'

'Fine,' Jamie said, not taking his eyes off me. 'You OK?'

I shrugged. 'Not bad.'

'Tom,' Jess said, standing up. 'Let's go and get some more drinks.'

'What? I've still got half a pint here. *Ow!* What was that for?' He rubbed his side where Jess had just poked him hard in the ribs,

'She wants to leave me and J alone,' I said wearily. I didn't have the energy to play games, no matter how small.

'Why didn't you just say so?' Tom said, still rubbing his side. 'I'm not an idiot. All you had to do was ask.'

Jess rolled her eyes and pulled him towards the bar where the two of them settled onto stools so they could not-so-subtly keep glancing over at us. Jamie gave me a small smile. I owed him an apology. On top of everything I had to apologise for being dreadful to him as well.

'J, listen, I'm sorry about Halloween. You were right about Brandon and I should've listened to you.'

'Don't worry about that right now,' Jamie said kindly. 'I really just wanted to see how you're doing today.'

Oh, God. Why is he being so nice to me? Tears pricked at my eyes, as they kept doing at the moment. I leaked frequently these days, without warning and without real explanation. I was a human sprinkler system.

'Honestly? I'm a mess. I've been hiding from everyone, and Karl won't leave me alone. And I'll never forgive Brandon but I still can't stop thinking about him. I know it's ridiculous and it makes me a mug but he was everything to me for a while and now he's gone I feel so empty.' It felt so good to talk to Jamie.

'Um, Amber—' he started.

'I know, I know. I'm a knob for even saying it but it's the truth. I should've walked away after the first time we were around drugs. He didn't care about how I felt, I see that now, but it's true what they say – love is blind. He swept me off my feet, charmed me, and I fell for it. I never thought I had such bad judgement but after what Karl did, I'm starting to wonder if I can trust my instincts any more. At least I have you, Jess and Tom. It's at times like this you learn who your real friends are.'

Jamie stared at me. He looked . . . well, kind of angry.

'Are you being serious right now?'

'What do you mean?'

'You think I want to know about those two bellends?'

'Eh? You asked me how I was.'

Jamie shook his head in disbelief. 'You are unbelievable.'

'J, what—'

'What day is it?'

'Wednesday.' I had no idea where this was going.

'The date, Amber. What's the date?'

'December twelfth.'

There was a beat of silence as the words hung in the air. December twelfth. December twelfth. December twelfth. My blood turned to ice and my hands flew to my mouth.

'Oh, God,' I whispered.

'You forgot,' Jamie said flatly.

'Please, no. No, no, no. I can't have.'

Today was the anniversary of Dad's death. It was the one day of the year that Mam, Rubes and I had promised we'd spend together. It didn't matter what else was going on in our lives, we'd all sworn we'd never be apart on this day. Until now.

'Do you remember last year?' Jamie said, his voice hard. 'Diana didn't want to give you the day off and you were ready to quit rather than let your mum and sister down.'

I nodded, tears streaming down my face. In the end, Diana had relented, but I'd missed my train so Jamie had borrowed his mate's car and driven me all the way up to Newcastle. And then he'd turned round and driven straight back to London because he knew he couldn't stay. The day was just about me, Mam and Rubes – and Dad.

'You were prepared to give up your job without hesitation because nothing was more important than your family.' Jamie shook his head. 'Where the hell has *that* Amber gone?'

The pain in my chest was so strong I couldn't speak.

'You've become so disgustingly self-obsessed, Amber. I never thought I'd see it, and I've tried to give you the bene-fit of the doubt, but this? This too much. It's been Brandon this and Brandon that for months – you've forgotten about your work, you've been a shit friend to Jess and Tom and you've shut me down every time I've tried to be a friend to you.'

'Stop. Please stop.'

'No. I've kept my mouth shut for too long, made excuses for you too many times. To be so full of yourself that you forget what must be the hardest day of the year for your family? It's unforgivable.'

'And you remembered,' I choked out through my sobs.

'I remember how quiet you were during the drive up to Newcastle. I remember how sad you looked. I remember the conversation you had with your little sister, promising her you'd be there for her no matter what. I thought you were the strongest person I'd ever met. What's happened to you? Who the fuck are you?'

'Help me. I don't know what to do.'

'Uh-uh.' Jamie stood up. 'You're on your own from now

on. You need to figure out how to fix this yourself. But, Amber, make this right. You'll never forgive yourself if you don't. I'm done with you.'

I tried calling Mam and then Rubes. Then Rubes and then Mam again. Over and over I tried them both, but neither of them picked up. I left voicemails, sent WhatsApp messages, but my phone remained silent. They didn't want to talk to me. I looked at my watch. It was eleven p.m. The day was almost over and I'd missed it. I'd been too wrapped up in my own trivial dramas to remember the one thing I'd promised never to forget.

Jamie was right – it was unforgivable. I really didn't know if there was any coming back from this. But I had to try.

Chapter Twenty-nine

I was in Alessandro's office. He was looking through a new set of my sketches, scrutinising each and every one of them. I felt like he was scrutinising me as well. I was a mess. I'd been trying to get hold of Mam and Rubes since last night but neither of them was returning my calls. I'd never felt shut out from my own family before and it was all my own fault.

Alessandro shut my sketchbook with a sigh. 'This is not your best work, bella.'

'I know,' I said. *No more excuses. If I'm about to get fired, then it's no more than I deserve.*

'What is going on, Amber?' Alessandro said. 'This is more than just man troubles, no? Today you look . . . so sad. Tell me. Maybe I can help.'

'I don't think anyone can help me. I've completely messed everything up.'

'Nothing is ever as bad as we first think it is. Talking about it might help.'

Slowly, I told Alessandro what had happened the previous

evening. Every time I thought about missing the anniversary of Dad's death a fresh wave of tears hit me. I couldn't help it: the guilt and sadness was overwhelming – I hated myself for deserting them so completely.

'I just need to talk to Mam and Rubes,' I finished. 'I can't start making things better if they won't even speak to me.'

Alessandro blew his cheeks out. 'That is quite the mess. But perhaps you're being too hard on yourself.'

'I don't think so,' I said. 'I was so wrapped up in my own life I forgot about what's important. There's no excuse for it.'

'You are so young, bella. This is not the worst thing you will do in your life, trust me.'

'That's not helpful, Alessandro.'

Alessandro laughed good-naturedly. 'What I meant was that we all make mistakes. But you must learn from them and try not to make the same ones again. Yes, you have done something that has hurt people you care about, but if they love you as much as I think they do, they will forgive you. It will just take some time.'

'It's too big a problem. I don't know where to begin.'

'And that is your real problem. You want everything straight away. With you, it is all or nothing. In love, in life, in work. You should enjoy the small things as well as the big moments. It all matters. There's inspiration in all things. Don't forget that.'

I was confused. 'But how does that help me now?'

'You have lost your way,' Alessandro said simply. 'This is not a criticism of you. We all lose our way sometimes, it's, how do you say it – human nature? Yes, human nature. You have to fix yourself before you can fix anything else.'

'I do feel lost,' I admitted. 'I don't know if I'm coming or going right now.'

'Your light has gone out, bella, and it is affecting every part of you. These sketches,' Alessandro pointed at my sketch-book, 'are good, but they're not outstanding. And you have the potential to be outstanding. That's what I expect from you.'

'Is there nothing in there you can use?' I asked, deflated.

'I do not compromise on quality,' Alessandro said a little sternly, though not unkindly. 'These do not have your spark. Why don't you take some time away from here? Go home, talk to your family, start fixing things. We have a saying in Italy – *famiglia è il cuore pulsante della vita.*'

'Eh?' I asked. My knowledge of Italian stops at 'bruschetta' and he knows this. *Why does he always insist on speaking Italian to me? Howay, I barely speak English for Christ's sake.* 'It means: family is the heartbeat of life. Spend some time with yours and get your passion back. The break will do you good and it could help with your work.'

'Don't you need me here? We need to finish the collection.'

'And we will. You can work from Newcastle for the rest of the year. Email me your sketches and we'll speak on the phone. Your heart is not in London right now. Go home, find it, fix it and come back when you're yourself again.'

'What if that doesn't work? What if everything I come up with is dreadful?'

Alessandro looked thoughtful. 'You say your theme is romance. But what is romance to you?'

'I thought it was what I had with Brandon.' Images flashed through my mind – our first date, the surprise trip to Paris, the gifts, the chauffeur-driven car, the parties. For a while, it

285

had been so perfect. Or so I'd thought. Looking back now, it was all so laughingly superficial. *Why did I think fancy presents and glamorous balls would inspire me?* It had been so outlandishly fake – and my designs reflected this. I sighed. They weren't authentic because I hadn't experienced genuine romance. 'The truth is I have no idea what romance is.'

'Grand gestures can be romantic, but they can also be quite meaningless.'

'Go on,' I said.

'Booking out an entire restaurant might seem romantic at the time,' Alessandro said wryly, 'but what does it mean to you now?'

'It means Brandon was a flash bastard who thought money could buy him anyone and anything.'

Alessandro pointed to my feather necklace that I'd been clutching. 'This necklace. You wear it all the time. It means a lot to you, yes?'

'Yes, my dad gave it to me.'

'Was it expensive?'

I shrugged. 'I have no idea.'

'Does it matter to you?'

'How much it cost? No, of course not.'

'Then why is it valuable to you?'

'Because it reminds me of him. I feel like he's with me when I wear it. But that's not romance.'

'No, bella. That's love.'

I felt like I'd had the wind knocked out of me.

The small things.

We sat in silence while I struggled to regain my composure. A whole different worry had just started stirring in my overworked mind.

'Alessandro, what does it mean if someone waited up with me after New York Fashion Week so I wouldn't have to read my reviews on my own? Or if he drove me to Newcastle one time because I had no other way to get home? Or if he kept trying to help me after I'd been a bitch to him? What does all of that mean?'

Alessandro frowned. 'Brandon did all of those things for you?'

'No. It was ... er, a mate.' *Smooth, Amber, really smooth.*

'Oh, bella. These things, these are love too.'

Bag of dicks ... I was afraid he was going to say that.

Chapter Thirty

I heaved my suitcase onto the luggage rack and then went to find my seat. Thankfully, because it was mid-week, the train wasn't that busy. Good. I needed some peace and quiet to think.

I settled down, pulled a magazine that I knew I wouldn't read out of my bag and took a sip of my hazelnut latte. I'd sent Mam a message, letting her know I was on my way home and that I'd be there in a few hours. I'd got one back, just saying,

Fine. See you then.

It wasn't exactly warm, but at least she'd replied. Right now, I'd take what I could get. The train pulled out of King's Cross and I looked out of the window. It had started to snow in London and a thin layer was beginning to settle. I'd always loved the way rooftops looked with a bit of snow on them, but the magic of the scenery was lost on me today. The train picked up speed and as we got further from the city, watching the world whizz by became gently therapeutic and the thoughts bouncing around in my head settled down into a rhythm of their own.

There was no denying it: I'd behaved like a twat. Ever since my conversation with Alessandro, I'd realised how wrong I'd been about everything. I should've told Mam about Karl the second he turned up. I thought I was protecting her, but she was the one who'd been protecting me all these years from the harsh truth that he'd never wanted me. I always thought I knew best, that I had all the answers, but there was so much I didn't know. If I'd come clean she could've saved me from making the mistake of trusting him, and in turn I wouldn't have been so preoccupied with my ultimately insignificant drama to have forgotten Dad's anniversary. I couldn't describe the feeling I got every time I thought about how I'd let Mam and Rubes down. It was like nothing I'd ever felt before. *Will I ever be able to make it up to them? I'm not so sure I can this time.*

It wasn't just recently that I'd been distracted. It had started long before Karl had appeared – it had started as soon as I'd gone on that first date with Brandon. He had swept me off my feet and I could finally admit it to myself: all the grand gestures had turned my head and I'd been blind to the truth of the situation. I hadn't been in love with him, I'd been in love with the idea of who I thought he was, of who I hoped he'd be. I thought we were supporting each other but it had just been me following him around, doing what he wanted, going where he wanted. None of it had been about me. I cringed as I thought about how I'd let him take over my life and push everything and everyone to the side. I couldn't even blame him – it was my fault. Our relationship had been all-consuming and I'd let that happen too easily because, for the first time since Dad died, I'd felt like there was someone looking out for me and looking after me. I'd had to be strong for Mam and Ruby for so long that as soon as there was a hint of someone doing something special for me, I'd fallen for Brandon's act hook, line and sinker. But the sad thing was that I'd had a string of people looking out for me all along and I hadn't even realised it – Mam, Jess, Tom, Alessandro, Jamie.

Jamie.

I screwed my eyes shut, trying to keep the tears back. I hadn't heard from him since that night in Jalou and he hadn't responded to any of the WhatsApp messages, texts, calls or Twitter DMs I'd sent. Every time I thought about the possibility of having lost him . . . no, I couldn't go there. The idea of never seeing him again, never speaking to him again, sent a cold chill through me. I pulled my phone out of my bag and tapped out another message.

> Hey you. You were right – I have changed. But I'm trying to fix things. I'm on my way home and I'll be there until Jan, but I don't want to wait that long before I fix things with you too. Please reply. I'm sorry. I miss you. Ax

I'd had it all twisted. I thought Brandon was a true gent and Jamie was the one sleeping around. All I'd seen was Jamie's easy-going banter and his flirtatious behaviour. I had overlooked his kind nature, his focused mind and his fierce sense of loyalty. Right now all I wanted was to turn back time and do the last six months all over again. *What would have happened if I'd just ignored Brandon's phone call that night in New York? Would I have taken it to the next level with J? Something had been happening between us but I'd been too quick to dismiss it as nothing.*

First things first, I thought. *Start making things up to Mam and Ruby. That's my priority. Maybe try thinking with your mind and not your minge, eh Amber? After all, that's why you're in this mess in the first place, you dopey tart.*

I didn't know how I was going to do that, but an honest conversation would be a good start. And then I'd take it one day at a time. Family, friends, work – that was going to be my life from now on. It was time to go back to basics.

I'd been staring out of the window for the entire journey so far but I was startled out of my reverie by someone sitting down in the seat opposite me. I tried not to feel annoyed but I hated it when people invaded my personal space on the train. Damn it! I'm trying to be sad here! Have some respect. I wanted to be alone. I looked up and saw a slim lass with long dark hair arranging her bags. I did a double take. *Was that ...?* The girl caught me staring and smiled.

'You all right, pet?'

'Er, yeah,' I said, flustered. 'Um, are you Vicky Pattison?'

The girl's smile widened. 'That's me, babe.' She studied me for a moment and then her expression cleared, as though something had just dawned on her. 'Are you Amber Raey?'

My heart sank. 'You've seen the papers?' I asked.

'Aye, unfortunately so, lass, but I actually recognised you from House of Rossi. I loved your first collection – I bought up practically everything you designed. I'm gonna have to up my game at Honeyz if I'm gonna compete with you! You're smashing it.'

I blushed. *Vicky Pattison is a fan of my clothes!*

'Thanks. I'm working on my second range now. We're planning to launch in February.'

'I cannae wait to see it,' Vicky said enthusiastically. 'Us Geordie lasses need to stick together.'

'You on your way back to Newcastle now?' I asked.

Vicky nodded. 'Aye. I'm there 'til Christmas now. No more work until after the New Year. I haven't had a break this long for years. I actually get to spend proper time with my family and I'm buzzing like an old fridge. I love Christmas – I'm going to make everyone wear Christmas jumpers and Santa hats! Me dad will hate it, the miserable barstard! But he's not getting out of it.' She laughed. She seemed so excited. It was a stark contrast to how I was feeling about going home.

I burst into tears. I was mortified.

'Whoa, steady mate!' Vicky exclaimed. 'What's wrong, Amber? You OK?'

'You saw the papers,' I sniffled. I couldn't believe I'd met Vicky Pattison and all I was doing was crying in front of her. 'My whole life is a total mess.'

Vicky reached forward and took my hand. 'Come on now, lass. I've been there, we've all been there! I mean, we've all had our share of Brandons. I know how you feel – like the walls are closing in on you?'

I nodded.

'Listen, pet, it's a setback, but things will get better. I've had so many people sell stories about me, it doesn't even surprise me any more. But it's all bollocks, man. You can bounce back from this. You can't let those oxygen thieves bring you down. Pricks! The lot of them!'

I felt as though I was in an episode of *Judge Geordie*. This was surreal. 'How do you do it?' I asked. 'How do you get over it? Being betrayed, having people know your innermost secrets and mistakes? How do I move on?'

'My family,' Vicky replied instantly. 'Just remember what's important in life. It's too easy to lose your head in this game, to have your head turned by a pretty face or have your interest piqued by sycophantic bellends who massage your ego but secretly only care about how you can help them. So my advice to you? Keep your circle small and tight and look after those who were there when you had nothing. If someone wasn't part of the struggle, don't dare let them be part of your success.'

Vicky's words resonated deep within me, but I still felt overwhelmed. 'I've really screwed up,' I said, looking out of the window. 'I've done something unforgivable and I've hurt the people closest to me. I'm going home to try to make it up to them but I don't think it will be easy.'

'Nothing worth doing is easy,' Vicky said. 'But they're your family – they'll forgive you for whatever you've done because they love you.'

'I hope so.'

'They will,' Vicky insisted. 'Family is all any of us have at the end of the day. Listen, it's not important that you fell, it's how you pick yourself up that matters.'

'Sorry,' I said, feeling marginally stronger. 'I didn't mean to cry all over you.'

'No problem,' Vicky said. 'Better out than in, I say! Mate, I cry all the time. I cried at *Bake Off* the other day. Did you see it?'

I shook my head, still a bit dazed at the situation I'd found myself in.

'Aw, lass, it was awful, man. One lady made a fantastic victoria sponge but her macaroons were soggy so she got booted off. Heartbreaking. I cried for at least fifteen minutes.' Vicky smiled and for the first time in weeks, I laughed. 'Pleased I could cheer you up, kiddo.'

'Thanks.' And I genuinely meant it.

We spent the rest of the journey alternating between chatting easily and falling into periods of companionable silence. By the time the train pulled into Newcastle, I felt as though I'd made a new friend.

Vicky gathered her things and gave me a hug. 'Remember what I said, pet. Keep your chin up and have a great Christmas with your family. Hey, maybe I'll see you out and about on the diamond strip!'

Chapter Thirty-one

For the first time in my life I felt like an intruder in my family home. I closed the door behind me. I could hear the sound of the TV coming from the living room. Usually Mam would've rushed out to greet me at the door – but not this time. I took a deep breath and tried to remember everything Alessandro and Vicky had said to me. This was going to be painful and difficult, but I would make this right. I had to.

Mam and Rubes both looked up when I walked into the living room but neither made a move to hug me. I felt a pang when I noticed the Christmas tree in the corner. We usually decorated it together. The glittery multi-coloured baubles swung gently, the foil-wrapped chocolate Santas glinted invitingly and the fairy lights were twinkling. It looked lovely and it made me feel so incredibly sad.

'Hi,' I said, sitting down. 'How are you?' I hated how awkward this felt.

'How do you think we are?' Ruby said.

Mam placed her hand on Ruby's arm. 'Love,' she said. 'Don't.'

'Why not?' Ruby said. 'She can't just turn up and expect everything to be normal.'

Mam looked at me. 'She doesn't expect that. Do you, Amber?'

'No,' I said quietly. 'I've completely messed everything up, and I'm sorry.'

No one spoke for a few moments.

'That's it?' Mam said eventually. 'That's all you have to say?'

I had so much to say, I just didn't know where to start. But how could I explain that to them?

'I know there isn't an excuse in the world that would justify my behaviour recently,' I began, 'and anything I do say will sound like an excuse. But I know that saying I'm sorry isn't enough.'

'It's a start,' Mam said.

Ruby looked at her sharply. 'You're buying this?' she said incredulously.

'Rubes, please. Tell me what to do to make it up to you. I'll be sorry until the end of time for not being here for you. Please just talk to me.'

Ruby wouldn't look at me. My heart broke a little more. I reached down for the bag I'd brought in with me and held it out to her.

'What's that?' she asked, not taking it.

'Some clothes,' I said. 'From work. I know you wanted some when you and Mam came down to London. I thought—'

298

'That you could *buy her off*?' Mam interrupted, her voice shaking.

'What? No. I just wanted to do something nice, something that would let you know how sorry I am.'

'And a bag of clothes is the best you can come up with?' Mam said, her voice rising.

'I don't know what to do for the best. I'm trying, but it's not easy.'

'This isn't about making things easy for *you*,' Ruby spat. 'Why is *everything* always about you, about how you feel? You only want to give me those things to make yourself feel better. It's got nothing to do with me.'

This was all wrong. I'd meant it to be a peace offering but I was just making things worse.

'Don't you see?' Mam said sadly. 'Being materialistic is what's got you into this mess. The fame, the parties, the fancy clothes – I didn't raise you to put those things first.'

'I don't! None of that stuff matters to me.'

'Then why did you think Ruby would want some free clothes instead of you talking to us?' Mam went on. 'Amber, you've kept a lot from us, and however misguided you were about ... Karl, I understand that you were trying to protect us. But somewhere along the way you just stopped talking to us about anything important that was going on in your life. We had to read about it in the papers. Can you imagine how that made us feel? And forgetting about this week – it's just not like you.'

'It *is* like her!' Ruby said, her voice rising. 'She hasn't been here for months! Too busy shagging that knob of a boyfriend to think about us.'

'That's not true,' I said as the tears began to fall. 'I think about you all the time.'

'Oh yeah? When was the last time you rang home for more than a few minutes? You've been too busy going to flash parties to care about us any more.' Ruby was shouting now.

'That's enough,' Mam said firmly. 'This isn't getting us anywhere.'

'So what do we do now?' I asked quietly.

'Let's take a break. We all need to calm down.'

'I don't care what you do. I'm going to my room,' Ruby said and walked out, slamming the door behind her.

'OK,' I said. 'I'm gonna go for a walk.'

'Be back in time for dinner,' Mam said gently. 'We've still got a lot to talk about.'

I had no memory of leaving the house or of how I ended up there, but I suddenly found myself walking along the Tyne. Dad used to bring me out here when I was younger, whenever I had a fight with Mam or Ruby. It calmed me down, soothed my nerves. Of course I'd end up here now, when things were so difficult.

The crisp December wind blew around me and I pulled my scarf tighter and buried my hands deeper in my pockets. Alessandro's and Vicky's words kept running through my mind.

Family is the heartbeat of life.

It's not important that you fell, it's how you pick yourself up that matters.

Enjoy the small things.

The clothes were meant to be a gesture, a symbol of my regret and how keen I was to make things better. But as with most of what I did these days, I'd misjudged the situation. I saw myself holding out the bag towards Ruby and I wanted to slap myself.

You tit, Amber. You complete and utter knob. Of course that wasn't the answer.

This whole year had been a whirlwind of change and opportunity and excitement. I'd attacked everything that was thrown at me with gusto, thinking that was the way to live life. *When had I stopped talking to Mam about my life? When had I stopped taking an interest in Rubes? Enough with the material shite*, I thought.

I reminded myself of what I'd told myself on the train. It was time to go back to basics. Only now I knew the basics meant just being there with Mam and Rubes, and talking to them about everything, no matter how painful or humiliating it was.

I'd been so lost in thought I hadn't realised that I'd made it to the Christmas market until a very happy-looking Santa wished me a merry Christmas. All around me people were buzzing with the festive spirit – I could practically see it in the air. Their cheeks were rosy from the cold and from happiness, and probably from the mulled wine too, people were calling out to one another and kids were pulling their parents along to stall after stall. The smell of sweet hot chocolate and cinnamon filled the air.

Christmas had taken on a bittersweet quality since Dad had died because there would always be one person missing. He had loved Christmas too and he'd passed that enthusiasm on to me and Rubes. Each year – the only day of the year I could manage to get up early – Rubes would crawl into my bed in the early hours of Christmas morning and we'd whisper excitedly about the day ahead. I wondered whether she'd do the same this year. I hoped so.

We kept Christmas Day for ourselves but on Boxing Day all of our neighbours and friends would come over for our annual leftovers buffet. Then one year Dad had watched *Bridget Jones's Diary* and insisted on adding a turkey curry to the feast from then on. Dad might be gone but that tradition remained – I made the turkey curry now.

Christmas was never about the gifts in the Raey household. It was about us all being together, making new memories and remembering the old ones. It was about family and friends and being thankful for each and every one of them. It was about love.

Love was what had kept me, Mam and Rubes close since Dad died. We may have lost him but we couldn't lose each other. I'd been a fool to think what I felt for Brandon was love. It was nothing like it, I saw that now. I had to show Mam and Rubes that I loved them and that they were the most important people in my life. I had to prove that I was still me, Amber, that I was back and that I'd never let them down again. I had to remind them that the love in our family was strong enough to overcome anything.

And I think I had finally worked out how to do it.

Much later, I emerged from the loft with the things I needed. Dinner had been a strained affair but there hadn't been any more shouting, just a lot of inane small talk. I brushed the cobwebs off me. I looked inside the cardboard box I'd filled up. I was pleased with everything I'd managed to find, and I hoped Mam and Rubes would be too.

I shut myself up in my room and got to work. I lost myself in the sorting and the arranging – I wanted everything to look perfect. By the time I was finished it was three a.m. and

I was exhausted but pleased with what I'd begun. It was going to look beautiful. Hopefully it would be enough to show Mam and Rubes I was trying to change.

I needed to show Jess and Tom I was back as well. I picked up my phone and sent them a WhatsApp message.

Hey guys. Missing you two so much! What are your plans for NYE? Do you want to come to Newcastle and spend it with me? Say yes! Invite the usual gang. Everyone's welcome! Ax

I hoped that by 'the usual gang' they knew who I meant. Because there was one more person I really needed to apologise to.

Chapter Thirty-two

It was Christmas Eve. The butterflies in my stomach were driving me mad. I'd decided to give Mam and Rubes the present I'd been making for them tonight, and I was so nervous about it.

Things between us were still tense. We'd had a couple more conversations about what had happened and I'd opened up a bit more about Brandon and Karl. Mam had started crying when I'd told her how deep Brandon had been into the whole drugs scene and Rubes had stormed out of the room. But the more honest I was with them, the better things became. Slowly, tentatively, we were all starting to talk a bit more. We were a long way from happy and there was no overnight fix but I was hopeful we were on the right path now. And I hoped their present would help us all move on more quickly.

Something I hadn't been expecting was my renewed energy when it came to work. While pulling together Mam and Rubes's present, whatever block I'd had when it came to being inspired had disappeared and I'd been sketching every spare moment I had. It felt good to have my head back in the game. I spoke to Alessandro most days and I kept him updated on my progress.

'Things are so much clearer now,' I'd said to him yesterday. 'I have so many ideas again. I'm excited to show you what I've come up with.'

'I am excited too, bella,' Alessandro had said. 'You sound much happier. Your voice is lighter.'

'It's still difficult. Every conversation I have with Mam and Rubes feels like an effort. It's not coming naturally yet but we're getting there.'

'Good, good. And you will get there eventually. Now, bella, go and have a nice Christmas. We will catch up after Boxes Day.'

'Boxing Day,' I'd laughed. 'It's called Boxing Day, Alessandro.'

Tom, Jess, Sam and Freddie had confirmed that they were coming up for New Year's Eve. I'd FaceTimed Jess and Tom a couple of times and things seemed OK there. I couldn't wait to see them. I had bottled out of asking if Jamie would be coming up as well. I was sending him at least one message a day but I still hadn't heard anything back. Every time I thought about him my heart ached a little bit.

'Hey,' I said, walking into the living room. Mam gave me a small smile and Ruby gave a sort-of shrug in acknowledgement. *Tough crowd.* 'Can I talk to you for a sec?'

'Sure.' Mam turned the TV off and Ruby sighed. Loudly. *Really tough crowd.*

I sat down, resting the package on my lap. 'I have something

I want to give you.' I saw Mam and Rubes exchange a look. 'No, no. It's nothing like that. It's not like last time. This . . . well, I made it. For you. For us. It's for all of us really, but mainly it's for you.'

For God's sake, Amber. Pull it together! Stop acting like a fanny!

'You were right when you said that I haven't been around much lately. I stopped paying attention to you and I'm sorry. I'll never forgive myself for forgetting about Dad's anniversary. I made you both a promise and I broke it and I suppose to a certain extent that's unforgiveable.'

'Amber—'

'No, wait,' I said, holding my hand up. 'Let me get this out, otherwise I might never say it. I've been thinking about a lot of things recently. So much has happened this year and it changed me without me even realising it. And by the time I did realise, it was too late – the damage had already been done. I hurt people I cared about and you'll never know how sorry I am for that. I've been a terrible daughter, a shocking sister, but I'm trying to get back to a better place. Lots of people have offered me advice recently but it all boils down to one thing: remember what's really important. Family. I forgot that and I took you both for granted. I'll never do that again.'

I took a breath. 'I wanted to do something special for you, so I had this idea of making something that would remind you of the good times, of our roots. I was going to give it to you tomorrow but I thought it would be better to do it now.' I thrust the wrapped present at Mam. 'Here. Merry Christmas.'

Rubes and Mam sat side by side and opened the package together. They pulled out the book and paused when they saw the words on the front.

Our Story.

'Whose story?' Ruby asked.

'Ours,' I replied. 'The three of us and Dad. It's our story.'

They started flicking through the pages and every happy exclaim, surprised gasp and delighted shriek told me that I'd done the right thing. The hours I'd spent in the attic, hunting for as many family photos as possible had been worth it. I'd found other things too – birthday cards from Dad to Mam, my old school reports, some of Ruby's drawings from nursery. They had all gone in. I'd arranged everything chronologically. The book opened with photos of Mam bringing me home from hospital as a baby and pictures from my early birthdays. When they got the page containing Mam and Dad's wedding photos, Mam burst out laughing. I'd sketched in a couple of speech bubbles above their heads. Dad's said: 'I'm the luckiest man alive,' and Mam's said: 'He's one fit bastard.'

'He was that,' Mam said, looking down at the page tenderly.

Our story continued and every moment, the small ones and the big ones, was in there. Me and Rubes meeting for the first time. Our old school pictures. Mam and Dad's anniversary photos. Birthdays, Christmases, school plays, family holidays. I'd even found a photo of all of us visiting Rubes in hospital when she'd had appendicitis. I'd sketched around everything so that each page was vibrant and full of colour.

'This must've taken you ages,' Ruby said, mesmerised. 'Oh my God! Dad had a tache?! He looks weird!'

'He didn't keep it for long,' Mam said, laughing. 'You were only a baby and it scared you – you wouldn't go anywhere near him. Oh, pet, this is beautiful. It's perfect. I love it. I'm going to look at it every day.'

Ruby flicked through to the end. 'Hey, these pages are blank,' she said. 'What are they for?'

'The rest of our story,' I said. 'We're not finished yet.'

Ruby burst out laughing and threw a cushion at me. 'You soppy tool!'

The three of us spent hours poring over the pages, remembering days out we'd forgotten and laughing over the ridiculous fashions of days gone by. There were some tears too but that was fine. They were good tears.

We were going to be OK.

I was woken up at around five a.m. by Ruby climbing into my bed.

'Merry Christmas, Amber,' she said, snuggling into my side.

'Merry Christmas, kiddo,' I said sleepily. I paused. 'You're not going to yell at me for calling you kiddo?'

'Nah. It's Christmas. No fighting today.'

'Sounds good to me. Is Mam awake?'

'Don't think so. Should we let her sleep?'

Rubes and I looked at each other and said together, 'No!'

I doubted very much that Mam would appreciate the two of us jumping on her in the early hours of the morning but, ah well, just another memory to add to the pile.

'I'm stuffed,' I groaned. 'I'm never eating again.'

'Quality Street?' Mam held the tin out to me. 'There are some of those green triangles left.'

'Ah, if you insist. Go on then.'

The three of us were in the living room. We were all in Christmas jumpers and Mam had been wearing a Santa hat all day. I had on the paper hat from my cracker and Ruby was decked out in a pair of elf ears. We looked ridiculous. I loved it.

We had just finished watching *Love Actually* and were now getting ready to watch *Home Alone*. I love a Christmas movie, me. Mam waved the Prosecco at me.

'Top up?'

'Aye.' I held out my glass. There's always room for Prosecco.

I checked my phone. Still nothing from Jamie. I pulled up the message I'd sent him earlier. Two blue ticks. He'd read it.

Things are getting better at home. You were right to call me out. It's been painful but we'll be in a better place by the end of it. You've always been there for me & I've never said thank you. I'm trying to be a better person, I just wish you were here to help me. Wherever you are, I hope you're having the perfect Christmas. You deserve it more than most. Ax

'Still nothing from Jamie?' Ruby asked. In the spirit of this new total honesty thing I was trying, I'd told Mam and Rubes everything over Christmas dinner.

I shook my head. 'I wish he'd reply just once. The silence is killing me.'

'Give it time, love,' Mam said. 'You can't push these things.'

310

'I can't fix anything if he won't speak to me,' I said sadly.

Jamie still hadn't replied by the time I kissed Mam and Ruby goodnight. I was happy that things were better with my family but I went to bed without the one Christmas kiss I so desperately craved.

Chapter Thirty-three

Mam and I were putting the final touches to our Boxing Day buffet. I'd made the curry extra spicy and there was a huge mound of rice on the boil, ready for when people started arriving. The poppadums were already on the table. Mam loved a retro buffet so there were also plates full of sausage rolls, mushroom vol-au-vents, cheese and pineapple on cocktail sticks, salmon mousse and cucumber, mini quiches, party rings and breadsticks. I rearranged the sarnies I'd made for our neighbour Betty – she couldn't handle spicy food. We'd thrown in a few pizzas and packets of Monster Munch for good measure too. I surveyed the table. *Yep, we definitely have enough scran.*

I'd been sketching all morning. I still hadn't been able to stop. I'd been looking through *Our Story* and it had got me thinking about the timelessness of love. Then I'd started looking at all the different fashions and I'd wondered if there was a way to combine retro styles with the idea that love never goes out of fashion. Suddenly, after months of feeling creatively useless, idea after idea had been popping into my head and my pencil had literally flown across the page.

I'd been trying to keep myself busy all day. I needed to take my mind off the fact that Jamie was still ignoring me. How could I have been so blind? I didn't know if he still felt the same way about me, but I did know that I couldn't lose him completely. He was one of the kindest, funniest – not to mention fittest – people I knew and I needed him in my life, even if it was as just a mate. It was no use going over everything in my head, though – I needed to say it to his face. I needed him to talk to me. Still, with the way things were, I wasn't holding out much hope that he'd be here for New Year's Eve.

On the other hand, I'd hardly thought about Brandon or Karl in days. They barely registered any more. It was weird how things changed.

The doorbell rang and a few seconds later I heard Rubes shout, 'Mam! Betty's here!'

Oi oi! Betty has arrived! Time to get this party started.

The house was heaving with people and I knew Mam wouldn't have it any other way. Everyone was tucking in to the food, the drinks were flowing and laughter filled the air. Half the street had arrived in their slippers and Betty was wearing what she called her housecoat. At one point, she'd taken me to one side, told me that she'd had her head turned by a cad once and given me a pound coin to cheer me up. *God bless, Betty,* I thought. *They don't make them like her any more. And I was thrilled with the pound as well.*

I was in the kitchen, looking for some ice, when I felt someone come up and put their arms around me.

'Hey, Mam,' I said. 'You all right?'

'I am, pet. Now that I've got you back, I'm doing just fine.'

I turned round to look at her. Her eyes were a little glassy and she had a lazy smile on her face. She was well on her way to getting well and truly smashed. She'd never looked more beautiful to me.

'I am back,' I said to her. 'A little wiser, a little bruised, but me.'

'Bruises fade. The wisdom doesn't.' Mam blinked. 'When did I turn into the bleedin' Dalai Lama? C'mon, pet, let's go find Rubes and get someone to take a picture of us. Those blank pages won't fill themselves.'

I stood back and took in the scene. Most of the food had gone but there appeared to be an endless supply of booze. Mam was dancing with Uncle Jimmy to some Rihanna that Ruby had put on, much to Betty's initial disgust. She'd demanded we put on some Frank Sinatra first, and had stamped along with her tiny slippered feet. But now those slippered feet were tapping in time to 'our rubbish pop', as she'd called it, without complaint. Mam's friend Lizzie was cuddling her bottle of Blue Nun while a couple of the lads from down the street were trying to get her to dance with them. She wasn't having any of it. Rubes and her friends were in a tight-knit circle, gossiping and laughing, so carefree. I looked at her fondly. She was growing up so fast and I didn't want to miss any of it.

I had a connection to every person in the house. Some of them I'd known since I was a child, some of them were newer friends, but they were all part of my history, part of *our* history. I loved that we'd kept this Boxing Day tradition going. We didn't even bother officially inviting people any more. They just turned up. Dad might be gone, but the memory of his love remained. I looked around the room with thoughts of Dad running through my mind, and I felt a sudden burst of inspiration. This was happening a lot lately. Alessandro had been right – I needed to fix myself and my family before I got my spark back. *That man*, I thought, *is a genius in many more ways than he knows.*

Hoping that everyone was too sozzled to notice, I slipped away to my bedroom. I grabbed my sketchbook, settled onto the bed and lost myself in my work. I pictured the faces of the people I loved and each one spurred me on – Mam, Dad, Rubes, Jess, Tom. Even Alessandro and Freddie popped up. And Jamie. Of course, Jamie.

I knew it was late and he'd told me we'd catch up after the Christmas break, but I sent Alessandro a message anyway:

Merry Christmas, boss! Thanks for sending me home. It was exactly what I needed. You're a very wise man. #amsketching. Ax

To my surprise, my phone beeped almost immediately.

Buon Natale, bella Amber. I am overly happy jumping the moon. I can't wait to see the new designs. Send me pictures when you're ready.

I continued to sketch. All the emotion poured out of me into my designs. They were full of heart. This collection was no longer about romance. It was about love. Because after all, romance fades, but love lasts forever.

Chapter Thirty-four

I was hopping from one leg to the other, trying to keep warm.
It was cold even inside the station. I was waiting for Jess, Tom
and the others – their train was due any minute now. I
couldn't wait to see everyone. I'd managed to have a brilliant
Christmas and now I was ready for New Year's Eve. I wanted
to start the new year right, and that meant making sure I was
with the right people. Squad goals achieved.

The previous day I'd sent pictures of my designs over to
Alessandro. He'd called back straight away – he'd loved them.
'Whatever has inspired you this time, bella, keep hold of it.
This is beautiful work.' I'd been buzzing like Brandon after a
trip to the men's room when I'd hung up. That's right, I was
making Brandon jokes now. That's how far I'd come. Fucking
helmet. And now I was going to have a night to remember
with my best mates. Things were getting back on track.

I saw Tom struggling through the barriers first. He was
hard to miss.

'What are you wearing?' I asked. He tried to give me a hug
but he couldn't move his arms much.

'It's a ski jacket. It's cold up north.'

'That's a *ski* jacket?' I didn't believe it. He looked like the Michelin man. 'Did you wear that on the train?'

'Yes, he did,' Jess said crossly. 'He refused to take it off. He almost knocked me out every time he turned around.'

'Oh, Jess.' I gave my friend a bear hug. 'I've missed you.'

'I missed you too, babes,' she said, returning my hug.

'Me next!' Freddie said, jumping around behind us.

I laughed and hugged him hello, then did the same with Sam. I looked around. There was no one else with them.

'Right,' I said, trying to hide my disappointment. 'Let's go back to mine. There's drinking to be done!'

'Mam!' I called when we arrived home. 'We're back!'

Mam came running down the stairs. She looked stunning. She was wearing a tight black Karen Millen dress that was the perfect fit for her, with some chunky vintage jewellery. She and Lizzie were going out for New Year and they clearly had plans to start the party early.

'Are you heading out now?'

'Aye,' Mam said. 'You just caught me. My cab will be here in a minute. Jess, Tom – hello! And you must be Sam and Freddie. Welcome. Is this your first time in Newcastle?'

We all stood in the porch and chatted for a few minutes while she waited for her taxi. I noticed Tom staring at her, his mouth slightly open. I tried to elbow him in the ribs but he didn't feel it. Nothing could penetrate all that padding.

'Tom,' I hissed. 'Stop staring at me mam!'

'I can't help it,' he whispered back. 'I'd forgotten she's so fit! She's such a MILF, mate.'

I was saved any further displays of embarrassment, and

Tom was saved from a punch in the throat, by the arrival of Mam's taxi. There were a flurry of hugs and 'Happy New Year's. Mam hugged me tightly before she left.

'He might still come,' she said quietly so the others wouldn't hear.

'I don't think so. But it's OK.' I plastered a smile across my face. 'I'm still going to have a wicked night with this lot.'

'That's my girl.' Mam gave me a kiss on the cheek. 'Happy New Year, honey.' She turned back around and called out to my friends: 'Have a good night. Remember, if you can't be good be careful!'

I closed the door behind her, a smile on my face. 'So,' I said. 'Wine?'

We were all lounging around in the living room. Jess, Freddie and I were working our way through a second bottle of Sauvignon blanc and Sam and Tom were lining up bottles of Beck's. I looked at my watch. We'd have to start getting ready soon.

'Where's Ruby?' Tom asked.

'She's spending New Year round a mate's,' I said. 'She'll be back tomorrow.'

'You look good, babes,' Jess said to me. 'Happy, more relaxed. It's nice to see the Amber we know is back.'

'I feel happy,' I said. 'It all got a bit messed up for a while.'

'Well, we missed you.' Tom planted a sloppy kiss on my cheek. 'Glad to have you back, mate.'

I screwed up my face and wiped Tom's slobber off my cheek. 'Er, thanks. I think.' My face turned serious and I looked at Tom and Jess. 'I never apologised to you guys properly. For getting so wrapped up in my own stuff that I disappeared for a while. And you were both so good to me after the whole Karl thing. I don't deserve mates like you.'

'No, you don't,' Jess said, but then she smiled and I knew she was kidding. 'But we're not going anywhere, so it looks like we're stuck with each other.'

'I know I neglected you,' I went on, 'and you must have been pissed off with me never being around and then just flying through for about half a second when I did show up. You have every right to yell at me.'

'Nah,' Tom said. 'That's not my style.'

'Just don't do it again,' Jess said. 'OK?'

'OK.'

'No more bellends!' Tom declared. 'That should be our New Year's resolution. Say no to bellends!'

'Love it,' I said.

'I'll drink to that,' Jess added.

Sam nudged Freddie. 'Are these three always like this?'

'Yep,' Freddie said. 'Welcome to the family.'

'So,' I began. I'd been dying to ask this question since we'd left the train station, and after a few cheeky glasses of wine I'd finally plucked up the courage. 'Did you mention coming up here to anyone else?' I was going for nonchalant, but Jess saw straight through me.

'I don't think Jamie's coming,' she said gently.

'J?' Tom said. 'Amber, mate, he's in Milan on some job. Didn't he tell you? I told him we were heading up here but it didn't sound like he fancied it, and I don't know when he's back anyway ...' Tom trailed off, realising he'd said too much.

'Oh, OK,' I said brightly. 'No worries. I just wanted to know if I needed to sort any more bedding.'

Jess raised her eyebrow at me. 'Bedding? That's the excuse you're going with?'

'Yes, yes it is and I am sticking firmly with it.' My face fell; I couldn't lie to this lot. 'I just want to see him,' I admitted quietly. 'He's not responding to any of my messages.'

'You fucked up,' Tom said, subtle as ever. Jess elbowed him in the ribs. 'Would you two stop poking me in the ribs all the time? I bruise like a peach!'

'I think my lady was trying to tell you to be a bit more sensitive,' Sam said. He smiled at Jess. It looked like she had decided that Sammy-boy was a keeper.

'Sorry, Amber,' Tom said, looking sheepish. 'Just give it some time, yeah? J can be a stubborn twat when he wants to. He'll come round.'

'Let's change the subject,' I said. I didn't want to talk about this any more. I looked at my watch. 'Actually, we should start getting ready. The Toon awaits and I can't wait to introduce you virgins to it! Brace yourselves, mind.'

I'd decided to take everyone to the Pitcher & Piano on the quayside. The place was packed, the atmosphere electric, and everyone was buzzing. This was the place to be. New Year's Eve was like no other night of the year – everyone was on top form, looking their best and hoping for the night of their lives. Christmas is about family, but New Year is about having fun. It's about getting drunk, kissing someone at midnight and making questionable decisions – and not necessarily in that order.

There had been a few stares and some glances in my direction but it was easy to ignore them when I was with my friends. Eventually they'd get bored and move on to talking about something else. Or someone else. I didn't really care.

'Here you go,' Freddie said, handing me my second mojito of the night.

'Everyone got a drink?' I said. 'All right. Before we get so smashed and forget our own names, let's make a toast.'

'Go on then, girl,' Sam said, putting his arm around Jess and pulling her into his side. 'What do you want to say?'

I thought for a moment. I didn't want to sound like a complete twat but I did want to let them know that I'd learnt some valuable lessons recently. 'Here's to friends becoming family,' I said. 'Here's to cheering each other on and making every second count. Let's smash it next year!'

Maybe it was the booze, maybe it was the atmosphere, maybe it was these people, but something was turning me into a total fanny. And I liked it.

I felt my phone vibrate in my bag. I pulled it out, hoping it was Jamie. It wasn't – it was Rubes.

Happy Nu Yr, sis! Love you more than I love Monster Munch! Rx

I tapped out a reply and hit send.

Happy New Year, little one. You and Mam are my priorities from now on. I love you more than I love mojitos! Ax

I opened up the message I'd sent to Jamie when we were on our way to the Pitcher & Piano. He'd read it but hadn't replied.

J, you have every right to be mad at me. I know now that things might never be the same between us again but I want you to know that if it hadn't been for you I might've carried on behaving like a twat. You set me straight & that's why I've been able to sort things out with Mam & Rubes. I want you in my life but maybe you don't feel the same about me any more? Give me another chance. I'm sending you a kiss for midnight x your Geordio Armani xxx

The five of us stood huddled together looking out at the Tyne Bridge and the Millennium Bridge. I may be biased, but it really was a beautiful view. It was ten to midnight and we'd managed to nab a decent spot for the countdown.

'Right,' Freddie said. 'Who's kissing who at midnight?'

'I'm all set, thanks mate,' Sam said.

'Me too,' Jess said.

'So the three of us should take turns, then?' Freddie said to me and Tom. Tom looked alarmed. My laugh died on my lips when I saw Freddie's face – he was deadly serious.

'Er, I don't think so,' I said, much to Tom's relief. 'A group hug will do.'

'But I have to kiss *someone* at midnight!' Freddie whined. 'It's tradition.'

'You've got ten minutes,' I said. 'Think you can put a shift in with someone in time?'

'Challenge accepted,' Freddie said, and he immediately disappeared into the crowd.

'We won't see him for the rest of the night now, I bet,' Tom declared.

'A hug for two?' I said to him.

'Hmmm, I think you might have other plans,' Tom said, pointing at something over my shoulder.

323

I turned round and my stomach dropped.

'Jamie.'

'Hey, Geordio.'

Somewhere in the back of my mind I was aware of Jess, Tom and Sam behind me but I only had eyes for Jamie. He was bundled up in a thick grey wool coat and it took all my willpower not to launch myself at him right there.

'What are you doing here?' I asked.

Jamie raised an eyebrow. 'I thought I'd been invited.'

'Aye, that's not what I meant. Tom said you were in Milan, working.'

'I was in Milan, and now I'm here.'

'How did you know where we were?'

'A floppy-haired bird told me.'

I turned to see Tom grinning from ear to ear. 'You're welcome, you Northern monkey!' he shouted.

I looked back at Jamie. He was so lovely. Why had it taken me so long to see it? I had so much to say but I didn't know where to start.

'Why did you come?' I asked eventually. 'You haven't responded to any of my messages. I thought you hated me.'

'I could never hate you,' Jamie said, taking a step towards me so he could tuck a strand of hair behind my ear. His fingertips grazed the side of my face and I felt a shiver run down my spine. 'I needed some time to think. The last few months haven't been easy, watching you with that dickhead. And then that night in Jalou . . . It was all too much. I needed space.'

'I'm sorry,' I said. 'You've always been good to me, and I didn't see it until it was too late.'

'It's not too late.' Jamie took a step towards me.

'It's not?' I took a step towards him our bodies were almost touching. A memory crossed my mind. 'But what about Portia?'

'Portia? We're mates, never been anything more than that. Amber, there's no one who can compete with how I feel about you. The question is, do you feel the same about me?'

'Yes,' I said immediately. *Nice work on playing it cool, Amber.*

'Then everything else can wait.'

And then he was kissing me. Softly at first, and then harder. I heard him sigh and I wrapped my arms tightly around him. When we broke apart, we were both breathing heavily.

'That was a bit premature, wasn't it?' I said, grinning like an idiot. 'It's not midnight yet.'

'No, Geordio, it was well late. Do you know how long I've been waiting to do that?'

'I have an idea.'

The countdown started up and everyone around us started shouting.

'Ten! Nine! Eight! Seven—'

Jamie didn't wait until the countdown had finished before kissing me again. The clock struck midnight and I could hear fireworks going off not just outside but in my pants as well! *Too much info there Amber, you sick puppy.* People were cheering all around me, but I didn't pull away. I was exactly where I needed to be.

Epilogue

I wasn't late, but I was definitely pushing it. *Old habits die hard*, I thought. I jumped out of the cab, paid the driver and quickly walked through Somerset House. The February wind was biting and my face felt numb from the cold. Still, I wasn't complaining – February meant London Fashion Week.

I was just about to head to the designers' waiting area when I heard a commotion behind me. I could make out a familiar voice above the din and a shiver ran down my spine.

'Can't you do anything right? You stupid little girl!'

I should've just kept on walking but something compelled me to turn around. As I expected, there, right behind me, was Diana. I smiled at her. She didn't smile back. I know she saw me – her steely grey eyes were looking right at me but no response. *Some things never change*, I thought. I caught the eye of the young lass who was the latest victim of Diana's wrath and threw her a sympathetic look. She looked terrified. I remembered feeling like that on a daily basis and I didn't miss it one bit. My gaze returned to my old boss. She was still staring at me, but when I looked back at her she suddenly turned on her heel and stalked through the door without so much as a backward glance. I shook my head sadly and continued on my way.

Freddie was waiting for me in the backstage area, and when I found him I threw my arms around him in a hug – I couldn't help it.

'What was that for?' he asked, surprised.

'You know how much I appreciate you, right?' I said, still clutching him close to me. 'We all do. House of Rossi would fall apart without you.'

'Yeah, yeah.' Freddie squirmed. 'Let go of me, crazy woman. I can't breathe! Plus I haven't been this close to a pair of tits since I was breastfed, and I'm not enjoying it!'

I let go, laughed and tried to pull myself together while Freddie updated me on the progress of the morning so far. I was so emotional these days. I felt so lucky; I was always telling people how much they meant to me.

'How are you feeling?' Freddie asked, cutting into my thoughts.

'Nervous,' I admitted. 'Excited but nervous.'

'What are you nervous for? You should be used to this by now!'

'It's only my second show,' I pointed out. 'I'm a long way off being used to this.' There are had already been some speculation about in the trade press. Expectations were high. So, yeah, excited but nervous just about covered it. 'Come on,' I said. 'We've got a lot of work to do.'

It was chaos. Hair stylists and make-up artists were rushing from one model to the next, design teams were pinning, tucking, accessorising and making last-minute alterations to their creations, hard-done-by assistants were doing their best to keep their bosses calm. Everyone had their own fashion-related drama to deal with and the buzz in the air was electric. *I live for this*, I thought happily.

Alessandro and I were double-checking the running order of the models.

'It is all fine,' Alessandro said to me. 'We've been over these things a million times.'

'Let's make it a million and one,' I responded.

Alessandro smiled and indulged my OCD behaviour. I did love that man. *Calm down, Amber, you over-emotional sap.*

'How's my Geordio Armani doing?' a voice said behind me.

I turned and let Jamie wrap his arms around me. Alessandro slipped away, muttering something about hair-pieces and shoes. I wasn't really listening.

'Everything going OK?' Jamie asked, smiling down at me.

'Weyaye,' I said. 'We're just checking through everything, but it all seems to be going to plan.'

Jamie gave me a quick kiss. 'You've worked hard for this. You're going to smash it.'

Jamie and I had only been together a couple of months, but though it was still early days it felt good to be with him. The last two weeks had been tough because we'd both been working so much. I had the show to get ready for and J was still the face of House of Rossi's menswear range so he'd been flat out too. But when I'd sat in the audience and watched him walk that catwalk a couple of days ago I knew it was worth it. I'd been so proud of him. And I'll admit it – I felt a tiny bit smug that he was mine.

We'd slotted into each other's lives seamlessly. It helped that we already had a lot of the same friends, but I'd worried it would feel weird being together with them. It hadn't been, though – nothing with Jamie felt weird. He'd met Mam and Rubes on New Year's Day and that hadn't been weird. Meeting his parents hadn't been weird. As for the sex ... Nothing weird about that either. Definitely not.

'I'll let you crack on,' he said. 'I know you need to focus. I just wanted to say good luck.'

'You'll be out there?'

'Of course I will! We're all out there. Tom thinks all his Christmases have come at once, with the amount of models running round.'

'You'd think he'd be used to models by now, working at Jalou,' I said.

'He said something about seeing them in their national habitat? I swear to God he thinks he's the David Attenborough of models.' Jamie pulled me in for a slow kiss. 'Own this, Geordio,' he whispered.

I watched him walk away. *That boy. The things I could do to him*, I thought. *Focus, Amber! Now is not the time to get in touch with your inner creep!*

'Bella,' Alessandro said, appearing at my side. 'It is time.'

The models began lining up and I stood at the side so I could give them a once-over before they stepped out onto the catwalk. I could see some of the audience from where I was, so I craned my neck. There they were. Mam, Rubes, Jamie, Jess and Tom sat a few rows back and they were all laughing at something Tom was saying. The audience was full of A-listers, fashion editors and press but I only had eyes for those five people. Mam turned her head slightly and we locked eyes. She smiled and nodded her head discreetly at me. I grinned back. There was one piece in my collection that she had inspired. I hadn't told her about it because I wanted it to be a surprise. I hoped she loved it as much as I did.

The show began and it whizzed by in a blur. It felt like only a few minutes had passed by the time Portia took her place. She was the final model and was wearing the dress I'd designed for Mam. It was based on her wedding dress. Mam's had been made from beautiful ivory lace, perfectly fitted to her, and I'd taken the cut and the same lace pattern and added a modern twist with a shorter hem and more open neckline. There was a burst of applause when Portia began her walk, but there was only one person's reaction that mattered. I peered out. Mam's mouth had dropped open and she was staring at Portia, tears in her eyes. Then she looked at me and mouthed 'I love you.'

No. I love you.

And suddenly I was taking my walk down the runway with Alessandro. Images of the last year flashed through my mind. So much had happened and I couldn't believe how far I'd come – and not just in my career. I'd made some terrible mistakes and trusted the wrong people. I'd been hurt and betrayed, and in turn I'd hurt and betrayed people that mattered to me. I'd met some complete wankers and I'd acted like a complete wanker. And yet, here we all were. Still together, still standing strong. I was going to make more mistakes, but a wise woman once told me that it doesn't matter if you fall, what matters is how you get back up.

Alessandro and I posed for photos and I clutched my feather necklace. None of us knew what was around the corner, but right now I felt like I could take on anything the world decided to throw at me

Bring it on. I'm ready for you, pet.

Acknowledgements

As always I would like to thank my amazing team at Little, Brown who continue to work hard on my projects and believe in me. The more time I spend in their offices and in their company, the more I love them and feel part of their family! So, with that in mind, huge thanks go out to Rhiannon Smith for all her editorial help, my marketer Sarah Shea, my publicist Jo Wickham, Hannah Wood for the beautiful cover, and everyone in the sales team, especially Sara Talbot, Anna Curvis, Jen Wilson and Ben Goddard. A very special thanks to the rest of my Little, Brown family too – Hannah Boursnell, David Shelley, Charlie King, Kiri Gillespie, Dom Wakeford and Linda Silverman. And finally, last but by no means least, thank you to my amazing editor and friend Manpreet (AKA Mannaz), who works tirelessly with me, has the patience of a saint and not only shares my love of biscuits, but also let me swear in the book!

Thank you to Faith Bleasdale for helping me shape my story.

To my amazing agents, Gemma and Nadia, for being supportive and understanding through the entire process – I love you ladies.

To my incredible family and friends who proofread my work, buy my books, turn up to signings and generally believe in me when no one else would! Mam, Dad and Laura – I love you so much, I don't know what I'd do without you.

And finally, to everyone who read *Nothing but the Truth*, *All that Glitters*, and now *A Christmas Kiss* ... Thank you! Books are something that I am so incredibly passionate about, and knowing that you enjoy my work and are allowing me to continue means more than you will ever know. I love you all.

Turn the page
for an extract from
Vicky Pattison's first novel,
All that Glitters

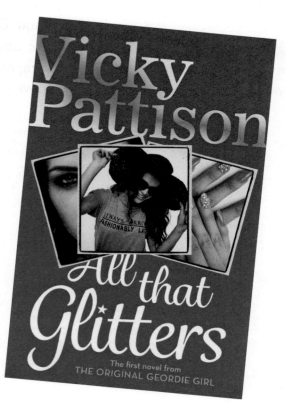

Bold, thrilling and romantic, *All that Glitters* is a
rollercoaster ride full of glitz, warmth and drama.
It's a must-read for fans everywhere!

Prologue

Issy Jones felt fat, warm tears sliding down her cheeks. She grasped her dad's hand tightly; it felt cold and unfamiliar. She barely recognised the man lying in front of her on the hospital bed, multiple tubes and wires attached to him. He had the same familiar dark hair and even features she knew so well, but his face was pale and so, so still. She squeezed his hand tighter as the machines continued to bleep around them.

'I promise I will do anything, absolutely anything if you get better, Dad,' Issy whispered, unsure if he could hear her. 'And I'll never leave you again. Just be all right. Please, Dad. *Please.*'

Still holding her dad's hand, she slumped down in the hard, uncomfortable hospital chair next to him and rested her head on his arm, remembering how safe she used to feel when he hugged her as a child. She didn't want to let go, afraid if she did she would lose him forever, and she wouldn't be able to bear that. Even the thought of it brought tears to her eyes and Issy breathed deeply, trying not to despair.

It had all happened so suddenly. Only the day before she'd

been working on an assignment at her hairdressing college in London, when she got a call from her brother, Zach, shakily telling her that their dad had suffered a heart attack. She'd dropped everything, rushed to the station and caught the first train she could home. A tear-filled three hours later, Zach had met her at Manchester station and had warned her that their dad was in a bad way. But nothing could have prepared her for seeing him look so frail.

The man in the hospital bed, wired up to machines, wasn't the gentle giant who had cared for her growing up. Issy's dad was a tall, handsome, muscular man, the years working in his garage had seen to that, but the figure in front of her seemed smaller and older than the man she knew.

The change in him had been so shocking her legs had almost given way when she'd first seen him. Zach had grabbed her to stop her from falling, and then held her while she cried. Her mum, Debs, who always had something to say, was silent as they stood together watching his chest rise and fall.

The three of them stayed by his bedside all night. At some point Zach had dropped off to sleep, and while he softly snored Issy and her mum had talked for hours, trying to keep each other's spirits up. But it hadn't worked. The fear was visible on their faces and in their trembling voices. Neither of them had wanted to think about what life would be like without the man who made them feel safe.

Issy took another deep breath, reminding herself to stay positive.

'Issy?' a husky voice said. She lifted her head off her dad's arm and tried to blink the tears away.

'Dad?' She wondered if she had imagined it. She felt a rush of hope as she saw his eyes flicker towards her.

'Isabelle, are you crying?' His voice was croaky and full of concern.

'Of course not,' Issy replied, brushing her cheeks. 'What's with the Isabelle? You only call me Isabelle when I've done something wrong.'

'I don't want you crying, kiddo. Help me out and find someone who can tell me what's really going on here, will you . . . ?'

'I'll call someone and get some help,' she said, getting up and reluctantly letting go of his hand.

She walked out into the corridor and took several long, deep breaths. A few hours after he'd been admitted the doctors had declared her dad 'stable', but she hadn't believed them. Not until now. This was what she'd been praying for, yet she still couldn't quite believe it.

After steadying herself, Issy grabbed the first nurse she saw, a young woman about her own age who looked perky enough to be early in her shift, so when Issy explained that her dad was awake she followed right after. She was the only member of the family left at the hospital and felt like a child, hopelessly out of her depth. Her brother had gone to check on the garage their dad owned and ran, while her mum had gone home for some rest. She wished they were both here.

When Issy followed the nurse back into the room, her dad had barely moved but his eyes were wide open and there was a sense of awareness about him. Relief flooded through her. He really was going to be all right.

'You gave us quite a fright, Mr Jones,' the nurse said sternly but with a smile.

'Yes you bloody well did,' Issy added, flashing him a beaming smile.

'Hey, love, sorry about the fright, but please, call me Kev.' He winked at the nurse.

'Really, Dad? One minute you're at death's door the next you're putting a shift in with a nurse!' Issy shook her head but she was still grinning.

Before he could reply the door to the ward burst open and her mum ran into the room clutching her yapping little dog, Princess Tiger-Lily, followed closely by Zach. She immediately launched herself on her husband, showering him with kisses.

'Debs!' Kev spluttered.

'You can't have dogs in here,' said the nurse sounding shocked and angry. 'We don't allow animals in the hospital and your husband is still *very* ill.'

'You shouldn't have brought her in here, love,' Kev said quietly. It was an effort to lift his hand but he gently stroked the side of Debs's face.

'I did try to stop her,' Zach said, turning his attention to the flustered nurse. He mouthed a silent 'sorry' at her and she visibly melted. Issy rolled her eyes. Her brother could charm his way into a nun's pants.

'Oh for God's sake, he's alive, that's all that matters. And surely you know how important pets are for patient rehabilitation?' Debs said, wagging a finger at the nurse.

'Just be careful. There are a lot of wires,' she simpered, eyes still fixed upon Zach. 'I'll go and see where the doctor's got to.'

'You do that, love,' Debs replied with a smile before carefully placing Princess at the foot of the bed and launching herself onto Kev again.

'Mum, you'll give him another heart attack carrying on like that,' Zach half-joked.

The nurse backed out of the room, her gaze firmly fixed on Zach, who had been pretending not to notice.

Issy stood in the small, grey hospital room surveying her family. She couldn't believe all their happiness had nearly been taken away from them. A rush of pure love filled her as she looked around at them all; her dad, her mum, Zach, even Princess Tiger-Lily, right now she'd even forgive all those times her barking interrupted a much-needed Saturday morning hangover lie-in.

It wasn't normal, it was quite far from normal, but they were hers and she loved everything about them. She meant what she had said before her dad had woken up; she would never leave them again.

Chapter One

THREE YEARS LATER

'So, what are we doing today, Vi?' Issy asked, wielding a pair of scissors and standing behind Violet, one of her regulars. They were in A Cut Above, her mum's hairdressing salon in Salford, on the outskirts of Manchester. It was the most popular salon in the area but that was because most of the clients belonged to the blue rinse brigade. Although there were a few younger customers, it wasn't exactly what you'd call edgy, and Issy longed to get her creative hands on people who wanted more than a trim and tint. Issy had asked what Vi wanted, already knowing the answer. She'd known Vi and many of her mum's other clients since she was a little girl.

'I just want a little bit off, duck. Not too short, mind. I don't want to look like a poodle,' Vi replied. Issy nodded. With her tightly permed white hair, no matter what she did Vi *always* ended up looking like a poodle.

'Of course not, Vi, God forbid,' Issy said, smiling warmly at Violet in the mirror.

Issy got to work on Vi's hair when suddenly a wave of nostalgia hit and she was catapulted back to her days at The Hair Academy. It felt like a lifetime ago that she'd walked away from her course.

The Hair Academy was the most illustrious hairdressing college in the UK, and Issy had worked her arse off to get a place on one of their courses. They only took a handful of students each year so competition was fierce, but back then Issy was full of confidence – and had the talent to back it up. Prior to her dad's heart attack, she'd been so driven and ambitious. Whether she ended up styling hair for magazine shoots or working backstage at fashion shows – one way or another she had been determined to make a name for herself.

It was a far cry from where she was now.

Issy looked around the salon. She'd practically grown up here – hairdressing was in her blood. Her mum had started teaching her how to style hair when she was barely a teenager. She'd practised on dummy heads, swept up hair, made notes – whatever it took to learn the trade. As a young girl, it had amazed Issy that people could come into the salon looking pretty ordinary and leave feeling amazing. Hair was powerful, she truly believed that. Hairdressing was about more than just the physical, there was a psychology to it too. People poured their hearts out when they sat in the hairdresser's chair and Issy understood that she was much more than a pair of scissors to them, they put their trust into her when they sat down in her chair.

Issy shook her head to dispel her nostalgia and tuned back into Vi's chatter about her latest ailments. Issy missed the glamour and the creative challenges of The Hair Academy, but her mum's salon had heart and the clients were important to her. They needed her and so did her family. Readjusting to living at home again had been hard but Issy had never once doubted that leaving her course and coming back to Salford had been the right decision.

A melodic hum of chatter filled the air. A Cut Above was a medium-sized salon and as well as Issy and her mother, Karen and Brenda, two other stylists, also worked there. Alice, their trainee, completed their small team and though at the moment she was shampooing, sweeping up hair and making tea, she was bright and good with the clients so Issy knew it wouldn't be long before she had the skills and confidence to start tackling cuts on her own. It was how they'd all got their start.

'Thanks, Alice,' Issy said as Alice delivered a cup of milky tea to Violet. Alice smiled back at Issy and said hello to Vi, before going off with her broom.

There was a commotion as the door opened and Issy turned to see Zach walking through the salon. He'd clearly come from the garage – it was just around the corner so they were always popping in and out – as he was wearing his oil-covered overalls, and his cuffs were rolled up to reveal his full-sleeve tattoo. Since their dad's heart attack, Zach had taken charge of all the manual labour at the garage and Issy's dad had taken a step back and focused on the office work. Kev insisted that he didn't mind the change but Issy secretly thought that he did miss getting his hands dirty.

'Ooo,' Vi said, turning her head suddenly and almost losing an ear in the process. Issy pulled her scissors quickly out of harm's way, she knew how Vi could get around Zach, or any young man, in fact. 'Zach, hi!' Vi waved flirtatiously as Zach made his way over to them.

'Hey, gorgeous,' he said to Vi. She blushed like a girl a quarter of her age and Issy shook her head.

At six foot two, Zach shared the same dark hair as Issy and their dad. He was definitely a good-looking lad, and had been for as long as Issy could remember. She'd been one of the most popular girls in school simply because girls thought they could get close to Zach through Issy. And he was still one of the fittest lads in Salford – not that Issy would ever tell him that. Zach definitely didn't have confidence issues.

'What are you doing here?' Issy asked.

'I had a few minutes so I thought I'd pop in for a sunbed.'

'Are you going to be naked?' Vi asked hopefully.

Issy's eyes sparkled with amusement. 'Vi, you're old enough to be his nan,' she rebuked.

'I am not,' Vi replied indignantly.

'No, Vi, I wear boxers in there,' Zach said conspiratorially, lifting his T-shirt to snap at the waistband of his Calvin Kleins and exposing a strip of muscular stomach as he did so. 'Got to protect little Zach!'

Issy looked around the salon. Alice was almost the same colour as Issy's crimson nails, Vi was grinning from ear-to-ear and Karen couldn't keep her eyes off Zach's groin.

'Right, that's enough,' Debs shouted, coming out from the back fresh from cleaning the sunbeds. 'Zachary Jones, get into that sunbed and leave everyone else to cut hair.' Zach threw Vi a final cheeky wink and then disappeared.

Vi chatted non-stop about Zach for the rest of her haircut. Issy shared a smile with her mum who was sorting out accounts and manning reception. Zach had taken on the lion's share of the work at the garage for the last three years and she was proud of him – despite the fact that he flirted with old ladies. Although in fairness he flirted with everyone and everything – dogs, pot plants, a packet of chocolate digestives. Nothing and no one was immune to Zachary Jones's charms.

Issy was just finishing up with Vi when the salon door banged open again and her father appeared.

'Hello, gorgeous,' Debs said coming round from the reception desk to kiss her husband, wrapping her arms around him in a display of affection that made Issy feel like an awkward teenager.

'Hi, love.' Kev looked around the salon and smiled. 'Hi, ladies.'

'Two handsome men in one day,' Vi said. 'I shall never recover.' Issy thought, not for the first time, that despite her age, Vi was still a saucy old flirt.

'What other handsome man?' Kev asked, sounding perplexed.

'Your son, love. He's having a sunbed.'

'*That's* where the bugger's got to. He said he had to pop out for teabags half an hour ago. I should have known where he'd be.' Kev looked annoyed but deep down he was more amused by Zach than angry. Father and son were like peas in a pod, but Zach was the new generation, for sure. He took care of himself in a way that Kev could never understand. Zach was a man's man, but a well-groomed one.

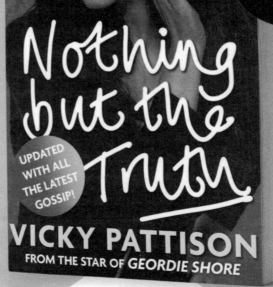